## ACKNOWLEDGMENTS

Sabre, Brax and the Reluctant Royal crew have been a long time coming and owe their inception to the infamous Max from my Elemental Paladins series. Thank you, Max!

With thanks to the 10 min sprinting team.

With thanks to my 'nitpickers'.

Dra'mon thanks Kohbi, Casey, and Lauren ;)

# CHAPTER ONE

**B**rax winced in sympathy as the poor schmuck landed with a painful thud against the concrete floor. He did not get back up. Shifting his weight from one foot to the other, Brax hoped he had been subtle enough to make room in his pants for his inappropriate and untimely erection.

"Please tell me this isn't turning you on."

Brax rolled his eyes, of course he hadn't been successful. Draven never missed anything when it came to him. Choosing the path of least resistance, Brax simply remained silent.

"It is, isn't it? You're horny! Unbelievable. That woman is a menace – a very sick, twisted menace if that guy's grey matter spread all over the ground is any judge. And here you are, lusting after her like some adolescent demon," Draven shook his head, disgust over the situation plain as day on his handsome features.

Brax cast a quick glance at the pristine angel standing next to him. Draven stuck out like a sore thumb in this environment. Well, to be fair, he pretty much stood out anywhere. He was everyone's clichéd version of what an angel should look like; tall, built, blond-haired, blue-eyed, and stupidly handsome. And although angel wings came in all sorts of shapes, sizes, and colours, Draven's were a pure snow white and reached from his shoulders to his ankles when they were out. It was truly a sight to behold. He was casually dressed in dark cargo pants and a t-shirt, as well as sensible running shoes, at the behest of Brax. But considering the clothing didn't stink of garbage, contain a multitude of holes, and look like it had been run over by a truck, the angel looked like a shining star in a pile of trash. Abraxis, on the other hand, probably fit in a little better. He was wearing his old army fatigues, a plain black t-shirt, and boots that had seen better days but had saved his butt on more than one occasion. He was also carrying an array of weapons that he hadn't bothered to conceal. But the one thing that had him fitting in with their surroundings the most? The dead look in his eyes and the rage coursing through his system, no doubt giving a whole new meaning to the term *resting bitch face*.

They were standing in the middle of the old warehouse district where illegal dealings, the homeless, and the derelict frequented. Back in the day, when he had been a newbie General to the Demon Horde, one of their tasks had been to clean up the area and wipe out the rampant criminal underbelly. His father had believed the area to be depressing rather than a violent cesspool of humanity and had wanted to help the people living within the chaos. The clean-up effort had worked – for about ten minutes. Then the criminals and the desperate scurried back to do what they did best. But his father had persevered and Brax knew his efforts had not been in vain. Maliq had been a good ruler, one of the best, and he had been well-loved by the people. But he'd never understood something which Brax had learned very quickly as a young soldier; you can't save everyone. Especially those not wanting to be saved.

Brax reined in his wayward thoughts; thinking of his late father was not wise given his current surroundings and caused a growl to rumble in his chest. Several crowd members next to him cast him concerned looks before quickly moving out of arms-reach. *As if that would save them*, Brax thought, a small, unpleasant grin kicking up the corner of his mouth. Draven placed a soothing hand on his forearm and Brax immediately felt calmer. But that wasn't what he wanted. Brax wanted to hold on to his pain and anger. He *needed* to.

It was all that he had left.

"It's not all you have left," Draven murmured. "You have me. You have the people."

Abraxis gritted his teeth, prying his arm out of the tender touch of the angel. Draven had the ability to read emotions when he was in physical contact with a person. It was a part of his angelic power of healing, including being able to calm as well as energise. After all, it paid to know what your patient was thinking and feeling as well as where and how severely they were hurt. It came in handy on the battlefield and when they were policing the supernatural population of Purgatory. But Brax more than resented it when it came to situations like now.

"Draven, you know I love you. But you gotta cut that shit out. I hate it," he informed his guardian harshly.

"I know you do," came the unflappable reply.

Brax grunted, "And the people hate me."

That had a frown creasing Draven's usually smooth brow, "They don't hate you. They just don't know you. You weren't groomed for the throne, Abraxis. Not like Mikhail was. And you weren't a notorious playboy and in the tabloids like Zagan either. Your focus was on warring, protecting, and policing the people of Purgatory. A thankless job but an important one. Besides, it is your responsibility to be there for your people, not the other way around."

Brax rolled his eyes. Draven sounded remarkably like his father and older brother. Both men perfectly suited and deserving of the title of King. Yet, here Brax was, the reluctant king, dressed in his soldiering uniform and surrounded by a cheering crowd of bloodthirsty supernaturals as they bet on who would get the shit beat out of them in the centre of the makeshift ring while his family waited to be avenged from their graves. And with that happy reminder, Brax returned his attention to his surroundings.

It hadn't been all that hard to track down the illegal cage fighting arena – and not because Brax was now one of the only demons of royal blood left living and everyone technically had to obey him. No, Brax had used his well-established and trusted contacts from his army days. Some of his soldier buddies had scouted several locations over the past few weeks, and although they had identified many people in need of being arrested for a plethora of illegal activities, none had yielded what he desired. A woman rumoured to be pure sin.

Focusing back on the continued death match in front of him, Brax knew that description was both figurative and literal. Not only was she an assassin, forged within the depths of the most notorious assassin den in Purgatory and therefore responsible for untold atrocities, but she was also an angel. Definitely a fallen angel with not a speck of Grace left in her tarnished wings, but an angel nonetheless. It should have been impossible for an agent of the Heavens to willingly kill in cold blood let alone submerge themselves in that life day after day. But the angel known only as Sabre certainly did. Brax had grown up hearing stories about the lethal angel, and over the course of his career had seen the result of many of her undertakings. But he had never seen her in person before, let alone met her. That was something he was intent on changing that night.

As yet another victim fell with a nauseating crack onto the naked concrete floor, Brax was relieved her reputation was not all bullshit. Being the intelligent demon that he was, he wasn't one to listen to rumours and tales. He had to see it to believe it. Maybe that was ironic considering he lived in a world made up of supernatural creatures. No doubt the human realm would find it laughable. But Brax could count on one hand the number of people he could still rely on for their word and when one of those people had suggested seeking out the notorious angel in order to aid his endeavour, Brax had quickly agreed. And now, he was definitely seeing the merit of his decision. Of course, he was also rapidly realising the assassin could potentially come with some unexpected problems.

*Like the fact that she is fucking sex on legs,* Brax acknowledged silently, thankful Draven hadn't caught his wayward thoughts this time. Watching the woman fight turned him on, there was no doubt about that. Sabre was dressed in tight leather from collarbone to ankles, showcasing her incredible body of subtle curves and flexing muscles. She had sharp cheekbones, a straight nose, and surprisingly full lips. Why the sight of her pummelling some poor vampire had his inner beast rumbling with approval, he wasn't sure. He had always preferred strong women, not the tittering, lace-clad society ladies that frequented the upscale bars and parties he had been duty-bound to attend. But he had never had the privilege of witnessing anything quite like he was now. He felt his eyes flare and knew they would be reflecting the light like an animal – a gift thanks to his shared bloodline with Cerberus. Though, not a very subtle one because Draven immediately began swearing.

"Don't even think about it. I'm serious, Brax. That woman is more trouble than a roll beneath the sheets would be worth. Trust me. She can't be saved."

Brax laughed a little at that; "Draven, that is the last woman in all the realms in need of saving. Don't worry," he assured his friend, "my need for information far trumps my need for sex."

Draven looked at him like he didn't believe him but thankfully let it rest. "Are you sure you want to do this?" he then asked for the millionth time.

Brax sighed, pushing his hands through his hair roughly and turning his back on the crowd who were now dispersing after the final fight. "What choice do I have, Draven? The royal family is all but eradicated, assassinated by a mysterious rogue we literally know nothing about other than the fact they have a sociopathic need to topple the line of Cerberus. Civil unrest is gaining momentum and all my months of hunting have been pointless." Draven was kind enough not to correct his timeline – *months* had recently turned into a *year*. "My spies have found exactly nothing and anytime we get a tiny lead, it turns to shit. We're not just one step behind this fuck – we're light years!" He ended in a growl, the sound rumbling through his chest like the demon-beast he was.

Training his eyes on the leather-clad, fallen angelic prize in front of him. He said decisively; "I'm doing this. I'm hiring Sabre."

CHAPTER TWO

It was some thirty minutes later, when the majority of the crowd had left and only a handful of various creatures remained that Brax and Draven made their way over to a very relaxed-looking assassin. She was sitting at a scarred table – one of only three in the entire open area of the warehouse – with a very pretty, young-looking woman and a man who at first glance, appeared human. There was a total of six chairs in the vast space, two small round tables and one long, solid block of timber that looked a little like a bar. Unfortunately, the stains on top of it told a different story and Brax just managed to stop his nose from wrinkling in distaste. Draven had no such restraint and he pursed his lips, shaking his head in disgust. Draven was a rather fastidious angel and Brax could see him cataloguing germs even as they waited next to where Sabre was merrily telling a tale to her two companions.

"So, anyway, I knocked on his door and I hear this scared little voice from the other side say, 'who's there?'" Sabre was explaining.

The young woman snickered before asking, "What did you say?"

Sabre's grin was decidedly evil as she answered, apparently completely unaware of their presence behind her. But Brax wasn't fooled. He knew the dangerous woman was well aware of her surroundings. No, Brax thought, she just didn't give a shit they were there. Why he found such irreverence appealing, he really had no clue. Usually, such casual disregard would piss him off. His demonic nature was all alpha and demanded respect and acknowledgment. Yet, the leather-clad, blood-covered female currently ignoring him in favour of continuing her chat with her companions was causing his beast to purr instead of growl. It was disconcerting to say the least. He managed to catch her answer and it had his eyebrows rising.

"I said *'Destiny, motherfucker!'* Then I bashed the door in and gutted him from back to front as he attempted to run away, screaming like a banshee the entire time. No easy feat, I assure you," she shook her head.

The two people with her laughed uproariously as if it was the funniest thing they had ever heard. Draven shifted uncomfortably from foot to foot, and Brax wasn't sure what to think. Was Sabre telling an exaggerated barroom tale? Or did she truly find humour in killing someone from behind?

"You really said it was Destiny at the door?" The other female asked between giggles.

"You bet your stripes I did," Sabre confirmed.

The dark-haired man with them simply shook his head, a smile lighting his face – but not his obsidian eyes. "Classic," he said.

Apparently, Draven had reached his limit on patience – and no doubt tolerance as well. He stalked forward, practically yelling; "Are you being serious right now?!"

The trio finally deigned to give them the time of day, and Brax was faced with three sets of hardened, judgemental eyes.

"Excuse me?" The odd human man asked.

"Do you really think that tale is humorous?" Draven asked, voice incredulous. "And do you really think such a story is appropriate for one so young?" he added, pointing to the black-and-white-haired young woman in their midst.

The teen in question rounded her eyes in surprise – one a startling blue and the other a bright green – before looking back at Sabre. She coughed, covering her smiling mouth with her hand, "Yeah, do you really think that is appropriate for my innocent ears?"

She was clearly being sarcastic, and Draven realised it too, for his hands clenched by his sides. Brax brushed against him subtly, knowing such a tiny movement would be enough to have him stand down. As an angel, it was a part of Draven's innate nature to care for and protect the young. The young adult he saw sitting in front of them looked fragile enough but Brax had a feeling it had been a long time since she was innocent. Or had the chance to be a child. *If she ever had,* Brax tacked on silently. If she was hanging out with the likes of the notorious Sabre at an underground cage fighting facility, then she was very likely to have just as much blood on her hands as the deadly woman sitting next to her.

"To answer your question; yes, I think it's funny. You see, it works on multiple levels. Because this –" Sabre quickly whipped out a knife the size of her forearm causing both Brax and Draven to take a defensive stance and pull out their own weapons. "This blade is called Destiny," Sabre continued, completely unconcerned by their arsenal, as if they weren't true threats. "Plus, his death by my hands was also his destiny. Get it?" she asked.

Draven blew air out of his nostrils in a rush and Brax was

surprised there was no accompanying fire. The woman in front of them was the very epitome of everything Draven scorned. "Oh, I get it," the angel promised. "I get that you're a travesty to every angel alive! You're sick! A disgusting example of –"

Sabre looked bored as she held up a hand for silence, "I'm sorry, who are you again?"

Draven drew himself up to his full height of six-foot-five inches – a good two inches taller than Brax's own solid frame. Draven was also well-muscled with broad shoulders and bulging biceps. He might act and sound like a British butler most of the time, but he was a warrior and a guardian to his core. Brax knew that Draven could throw down with the best of them and had, in fact, witnessed him doing so many times. As a royal guardian angel to the General of the Demon Horde of Purgatory, the angel really didn't have a choice. Not that the man wanted one, Brax knew. Being Brax's guardian, his mentor, his best friend, and his advisor was more than Draven's job. It was his calling, his purpose. It was the reason why his Grace was bestowed upon him and why he found himself on one of the middle planes instead of remaining in Heaven.

"I am Draven, Guardian Angel to Abraxis, King of Purgatory."

"Uh huh," the notorious assassin yawned. "How nice for you. And you are?" she directed her eyes toward Brax next.

Brax felt his lips twitch despite himself. The woman had balls he'd give her that. "That would make me the King," he answered, drolly.

"Well, well …" she murmured, before using a foot to push out a chair. "Take a seat," she said, just as the chair slid to a stop with a millimetre to spare in front of his steel capped boots.

Brax made no effort to take the disrespectfully offered seat, instead he took the opportunity to observe Sabre close up. She was long and lean, perhaps coming up to his shoulders, which would make her around six-feet tall, he thought. Perhaps on the taller side for a woman, but angels – both male and female – were typically tall beings. Her sleeveless leather vest showcased muscular biceps and skin the colour of milk. The paleness of her skin was a striking contrast to the dark, blue-black of her hair, which was cut in an almost masculine style. It was short at the back and at the sides but still held enough length on top to be styled. No doubt the short locks were for ease of maintenance. As a soldier, Brax could appreciate that. He himself habitually cut his hair so it would stay out of his eyes when fighting. Unfortunately, his demonic nature caused his hair to grow incredibly quickly. And since he was no longer fighting on the front lines, it had gotten substantially longer. He even had to use a band to tie it back these days. Something his father would have scolded him for and something his brothers would have teased him about. Why did he keep reminiscing about the good old days? Such memories were useless. He continued his perusal and noted small breasts that were encased in black leather, dipping enticingly into a small vee at the front, giving a hint of subtle curves. He had no doubt those curves would be a perfect handful. A tucked in waist, lean, long legs that ended in desert style black boots completed the entire look. But it was her eyes that had his breath stalling in his throat.

Her eyes were the intriguing colour of plums; purple, maroon and cream all mixed together. *Fuck,* Brax thought, irritably. *I love plums.* He immediately scolded himself because the unexpected attraction could very well be the death of him. Literally. A few short months ago, such a thought wouldn't have bothered him. He had hit rock bottom and was well past depressed and into drowning. He had felt the fruitless nature of his search reflected like a mirror; meaningless, barren and with no end in sight. But a few well-chosen words from his soldier buddy and quite an elaborate arse-kicking by Draven had given Brax a new, small spark of purpose and hope.

"You going to sit down or what, Abraxis?" Sabre questioned, plum eyes lighting with both humour and challenge.

"That's King Abraxis to you," Draven corrected immediately.

The assassin raised her eyebrows, "Oh, that's right … *King*."

Eyes of maroon swept him from head to toe and the slight crinkling of her nose along with the flat look he received left no doubt in his mind that she had just weighed and measured him – and found him wanting. Why that pissed him off so easily and so swiftly, he didn't know. He had never cared for the opinions of others and certainly had never cared to impress anyone. Other than his family, whose pride and affection had meant the world to him. *All for naught now,* he thought, bitterly. The sharp stab of pain in the centre of his chest was a welcome reminder of why he was skulking around the underground fight club to begin with. Manoeuvring the chair, he finally sat down.

"Your Majesty," Sabre mocked, bowing her head. "I had no idea the King would be gracing me with his presence. Had I known I wouldn't have spilled brains all over the floor."

"Somehow I doubt that," Brax said, dryly.

Sabre smiled, a look that was particularly becoming on her face. "Meh, you're probably right. So … to what do I owe the pleasure?"

"I want to hire you." His words garnered no reaction at all, and he found himself gritting his teeth. He had expected at least surprise from his announcement. The woman seemed unflappable, and he had to force the beast inside of him down, warning it not to take it as a challenge. "Did you hear what I said?" he asked, allowing the words to emerge with a hint of fang. Unlike were-wolves and vampires whose fangs elongated from their upper incisors, his fangs were actually embedded in his lower jaw, causing all sorts of issues with his speech when he was growing up before he managed to control them better.

Sabre eyed him for a moment before sitting forward, "I heard you. Why would the King need to hire me? For what?"

"What do you think?" Draven sneered from behind Brax's right shoulder where he stood like a sentinel, "Killing."

Sabre scrunched her nose up, "Killing, huh? Don't you have an army for that? Or is this entrapment? Maybe you want me to confess to crimes so you can have me arrested and thrown in jail."

Brax leaned back in his chair, shaking his head in disbelief, "Really? I just saw you kill a guy in front of me not thirty minutes ago. I don't care about your little death matches –" he managed to get out, only to be interrupted by the, as yet, silent man.

"Hey! These are the best cage fights in all of Purgatory – minus the cage of course. That's kind of metaphorical, you know? Anyway, I worked hard for its reputation," he pointed out.

Now that the man had his attention, Brax narrowed his eyes, taking a deep breath in and trying to gauge the being's scent. He really did look and smell human. If it wasn't for the black eyes, Brax would have believed there was nothing supernatural about him. Although humans were scarce in Purgatory there were a few around. Most of them were magic users like witches, mages, and voodoo practitioners who were able to cross the veils between realms. Not many humans – even those with magical abilities – knew there was more than one plane of existence, let alone how to access the veils. But in fact, there were four planes; the human realm – Earth – as well as Purgatory, Heaven, and Hell. Out of all the realms and all the beings that existed, humans were the most ignorant to what was really going on. Purgatory taught the history of all the realms as a part of their schooling in adolescence. Brax wasn't sure what went on in all the levels and dimensions in Hell, but he knew they were aware of the veil and the realms. And as the first realm to explode into existence, Heaven pretty much knew everything. He had no doubt humans would be surprised to learn that Purgatory was a world in its own right, with living, breathing beings and was in no way a waiting room for the dead. Purgatory was merely a world filled with supernatural creatures and was parallel to Earth. In fact, it was almost a direct reflection of Earth, with televisions, movies, phones, and cars. The universe was big on balance; two living realms sandwiched between two death realms. Heaven and Hell housed the dead, while Earth and Purgatory housed the living.

"And who are you exactly?" He eventually asked the man; certain he wasn't a magic wielder but clueless about everything else. "*What* are you?"

"Gage," was the only reply he received before the man stood up. "If you're going to talk shop, me and the kitten will take our business elsewhere. Jinx, come with," he motioned toward the long slab of wood a small distance away.

The girl – Jinx – opened her mouth, no doubt to argue, but quickly shut it when Sabre gave a small shake of her head. Huffing and rolling her unusual bi-coloured eyes as only the truly young can do, Jinx pouted as she was quickly led away. Once alone, Sabre returned her gaze to him.

"What exactly do you want from me? You're the King. You have resources I could never have. Why have you come to me?" Sabre asked, bluntly.

"I've been led to believe you are one of the best assassins and mercenaries for hire in Purgatory," Brax began, only to be interrupted.

"Not one of the best. I'm *the* best," Sabre boasted.

Usually, Brax would have taken such words as arrogance but in Sabre's case, he felt they were probably true. Still, he ignored them as he continued on; "And I need information. Information that people won't tell me because of who I am."

"Ah, I see. You need intel from the slums but you live in a palace. I'm guessing even your reputation as a leader of the Horde can't unlock some doors for you," Sabre said, eyes directly on his.

The words annoyed him because they were true. Instead of growling like he wanted to, he simply agreed, "Right."

Sabre leaned back in her chair and kicked her long legs out in front of her under the table. "Okay. You need information. What about the killing part? Oh ..." her eyes suddenly lit with an inner fire, "do I get to torture them for information *before* I get to do the killing? Appetiser and a main – my favourite."

"You are horrible," Draven whispered, his voice sounding incredulous.

"Yeah? Well, so's your face," was the decidedly lame comeback from the assassin in question.

Brax held up a hand, silencing the duo who, for all the world looked and sounded like a pair of bickering siblings. "Will you two quit it? Sabre, I don't care how you get me the goods. Just as long as you do. And at the moment, I don't want any primary players killed."

"And why is that?" Sabre inquired.

Brax allowed his eyes to flare, the demon-beast within him rising to the surface. "Because I intend to kill them myself."

Sabre perked up like a dog being offered a treat, "Going to get those royal hands dirty, Your Majesty?"

Brax snorted, "My hands haven't been clean for a long time."

Sabre held out her fist, "Right on. Come on, fist bump. You're not gonna leave me hangin' are you?"

Brax raised his own fist as if drawn by a magnet, only to have it slapped back down by Draven. "Don't even think about it," his angel warned. Glancing at Sabre, he saw her roll her eyes and noted that her lips were quirked in humour. But he also saw what he thought was a hint of respect in her eyes. *The woman respects violence and death. Go figure,* he thought. And apparently his dick respected women who respected violence and death. It was still sitting at half-mast from his earlier inspection and the longer he sat in the presence of the wicked angel, the more it tried to twitch its way out of his pants.

Draven cleared his throat, "Business, Your Majesty?" he prompted.

Brax nodded once. Draven was right, time to get down to the nitty gritty. "Right. I want you to find the person who took out the hit on my brothers. As well as any other information you can find as to why someone would even want to topple the line of Cerberus."

Sabre's lashes twitched minutely even as her face remained impassive. "Wow. Want me to find Santa Claus for you too? Because I have a feeling it will be just as impossible."

Brax clenched his fists, his claws piercing his palms as he made to stand, "If you don't think you're up to it –"

"I didn't say that." Sabre tapped a finger against the beaten-up wood of the table, apparently considering his words. Finally, she sighed, "What's in it for me?"

"How about a good deed? The sense of accomplishment that comes with doing something right and noble?" Draven offered, sarcasm dripping from his words.

This time, Sabre made to stand. "Sorry, feather-brain. I don't work for free."

"If you get me the information I want, you can name your price," Brax interjected.

Sabre sat back down slowly, eyes narrowing in his direction. "Tempting. Very tempting. Question: what makes you think I'm not already a part of the conspiracy?"

Brax couldn't say why, and it was probably the stupidest feeling he had ever had, but he was pretty sure Sabre had nothing to do with wanting his family dead. Still, he allowed the scene to play out; "Are you? If you are, I won't have any need to hire you of course. Although, I'll still consider it a good evening out because I will get the information I need from you. One way or another."

Sabre looked amused by his last threat, but she surprised him when she looked him in the eye and gave him a genuine response; "That won't be necessary. I currently know nothing. My allegiance is to the Blue Devil Den. In turn, that means my loyalty goes to the employer of whatever job I am hired to do at the time. If that is now to be you, then you have my loyalty for as long as it takes me to fulfil the contract."

This time it was he who raised his hand toward Sabre. "Consider yourself hired."

## CHAPTER THREE

"How'd I do?"

"You totally pulled it off. If I didn't know you had been making moon eyes at him for years now, I would have been convinced that you didn't know who he was," came Jinx's prompt reply.

Sabre pursed her lips and responded primly, "I do not make moon eyes at anyone. Least of all the last remaining official heir to the throne of Purgatory."

Jinx snorted, boosting herself up to sit on Gage's combination bar, office desk, mortuary table, and hospital bed. The solid timber bench performed many uses faithfully and never complained about what was put on it, whether it be money, blood, sweat, or tears. "Gage?" Jinx inquired, casting a quick look in his direction.

"Major moon eyes," Gage confirmed, not even looking up from the money he was counting.

"To be fair, you stalk the entire royal family equally," Jinx pointed out, before Sabre could do anything more than growl in annoyance. "It's only the middle one you swoon over."

"I don't stalk the royal family," she immediately and automatically denied. "In my line of work it's smart to take an interest in monarchy and politics." And it was, though that wasn't the main reason for her stealthy focus on the descendants of the line of Cerberus. That was something she could never speak of. To anyone.

"I must say, he sure looks good close up," Jinx confessed with a small sigh.

*Indeed he does,* Sabre agreed. Abraxis, the demon who would be King, looked to be around three or so inches taller than her. He was at least twice her width though and all muscle. Years leading the most elite military force in Purgatory no doubt had a hand in that, she mused. The tight shirt he was wearing left very little to the imagination, showcasing muscled biceps and forearms, and a lean, strong torso. She wouldn't be surprised if the man was hiding an eight-pack beneath his shirt. His eyes were an astounding canary-yellow, often reflecting the light like a beast. Brax's thighs looked to be as solid as the rest of him and Sabre thought she would be able to climb him like a tree with no hardship. Not that she would be climbing him at all, considering she was officially under his employ. And that little fact was a kick in the pants. The irony would be funny as fuck if only the implications of the situation weren't so … fucked.

"What did he want to hire you for, anyway?" Gage asked. He was now leaning over the bar-like table, head cocked in interest and dark eyes intense on hers.

Sabre puffed up her cheeks before expelling the air out in a rush, "He wants me to find the person responsible for exterminating his family." Her words were met with beats of silence before the inevitable eruption occurred and Jinx and Gage began to talk over the top of one another.

"What?!" Gage glowered.

"You can't be serious! What did you say?!" Jinx demanded.

"I am very serious. And I said yes, of course," Sabre responded, wincing when Jinx practically shrieked.

"You said yes?! Sabre, you can't be serious," she repeated. "Do you have a death wish?"

"Sometimes," Sabre replied with honesty. "But not today," she assured her two companions who were still looking at her like she was crazy. "What exactly was I supposed to say? It's the King."

"Exactly," Gage said, dark eyes direct on her face. "It's the King. And you could have said no. You say it often enough."

That was true, Sabre admitted. She was approached all the time by people wanting something from her. She had no issue turning them down and sending them on their way – often with a fresh perspective on the meaning of fear. But there were a multitude of reasons why she couldn't deny the new king. *Abraxis,* Sabre said his name silently, doing her best not to sigh. The man had a very sexy name. One she was sure would sound perfect when echoing throughout her bedroom in the throes of passion. *Wait, passion? No Sabre, there will be no passion!* She didn't even know where that thought came from. Unless they were with their chosen mate – or mates – angels had a notoriously low sex drive. In fact, angels in Heaven never engaged in any form of sexual interaction. Lust simply didn't exist in that realm. But once an angel found themselves on a different plane, like in Purgatory or Earth, human and animal emotions of lust, affection and even love, tended to make themselves known, and angels often partook in the pleasures of the flesh. Most of the time it was experimentation with a true sex drive only rearing its orgasmic head when they met the person – or persons – they fell in love with.

Sabre had tried the whole sex thing once – years and years ago – just to see what all the hype was about. Needless to say, it didn't live up to the propaganda and she hadn't bothered with it since. That's not to say she didn't indulge in a few *private* fantasies every now and again. And if the new king happened to be in a couple – or a thousand – of those fantasies, Sabre figured there was no harm in that. Until, of course, she became employed by him and would now be in closer proximity to the gorgeous demon-beast.

"It's not going to be an issue," she said firmly out loud. The benefit was for herself as well as Jinx and Gage who were still staring at her askance.

"But if he finds out –"

Sabre cut Jinx off before she could finish, "He won't find out."

"Sabre …"

Jinx's voice was worried this time and Sabre melted a little from the obvious concern and affection the weretiger had for her. It was more than reciprocated which was another reason why Sabre needed to take the job. She needed her part in all of this to be over. She yearned for the day when she no longer had to lie and keep secrets from the two people who had attached themselves to her – whether she liked it or not. And in the early days, it had most definitely been *not*. Gage had come along first, almost fifty years ago, and declared that Sabre needed him whether she wanted him or not. The man was perhaps the stubbornest person she had ever met, and she had given in gracefully – after a few years. Jinx was a newer acquisition to the small group, but no less important. Sabre would never say so out loud, but the weretiger and the akuji were family.

"Just be careful," Gage warned her, presently. He was a smart man and knew when he wasn't going to win a fight. Which, when against her, was never. He continued, "If he finds out your secret, he'll rip you to shreds."

Oh, Sabre had no doubt about that at all. The new king wasn't like his predecessors, groomed and educated from birth to ascend to the throne. He was the 'spare heir' and had thrown himself into the hands-on work of policing their people. It was no easy task, considering their people could tear each other limb from limb or drain each other dry. It was also messy and Sabre knew Abraxis would have no problem getting his hands dirty. She recognised a warrior when she saw one. And a beast. The broody new king was both.

Ignoring the delightful little tingle that knowledge wrought, Sabre exhaled roughly, "And with that happy thought …" she uncrossed her ankles and drew herself up straight from where she had been leaning on the bar. Standing, she stretched her back, over-worked muscles from the evening's matches making themselves known.

"Where are you going?" Jinx asked, frowning.

"Back to the Blue Devil," Sabre replied, already turning and walking away from the inevitable argument to follow her statement.

"Why? Sabre, why don't you stay in your studio? Or better yet, come home with me for the night," Jinx implored from behind her.

Sabre sighed, pausing in her tracks but not turning around. The last thing – the *very* last thing she wanted to do was return to the Blue Devil. The Blue Devil Den was the most notorious assassin den in all of Purgatory for all the wrong reasons. The assassins who called the Blue Devil home were known for their cruelty and ruthlessness, willing to do anything to get the job done. And since the age of eight, Sabre had been one of them. The proprietor – or the pimp in Sabre's mind – of the Blue Devil had the nasty habit of stealing children from the most powerful supernatural races and training them from childhood. The term *training* was as loose as the term *proprietor* and was more like conditioning young, vulnerable and malleable minds and bodies until the lines between right and wrong were not just blurred; they were erased. Endless days and nights of torture, schooling, and training resulted in mercenaries with poor impulse control and a thirst for blood. There were no exceptions; not even angels. Of course, angels were probably the only supernatural race never to have succumbed to the harsh, yet effective, training regime of the assassin den. Until Sabre of course. She had been taken before her true path had been laid, thus derailing her angelic purpose. Now, one hundred and ten years later, her angelic purpose was nothing more than an annoying buzz in her head as she carried out the demands of her employers.

Sabre might have been resigned to her fate. Hell, she might even enjoy it some of the time. *Okay, most of the time,* she admitted. But one thing she absolutely loathed with every fibre of her being was the mansion that was the Blue Devil Den. The only thing she despised more was the owner – *her* owner – Carlisle. Although she had never said anything out loud – she was really fucking good at keeping secrets – Jinx and Gage knew she hated going back there. Unfortunately, it was as inevitable as the sun rising in the North. She could spend days and even weeks away from the Den, checking in with sporadic messages and phone calls. But she couldn't stay away forever. No matter how much she wanted to. Her sense of responsibility and deep-seated work ethic guaranteed her continued acquiescence to the brutal life of an assassin. The fact that she was once supposed to sport feathers on her back didn't mean jack-shit. Sabre was a killer now. It wasn't just something she did; it was something she was. One death, let alone hundreds, had been enough to seal her fate.

"I haven't been back for over a week," Sabre finally pointed out. She turned around only to be confronted with a five-foot nothing tiger cub and a zombie-man looking pissed and as unmovable as granite. "Guys, I'm serious. I'm beginning to feel itchy." And she was. The bond with the den and the den's master was soul-deep. "Look, I agreed to meet with our esteemed king and his stuck-up guardian tomorrow to get more details. I'll only be there one night." It was a compromise and the best she could do under the circumstances.

"Fine," Jinx grumbled before leaning in for a hug.

Sabre allowed herself the brief moment of affectionate contact, breathing in deep and hoping some of the goodness within the small body plastered against hers rubbed off on her. A fruitless endeavour, but one Sabre continually attempted. The young weretiger was goodness personified with the heart and constitution of a queen. One of the best things Sabre had done out of the million terrible things was rescuing Jinx four years ago when she had been just fifteen years old. She had been sold as a sex slave into the harem of a particularly disgusting lust demon who coveted beauty.

The lovely Jinx never stood a chance against him with her delicate Asian features, unique striped hair that mimicked her tiger form and unusual eyes of one blue and one green. Although Jinx was capable of shapeshifting into a 200 kilogram, nearly three-metre long white Bengal tiger, she had been a mere child of thirteen when her parents had sold her to Asmodeus for the cost of their next hit of Hype – the drug of choice in Purgatory. As such, Asmodeus had been able to collar Jinx before she could even think to shift and defend herself. Sabre had happened upon the demon's sex-nest by accident when she had been tracking a target. It had taken her all of five seconds to judge the clichéd harem-style tent for what it was; a lust demon's wet dream and a place of evil acts against the unwilling. Sabre had slaughtered everyone there except the sex slaves before emptying her stomach in a nearby bush. She had given Jinx the opportunity to exact her own vengeance on her captor before the young weretiger had somehow bonded to Sabre, declaring her a part of her Tribe. That Tribe had grown to encompass Gage as soon as the man had laid eyes on the malnourished and horribly treated teen. Now, five years later at nineteen, the shadows in Jinx's eyes were all but gone, but her gratitude for Sabre remained. Even as corrupt and criminally inclined as Sabre was, she didn't have it in her to chase the girl away. Not that Jinx, nor Gage, would let her.

Finally pulling back, Sabre mock-punched Jinx in the shoulder, "Later, tiger." She nodded at Gage, "See ya 'round, dead-man-walking." This time she didn't look back.

## CHAPTER FOUR

Sabre steeled herself before looking up at the mansion which housed around twenty assassins and mercenaries, perhaps double that in staff, one truly horrible incubus owner, and the resident torturer – a pain demon by the name of Mercy. From the outside, the building was a thing of beauty, with curved balconies, a wrap-around porch, and three-stories of pristine, white render. Dozens of windows and a double door at the end of a horseshoe driveway created the illusion of welcome. But there was nothing welcoming about what was inside those ornate doors with the crystal handles. Inside, a nightmare awaited – one she couldn't wake up from. A nightmare she wasn't *allowed* to wake up from. A simple promise made as a child was as binding as a pact with the Devil himself. Such was the curse of her race.

Angels were either born or created. Those born had more options and were free to choose their own righteous paths. Though, their word, when given freely, was still binding. But those who were created in the Heavenly plane, designed to guide and guard those with important destinies, had to be even more careful with their words. Sucking up her instinctive hesitation, Sabre gave herself a mental chiding as she trudged up the long driveway, reminding herself that it didn't matter how her innocent words were intended. All that mattered was what they had wrought – the first ever angel assassin in the history of the four realms. Leaning into the retina scanner, Sabre waited for the light above the door to turn from red to green before she then placed her right hand onto the palm plate next to the door handle. A second later, a happy little beep followed by a click of the door lock finally allowed her to enter. The sounds that afflicted her ears had her wincing and focusing her gaze on the floor in front of her, not even tempted to look at what the 'family' of killers found so damn entertaining.

"The prodigal daughter returns!"

The snarled, resentment-filled voice coming from the great room to her left didn't cause her even a moment of pause. She simply flipped off the surly werewolf, following it up with a; "Fuck you, Wade," as she climbed the stairs to her room. The alpha wolf growled behind her, no doubt upset about her lack of fear and respect. But Wade was a sadistic arsehole, much like the vast majority of the mercs and killers under the employ of Carlisle, completely undeserving of her respect. She was also completely and wholly unafraid of the seven-foot, muscle-bound creature, knowing she could take him with one hand tied behind her back.

It wasn't arrogance that had Sabre trusting her skills and powers, it was experience. In all her one-hundred-and-eighteen years, she was yet to come up against an opponent she couldn't beat – one way or another. As she trudged up the clichéd mahogany-carpeted staircase, Sabre acknowledged that it was also her biology that allowed her to flirt with danger and death so much. As an angel she could heal from practically anything –

though she wasn't immune to pain. She was stronger, faster and had more endurance than nearly any other supernatural creature because the power that flowed in her veins was gifted from the Heavens.

Grace was the very essence of an angel and was what their powers were made of – as well as their wings. The more Grace bestowed on an angel from the Gods, the more powerful the angel was and the more incredible their unique abilities were. The other side to that, of course, was when an angel became fallen, whether it be on the human plane, in Hell or in Purgatory, their wings slowly lost their Grace. And with it, their powers, essentially making them nothing more than glorified humans. Although, a fallen angel still retained what their genetics decreed; strength and longevity. But their Heaven-gifted magic was denied to them as their Grace diminished and their wings eroded one feather at a time. The number of times fellow mercenaries and victims had asked her what colour her feathers used to be was ridiculous. It was also annoying as fuck and highly private. She always made sure to get in a few extra stabs whenever one of her hits asked.

Once at the top of the stairway, Sabre turned left and made her way down the long hallway. She had her own room right at the end of the hallway, and as a result thankfully only shared one wall with another assassin. The noises that echoed along the hallways, not to mention through the thin walls of her room, were enough to make her shudder. At least she wasn't subjected to surround-sound like most of the others. Using her microchipped keycard, she swiped it through the lock, pausing in her doorway to make sure nothing had been disturbed in her absence. The single bed was still neatly made, dresser drawers and wardrobe door shut tight, and the rough rug looked like it hadn't been walked on. Determining no one had been inside, Sabre stepped in, turning and immediately locking the door. She began stripping off her clothes as she walked straight into the attached tiny bathroom. A small, free-standing sink, toilet and corner shower stall were the only things in the florid green bathroom. Still, the water pressure was decent and Sabre more than needed the hot spray to help wash away the invisible ick she felt all over her skin.

Sabre enjoyed the hell out of the fight-nights at Gage's warehouse. She was a frequent contender in the matches and Gage always raked in the money whenever she showed up to fight. Usually because some fucking idiots who thought they were Superman reincarnated believed they could beat her in a fight and bet against her. Gage and Jinx knew better than that but often encouraged such moronic lines of thinking in order to hike up the bets. Gage then bet on Sabre and, *boom*, Gage had a month's worth of income from one night. Sabre also used the warehouse arena for work, often luring her hits in with a challenge; if they could beat her in a fight, Sabre wouldn't kill them. Of course, that never happened either. Like the Djinn from that evening.

She had been tracking the Djinn for a week before she was able to capture him and issue her challenge. Seeing his grey matter spread all over the concrete floor had been more than satisfying, considering he'd had the nasty habit of making children's nightmares come true. Djinn were one of a handful of supernatural creatures who could cross the veil into the human realm, and this particular arsehole had already killed two human children as a result of his sick games before Sabre was able to track and kill him. Sure, she could have killed him elsewhere, but she liked to help out Gage when she could. Because the fights served multiple purposes; money, catharsis, work … and food. Djinn were a particularly rare delicacy and she was more than happy to ensure Gage was well fed.

After three full-body scrubs and washing her hair twice, Sabre stayed under the spray until the water began to cool. Finally stepping out of the shower, she felt the shift in the air immediately and knew someone was invading her personal space. Not that her room was really *hers*. Nothing in the Den belonged to her, as Carlisle liked to remind them all. *Like I give two shits,* Sabre snarked internally. She wouldn't claim anything at the Blue Devil even if her life depended on it. *Maybe two somethings*, Sabre corrected, thinking of two other residents of the mansion whom she considered trustworthy.

"Where have you been?"

The voice was like honey, sweet and dripping with promises of pleasure. The sound caressed Sabre's naked skin, causing goosebumps to flare to life. Sabre ignored her body's automatic and forced reaction with practiced ease, throwing off all hints of arousal before they even began. Taking her time, she wrapped herself in the plain white robe she had thrown over the sink prior to stepping into the shower before looking up at the trespasser standing at the foot of her bed and staring openly at what was her naked form just seconds ago. The man was as beautiful as his voice; deep brown eyes, messy blond hair, square jawline, and a body to die for. Sabre smirked, knowing that hundreds had in fact died for just such a treat. Sabre had never been one of them and never would be. She would sooner cut off her own arms than voluntarily touch Carlisle.

Her employer.

Her owner.

Her worst nightmare ... and greatest desire.

Not desire to fuck, no matter how much sexual charisma the incubus seeped from his pores. Oh no, Sabre wanted to gut the sex demon and dance in his entrails. Literally. He had been the one to find her when she was eight, his good looks and soft voice garnering her trust with the illusion of safety and warmth. That illusion had lasted only as long as her first night spent in the mansion. But by then it had been too late. A deal had been made.

"I've been busy," Sabre finally replied to the Den Master's question.

"Doing what?" The silky voice asked.

Sabre gave Carlisle a droll look, "Killing people. What do you think?"

"You only had two contracts in the last ten days and you fulfilled one five days ago. I understand the other was completed tonight," he said. Carlisle always knew when a contract was completed. "What have you been doing in between?"

Sabre ran her tongue along her teeth, curbing her impulse to tell the sociopath in front of her to jump off the nearest bridge onto a pile of jagged rocks covered in acid. *Lots and lots of acid,* Sabre thought, gleefully picturing the golden Adonis's screams of pain as he writhed and burned from the outside in.

"What are you smiling at? You never smile at me," Carlisle added, sounding intrigued and pissed off at the same time.

"Was I smiling?" Sabre deflected, giving herself a stern warning to dial back her fantasies.

Carlisle grunted, walking to within arms-length of her position near the open bathroom door. "You haven't answered me, Sabre."

Sabre unclenched her teeth, loathe to follow any orders from him – even if it was answering a simple question. But she did – just like always, "I've been travelling around and then staying with a source. It took some time to find that damn Djinn. He was in the human realm. I had to wait for him to get back."

"And you couldn't just kill him when you caught him?" Carlisle inquired, looking suspicious.

Sabre grinned once more, "You know me; I like to play with my prey first."

Stepping into her personal space, Carlisle crooned as he

stroked a patch of skin on Sabre's vulnerable neck, "That you do. You know, you really are my greatest success story. Angel turned assassin. Agent of Heaven turned merciless killer. It makes me hard just thinking about it." Sabre kept her mouth shut, not reacting to the man's touch – or his words – in the slightest. The incubus finally sighed, "Well, I have a new contract for you."

"Sorry. Can't. I've already got a new job," Sabre was quick to say.

Carlisle pulled back abruptly, "What? What the fuck are you talking about, my pet?"

"Private deal." Sabre knew she was on shaky ground and reminded the impulse control section of her brain to take it easy and not let her viper tongue run away with her. Sabre was one of the only assassins in the employ of the Blue Devil who was permitted to take on private contracts. The contract she had renegotiated when she had reached one hundred years of service had included a clause which enabled her to accept private offers. As long as the Blue Devil Den and Carlisle received a large percentage of the commission of course. She had fought long and hard for the irreversible clause, knowing it was an integral part of her long-term plan. The *end game* depended on it.

"Private deal? Another one?! You're getting dangerously close to your quota," he reminded her, a growl falling from his pink lips.

"I'm aware," Sabre said simply. She was allowed four private commissions a year. Just one per quarter. This was her last available spot. Thankfully, she had been leaving it open for just such an opportunity. It was the only reason she had been able to say yes to Abraxis.

"Well? Don't be coy. Who is your temporary employer and who are you supposed to kill?" Carlisle urged her to speak.

There was no point trying to lie to Carlisle. He had more

sources and spies than even Sabre herself, so she simply went with the truth; "The new king wants me to find out the mystery conspirator who is knocking his family members off the perch. It's kind of more mercenary work than assassination at this stage. But –"

"Did you say the King?" Carlisle breathed, a strange look of both fear and excitement on his face.

"Yes …" Sabre responded, warily this time. She had seen that look on the incubus's face a few times and it was never a good thing.

Carlisle rubbed his hands together, "This is good. This is really good. We can use this."

"This is a private gig. There is no *we*," Sabre swiftly responded.

The incubus moved fast, almost as fast as Sabre was able to, and grabbed her hair in a punishing grip within a second. "There will always be a *we*, my pretty little fallen angel. At least for the next ninety years," Carlisle amended, referring to her renewed contract.

All contracts lasted for one hundred years before they expired and needed to be renewed. Her original contract had been written in the blood from her veins, and signed in the blood from her arteries, binding her body and soul to Carlisle and the Blue Devil Den when she had been but eight years old. She knew Carlisle had been sweating the time when her original contract ended, no doubt worried about falling victim to the monster he had created with his own two hands. Because as long as she was under his employ, she could not physically harm him. To say the incubus had been pleasantly surprised when she said she wanted to renew her contract was a vast understatement. With bile in her throat and shaking hands, Sabre had signed her life away once more ten years ago. Unfortunately, the end game had not been upon her and she'd had no other choice.

It was times like these when she regretted it the most. Times when she wanted nothing more than to shove her fist into Carlisle's ribcage and rip out his heart, squeezing it so hard it exploded into pulp. Instead, Sabre kept her face bland, ensuring her homicidal thoughts stayed well hidden. "Whatever you say, Carlisle," she finally said, meeting his gaze.

"That's right. Whatever I say." He sniffed at her, his tongue coming out to lick a long line up her neck, coming dangerously close to forfeiting their contract.

Sabre held her revulsion inside. The man wanted her desperately – almost obsessively. It hadn't always been the case. Thankfully, Carlisle wasn't interested in children sexually. If the incubus had one thing going for him, it was that he wasn't a paedophile. Her original contract, having been signed when she was so young, had a 'no sexual contact or training clause' in it. Along with the freedom to take on four private clients a year, Sabre had also made sure that same special clause had been transferred to her new contract. It pissed Carlisle off to no end. He had lusted over her the second she turned twenty. Yet, here he was, almost ninety years later with a major case of blue balls. She could go to him willingly but he could not force her. Even his powerful incubus pheromones couldn't persuade her to sleep with him. He blamed it on the angelic low sex drive thing. But it wasn't about that at all. Sabre simply had standards.

Receiving no response, Carlisle grudgingly pulled back, letting go of her hair, "You will report back any and all findings to me. I have an … interested party who will pay handsomely for such information."

Sabre frowned, "You know someone who wants to protect the new king?"

Carlisle laughed, "Oh, my dear. Still so sweet and naïve after all these years. No, not protect. Destroy."

Before Sabre could question him any further, he swept from the room, slamming the door. Sabre spent the next few hours wondering who Carlisle could be referring to and exactly how much Carlisle knew. She also started plotting how she would get the information out of the incubus.

## CHAPTER FIVE

Brax's night had been largely sleepless. Something he had grown used to over the past year, but something he resented nonetheless. His eyes felt gritty and his skin too tight on his face as he stumbled into the bathroom. Looking into the mirror above the sink, he recoiled. "Ye, Gods," he muttered, shaking his head at his dishevelled appearance. How his hair managed to stand up that high, he had no idea. *And this is exactly why I like my hair shorn,* Brax thought to himself. Deciding that he couldn't be bothered with the clippers that morning and that dunking his head under the sink was simply not going to cut it, he moved to the large marble shower that took up nearly the entire length of his ensuite bathroom. The giant tub took up the other wall, leaving only minimal space for the double vanity and the toilet.

There were bigger and grander bathrooms attached to more luxurious suites in the palace, and Brax had his pick of all of them. But he had chosen his suite of rooms because it was the only part of the palace that had its own turret. Yep, his bedroom was like his own private little castle. As a child, he had begged and pleaded with his parents for the four-room suite. But it had been at the opposite end of the palace from the First Family's and he'd had to wait until reaching maturity to claim the magnificent space. It overlooked a private garden and Brax had spent many a morning sipping his coffee from the secure balcony.

The royal palace was a grand old building, situated in the heart of the main city, looking much like it did when his ancestor, Cerberus, had it built thousands of years ago. It had been updated over the years of course, but there was a certain comfort in the fact that the old building had housed generations of his family. *A family that is now all but gone …* Brax cursed the sudden reminder, punching a hole in the grey-veined marble wall. "Well, fuck," he muttered, knowing Draven would have something to say about the new hole.

His family had slowly been dwindling in numbers over the past fifty years; his father, uncles and first cousins were all gone. But it had been the deaths of his brothers in quick succession just a year ago that had flipped a switch inside of Brax, causing numerous holes in the wall and lots of destroyed priceless antiquities. He and his brothers had been as close as three people could possibly be, sharing a bond like no other. Born just minutes apart, they had been triplets with Mikhail being the oldest and Zagan being the youngest. Brax had come screaming into the world in second place – a fact he had always been thrilled with, for he had no desire to be a king. That had been Mikhail's deal, and a calling well suited to him. Zagan would have suited the lifestyle of King even less, Brax mused as he shut off the water. He was the cliché party boy of the royal family, always in the tabloids for one stupid stunt or another. Still, Brax felt as if there was a literal hole in his chest where his brother's lives should be. If Sabre couldn't find any new information, Brax didn't know what he was going to do.

But it wouldn't be pretty, because he was hanging on to the ledge with just his fingernails.

Stepping out of the shower, Brax didn't bother grabbing a towel, preferring to air dry. Standing naked in front of the mirror once more, he was relieved to see that the hot shower had achieved the desired result – both to his hair and his half-awake state. But that didn't stop him from almost tripping over the damn mutt spread across the threshold of his bedroom when he walked out of the bathroom. How he missed the huge three-hundred-kilogram beast he didn't know, but now he was cursing and limping as he tried to protect his sore toe from further abuse. The hell hound's hide looked a lot like leather and felt like it too. As a result, it was decidedly unpleasant to kick. Styx, apparently thinking his master was playing a game with him, jumped to his massive feet and began to woof, nearly rupturing Brax's eardrums.

"Shit! Styx, quiet," he yelled over the echoing noise. Styx immediately quieted, looking dejected and Brax sighed. "You're not in trouble, you big oaf." Brax patted the beast's head, tugging on his ears until he groaned in doggy ecstasy. Styx had been a gift from Draven and other than the angel himself, was Brax's favourite being in all of Purgatory. "Come on, let's get organised. We have an assassin to meet."

Thoughts of said assassin were the culprit for his night spent tossing and turning in his bed. For some reason, he couldn't get the deadly, black-haired beauty out of his head. She had been different than he thought she would be. *Somehow softer,* he thought, surprising himself. Yet the more he rolled it over in his mind, the truer it sounded. Sabre had put on a good show with that sharp tongue of hers, leather-clad body and arsenal of weapons. But her eyes spoke of a vulnerability and a warmth that had nothing to do with the warm tones of her irises. Brax wasn't stupid enough to think she was a good person by any means, but she surprised and intrigued him in ways that he hadn't counted on … making her doubly dangerous.

A knock on his door had him looking up only to find a frowning Draven in the doorway. "Why aren't you dressed? That horrid woman will be here soon and you're still standing around in naught but your skin."

Brax rolled his eyes but finished his journey over to his walk-in wardrobe. Donning a pair of black cargo pants and a dark green t-shirt, Brax considered himself done and he stepped back into the room. Draven was smooching with Styx – he loved the hell hound just as much as Brax did – but looked up as Brax stepped out. The automatic frown over his chosen attire made Brax smile. Draven would have preferred Brax to be wearing something more befitting his station like designer slacks and a button-up shirt. But Brax was a soldier to his core and the familiar clothing bred comfort. Something he was in dire need of these days.

"Do you think –"

"I'm not changing, Draven," Brax stated as he pulled on socks and his boots. "Something tells me Sabre isn't going to care what clothes I'm wearing."

"As long as you make sure to keep your clothes on whenever she is around, I suppose I don't care what you wear," Draven's blue gaze met Brax's levelly.

Brax felt like a kid caught with his hand in the cookie jar. Draven knew him better than anyone else in the universe. As his guardian, Draven was all things to him – other than a lover. He was a protector, a friend, confidant, a guide, and a weapon. He had been with Brax for so many years that the two of them could communicate with each other without even speaking. A simple look or raise of an eyebrow and Draven knew Brax wanted the twelve-inch sword with the wooden inlaid pommel rather than the engraved one. Most of the time, Brax liked their closeness and appreciated the angel's intuitiveness. But he thought there were some things in life that were better left private; like who he did and did not become erect for.

*Yeah, boners should definitely be a private thing,* Brax decided. Out loud he said; "Relax. I like my head exactly where it is. I have no intention of hopping into bed with a known murderer."

Draven harrumphed as he made his way out of the bedroom and through Brax's living room, Brax and Styx trailing along behind him like good boys. "See that you don't," Draven tossed over his shoulder.

They continued to make their way through the palace in silence, until stopping to comment on the weather once they made it outside into the gardens. Sabre had agreed to meet them there at nine. Glancing down at his military grade watch, Brax noted that it was one minute away from that time and Sabre still wasn't there. If she didn't show, Brax was going to –

"Oh my Gods!" came a shrill, female scream, "Is that a hell hound?"

Brax spun around to see Sabre standing inside the still locked entrance to the gardens. How she had managed to get in without the guards notifying him of her arrival, he didn't know. But that wasn't his biggest concern right then because Styx was off and racing before Brax could stop him, massive jaws open and saliva dripping off his three-inch fangs. Growls could be heard over the frantic beating of Brax's heart as his dog, literally from the depths of Hell, attacked Sabre. Brax wasn't sure who he feared for more; Sabre or his dog. Because he knew both were completely lethal and at that moment Styx no doubt believed the loud female to be a threat. Styx believed nearly everyone to be a threat – other than a small select few. Hell hounds were notoriously grumpy beasts and were not often kept as pets, but Brax wouldn't choose another beast for all the money in Purgatory.

Brax launched himself after his mangy mutt, sadly unable to keep up with the hound even with his preternatural speed. He really hoped Sabre didn't kill his beast in self-defence before he could stop her. Suddenly, Styx leapt, his weight and massive form tackling Sabre and obstructing her from view. A series of growls and yips followed as Styx appeared to eat the angel whole. A flutter of wings had Brax looking up to see Draven moving above him in swift flight. His guardian landed next to the struggling pair a heartbeat before Brax finally reached them. Fearing what he would see, he stopped cold when a strange sound reached his ears. Was that ... giggling?

"Hi, big boy! Aren't you beautiful? Aren't you just the cutest?"

Brax stared in shock, the sound of baby-talk freezing him to the ground. Styx was not in fact trying to eat Sabre; he was licking her and dancing around her in joy. As for Sabre, she wasn't wrestling with Styx in order to ward him off or injure him, she was patting every part of him she could reach and grinning like a maniac.

"Oh, you're a sweet boy, yes you are, yes you are." Styx – killer of hundreds – flopped onto his back, dark blue tongue hanging out of his mouth as Sabre – also killer of hundreds – proceeded to rub his tummy. "You like that? Do you? What a good boy. What a good puppy you are."

"What is happening right now?" Brax whispered from the corner of his mouth.

Draven shook his head slowly, blue eyes opening and closing experimentally a few times. "This is worse than my original fears. The assassin is even more dangerous than I believed," Draven finally murmured, slowly tucking his wings away.

Figuring it was safe to take his eyes off the shared adoration he was witnessing on the ground, Brax frowned at Draven, "Worse? What do you mean?"

Draven turned to Brax, eyes wide and alarmed; "Brax! She turned a hell hound into a puppy! She is clearly a devil-woman with magic too horrible to be spoken of."

Brax snorted a laugh before rolling his eyes over his friend's theatrical words. Draven had a real flare for the dramatic. Unfortunately, Brax knew Draven was actually being very serious and he had no doubt the angel was planning an exorcism or something in his head right at that moment.

"We cannot allow this to continue," Draven stated.

Brax wholeheartedly agreed, but not for the same reason. The inane baby-talk coming from Sabre's mouth was just plain embarrassing. Even as he continued to watch, Sabre laughed and pushed Styx away playfully. "No licking the face, big man. Your breath smells like carrion. Have you been eating dead things? Have you?" she asked, in that chirpy, high-pitch voice again – as if eating dead things was cute. "I bet you roll in dead things too, huh? You know, I play with dead things all the time as well. Yes, I do. Yes, I do."

"Sire, please," Draven pleaded from beside him. "There is only so much madness I can take."

Shaking his head, Brax stepped over to the pair of idiots on the ground. "Okay, Styx, enough." To his chagrin, Styx didn't move, simply closed his eyes in apparent bliss as Sabre rubbed his muzzle roughly.

"How did you get a hell hound?" Sabre finally looked up at him, dimples teasing her cheeks as she smiled. "He's beautiful."

Brax tried to tell himself that calling his hell-dog beautiful was not another thing to like about the assassin, but as he watched the happy grin on Styx's face, he knew he was lying. Styx had loved Mikhail and their father but had hated their mother and also Zagan. Styx liked the kitchen staff well enough and tolerated the gardeners but that was it. Other than Draven and Brax himself, Styx wanted to kill then eat – or eat and then kill as hell hounds tended to do – everyone. Brax cleared his throat, determining it was better to answer Sabre's question than to focus on her appeal. "He was a gift for my eighteenth birthday from Draven," Brax revealed.

Sabre's mouth twisted as if she had a bad taste in her mouth. "Really? Who knew the scarecrow could be so thoughtful."

Draven took an aggressive step forward but Brax put an arm out in front of him. "Do you think you two could pretend to get along – just until our business is concluded?"

Sabre shrugged, finally standing up and dusting herself off. "I can play nice if feather-brain can."

Draven growled but remained silent when Brax pointed a finger at Sabre, "That means no name-calling."

The assassin deflated before his very eyes, her upturned lips morphing into a pout of epic proportions. "Aww, Your Majesty, why you gotta hate like that?"

Brax fought the twitch of his lips with all of his might. Sabre had a wicked sense of humour and a quick wit. Two qualities he loved in a woman. There was nothing worse than a woman with no brain in her head who couldn't string together an independent thought if her life depended on it. Brax had met more than his fair share of pretty faces and empty minds. He knew to look beyond the outside and see the person within. The only problem with Sabre was that she was a double whammy; pretty and smart. Brax quickly ran his eyes over her leather-clad form, noting an array of weapons including a small, fold-up crossbow strapped to her thigh … and was that a handgun?

Although their world mirrored Earth almost exactly, they had of course evolved separately. Supernaturals, being stronger, faster and having longer lifespans, didn't require the assistance of vast weaponry as much as humans did. There were no weapons of mass destruction in Purgatory. And as far as he was aware, there were also none in Heaven or Hell either. Curiously, the need to devise such weapons seemed to be a solely human failing. The weapons that *were* present in Purgatory were much more primitive in nature and consisted mainly of swords, daggers, clubs, and arrows. Guns were typically not seen anywhere but they were accessible to those who could access the veil or even teleport to earth. He shouldn't really be surprised that Sabre had a gun. She no doubt had a huge number of weapons he wouldn't even know the names of.

"Is that a gun?" Draven demanded, spotting the firearm just seconds after Brax.

Sabre blinked guilelessly at Draven as she replied; "Why yes, Draven, it is. Good observation skills."

Draven's own eyes narrowed and he commanded, "You cannot have a gun in the King's presence."

"Why not? It's not like I'm going to shoot him with it," Sabre graciously pointed out. "Besides, I'm just as deadly with the other two dozen weapons I have concealed on my body."

Brax groaned and hung his head, he had a feeling it was going to be a really long fucking day.

## CHAPTER SIX

Sabre patted the great beast's head as it leaned heavily against her side. The hell hound was much bigger than any normal dog, with a reddish, leathery hide, a dark blue tongue, and really big, pointy teeth. He was also the size of a pony, with his back reaching her rib cage and his head able to rest on her shoulder. Sabre had no doubt Styx would be well and truly taller than her six feet when he stood on his back legs. He was a sweetie though, and she couldn't believe Brax was in possession of one. Hell hounds were extremely rare in Purgatory because they tended to like warmer, dryer climates. Not to mention that they were rather testy animals and weren't known to be trainable. In Hell, they pretty much did what they wanted, when they wanted. The fact that Brax was currently shaking his head, yellow eyes warm and filled with humour as they gazed at the hound, made the man rise in her estimation. Anyone who was patient and kind enough to love an animal like Styx must have a good heart.

Shaking off her gooey thoughts, Sabre gave Styx a playful

shove, "Okay, buddy. Off you go. The adults have some things to discuss."

Styx seemed to groan in annoyance, but he dutifully trotted away to settle and keep watch under the shade of a large tree. The private royal gardens of the palace really were a rare treasure and Sabre had indulged herself in a leisurely stroll or two in the past. It was always easy to get past the guards unnoticed, given she had knowledge of and access to several secret passageways. She was wise enough not to say so in present company though, and she decided to get on with business.

"I am here as requested," she began.

"Yes, you are," Brax agreed. "How exactly are you here? My guards didn't announce you."

Sabre merely shrugged, causing Brax to scowl and cross his arms over his chest. Her eyes greedily took in the way the movement stretched his shirt over his broad shoulders, and the way his biceps flexed. She wanted to lick him everywhere. Her eyes widened with the knowledge and she kept her mouth shut in order to guarantee her tongue stayed well away from Brax and his sinful body parts.

"Not going to tell me how you got in?" Brax challenged.

"No. But I'll tell you what … I'll compromise. Ask me another time. Sometime in the future after I've decided whether I like you or not, and therefore want to be honest with you. In the meantime," Sabre rushed on to say, curbing any and all rebuttals, "I'm here for more information."

"What kind of information?" Draven, the ever-present, immediately asked. He was already eyeing her suspiciously.

Sabre huffed in annoyance, "Does he have to be here?"

"Yes."

"Yes." Draven and Brax responded simultaneously.

Sabre mock-pouted, "But he's so ugly."

Draven gasped in outrage and she was gratified to see Brax covering a laugh with a fake cough. Of all the things Sabre could say to the stuffy angel, she knew that would have to be top of the list to get a reaction. Draven was incredibly beautiful, from the top of his golden head – where she could almost see his fucking sparkling halo – to the bottom of his leather loafers. The angel was classically handsome and he no doubt knew it. Sabre also knew that he was likely quite vain, as most angels tended to be, and any slight against his appearance would be a massive insult.

Predictably, Draven ran his hands through his perfectly styled locks, arguing; "I am not ugly."

Sabre pasted a look of disgust on her face, taunting him further, "You are from where I'm standing. Which is downwind by the way," she pointed out, helpfully.

Draven's head snapped back, "Are you now suggesting I *smell*?"

Sabre opened her mouth to reply only to be interrupted by Brax, who growled low in his throat; "Would you children quit it? Am I going to have to separate you two?"

"Yes, please," Sabre promptly responded, smiling widely at the king.

"Sabre ..."

Brax sounded aggrieved, frustrated and tired. All things Sabre couldn't blame him for. She kind of had that effect on people. Cutting him some slack, she decided to stop fucking with Draven and get on with the job. "Sorry," *she was so not sorry,* "I'll behave," *for now,* "I promise," *not really.* "The sooner you answer my questions, the sooner I can get out of your hair." At least that final part was true.

*And what great hair you have,* Sabre mused, silently. It was rakishly long and decidedly wild-looking. She bet he hated it. But to her it looked appealing ... and like something to hang on to.

Thankfully, Brax chose that moment to speak, derailing her treacherous thoughts.

"What do you want to know?"

Breathing in deep, Sabre consciously shifted the part of her that hunted and killed for a living to the forefront, "As much as you can tell me about the death of your brothers, father and uncles." Brax winced, and though Sabre felt bad for the demon, she knew he could have some important information for her. "Start with the latest deaths; Zagan and Mikhail."

"I ..." Brax looked a little helplessly at Draven, who stepped forward and placed a hand on his arm.

"Zagan was killed while out nightclubbing about fourteen months ago. There were dozens of witnesses yet none at all. Nobody at the club saw who or what killed Z and his guardian angel – who of course had been with him at the time. His angel, Eli, was killed first – beheaded – followed by Zagan mere seconds later. He was doused in Hell fire and reduced to ashes in seconds," Draven explained, voice carefully even.

Sabre nodded thoughtfully, "I read about it of course. But I must admit, I thought it was the media catastrophising and dramatising the facts."

"Unfortunately not," Draven intoned.

"How could there be no witnesses? If a prince was there, I bet the place was packed," Sabre said, wheels turning.

"It was indeed. But everyone reports hearing the screams and seeing the bodies – and the flames – but nothing else. So many people were fleeing that the killer just melted into the crowd," Draven stated.

Sabre doubted that. If it was an assassin, they would have stayed to watch until Zagan was nothing but ashes. And a beheading? That was a messy business. Although, Sabre acknowledged that it was a very expedient way to kill an angel. With their speed, strength and rapid healing abilities, not much could kill their kind. Not to mention that nearly all angels created in Heaven – as all guardians were – were warriors by default and were extremely gifted fighters.

There were just as many types of angels as there were demons. Each were born or created with different abilities and each with their own purpose in life. Most angels were born in Purgatory as descendants of the original, powerful beings. That wasn't to say that born angels were in any way diluted or weak. They still held great strength and powers and were born sharing the abilities of their predecessors by blood – inheriting whatever power and purpose was tasked to the angel of their line. However, unlike demons and other supernatural creatures in Purgatory, there were still some angels who *were* created in Heaven. Such angels were fashioned by the Gods themselves with a specific purpose and were tasked with a higher calling. There weren't many around these days but the few that were, held great power. The guardians of the royal line were always such angels. So, to get past not just one guardian to kill Zagan, but also Mikhail's, their father's and their uncles' …? The chances of so many powerful angels being overcome was a statistical anomaly.

Sabre decided to continue the new avenue of thought, asking; "What about Mikhail's guardian? Was that angel killed before him as well?"

Brax made a strange noise in the back of his throat and scrubbed a hand over his face, looking dejected. "You've asked the one question I can't answer reliably. Mikhail … well, he didn't have a guardian angel."

Sabre shot him a look of disbelief, "Excuse me? What do you mean, he didn't have one? Every one of you royal demons gets a guardian angel, express delivered from the Gods themselves."

"Yeah, well, Mikhail didn't." Brax's response was flat, leaving no room for argument.

Sabre paused, taking in the serious countenances of both Abraxis and Draven, "How is that possible?"

Brax stuffed his hands into his pockets and rocked back on his heels, "We don't really know. Father and Mikhail had theories of course. But nothing they could prove. Like, maybe his angel was killed before they could find each other –"

"If that was the case, then another angel would simply be created to replace them. That's how it works," Sabre interjected.

"Right …" Brax acknowledged slowly. "How do you seem to know so much about guardian angels and the royal family anyway?"

Sabre kept her face carefully blank and ignored the looks of suspicion and curiosity on the faces of Draven and Brax. "I'm an assassin. It's my job to know stuff. And what I don't know, I find out. Isn't that why you hired me?"

"You're prevaricating," Brax stated. "But I'm going to let it slide. The other theory was that Mikhail just hadn't met his angel yet. Guardians are delivered to Purgatory only when they are going to be of most use. Angels no more know who their charge is than we as demons know who our angel is. But there is a recognition – a *knowing* – when we finally meet," Brax revealed. "Every demon in my family has met their angels at different ages. Although, Mikhail was the oldest by far. He was over one hundred when he was killed and still no angel. Mikhail never really seemed bothered by it – which I always found odd. Anyway, it's a moot point now. My brother is dead and if he ever had a guardian to begin with, he sure as shit doesn't now."

Sabre felt the line of questioning was pissing Brax off, so she quickly moved on, "Okay. No guardian angel. Whatever. Moving on; witnesses?" Sabre prompted, "Who found the body?"

"I did," Brax's response was cool and flat but the fire in his eyes was bright hot. "And the vision of seeing my older brother, so strong and noble and wise, bleeding out from a single cross bolt to the heart, still gives me nightmares a year later. How is any of this helping?!"

*Yep, definitely pissed,* Sabre thought. "I'm sorry. I know this is hard, but I need as many details as I can. Zagan and his angel killed in public, Mikhail killed in the palace with no angel and you found the body, your two uncles and father were killed over a period of about a decade – all within the palace walls. Correct?" Sabre recapped.

"That's right. No witnesses. Their angels all died protecting them. Father was killed by poison, Uncle Yuri's head was beaten in, and Uncle Sage was found drowned in his bathroom," Brax listed.

Sabre blew out a frustrated breath. Other than Mikhail not having a guardian, there was no new information there at all. Sabre already knew all of it. She had no idea where to start considering she had already pursued a lot of fruitless leads in the past. Not that she could tell the King that. She had five deaths, spread over fifty years and the only thing that linked them was the fact that they were royals. Thinking on her toes, she suddenly asked; "And you're sure it's the same person behind all these deaths?"

"You think the deaths are unrelated?" Draven sounded incredulous.

"Well, no," Sabre allowed. "But the deaths of your uncles and father were a whole generation before you. That is some long-term goal setting from our murderous villain. It makes me question their intent."

"The demise of the line of Cerberus isn't enough?" Brax asked, dryly.

Sabre shrugged, "Not really, no. I mean, to what end? You think they want to take over or something? Who inherits the throne if you die?" she turned to Brax.

"There are still quite a number of cousins about the place," Draven admitted, when Brax remained silent. "They are also eligible for the throne in the case of emergencies even though they are not in direct succession. But the very nature of how the descendants breed, ensures there are many others about with Cerberus blood in their veins."

"Right. The whole triplet thing," Sabre muttered. It was a freaky fact of nature that the ruling couple always produced triplet heirs. Male triplet heirs as a matter of fact, and the oldest male was the one to ascend to the throne. After the birth of a new set of triplets, that generation became the only ones able to claim the throne. So, even though Sabre bet there were dozens of second and third cousins, as well as a few great uncles around, they weren't in direct succession. Still, it wouldn't hurt to talk to a few of them, Sabre mused. As well as tug on the angel thread. Then there was Carlisle's offhanded comment the night before.

*Okay, maybe I have a little more to go on than I'd originally thought.* Feeling a surge of energy, Sabre asked one last question that had been bothering her, "What about your mother? Didn't she die just before your first uncle was killed?" Sabre didn't know that much about the former Queen. Only that she had been unwell for a long time and had retired from public life years before her death.

Brax immediately shook his head, "I can say with certainty that mother's death had nothing to do with it. She had a wasting disease that affected the females of her line – after giving birth. She and father knew about the risks and father was willing to abdicate the throne for her and stay childless. But mother pushed the issue. She wanted children she said."

Draven shifted minutely, but Sabre zeroed in on the telling movement, "Draven? You have something to add?"

Draven looked toward Brax who looked resigned as he nodded his head, giving permission for whatever Draven was going to say. "I don't like to speak ill of the dead, but I believe it was more a case of wanting to be the Queen than wanting to have children."

*Interesting,* Sabre thought. But Eronia wasn't the first person wanting to marry into a royal family for the prestige and power. "If she was willing to risk her life to have children and secure her position as Queen, then I'd say she was pretty dedicated to the cause." She looked at Brax, "She wasn't a good mother?" Sabre didn't really know why she asked that. It wasn't pertinent to her task. But she still held her breath, awaiting his answer as if it was important to her. Sabre herself had no recollection of experiencing a mother of any kind, and was a firm believer in the human adage, *'you can't miss what you've never had',* but for some reason thinking of a small yellow-eyed boy crying for a mother who didn't want him made Sabre see red.

"She wasn't a *bad* mother per say. Just a little … disinterested. At least, she was to Mikhail and me. Now Z, she adored Z. Her baby was definitely her favourite and she spoiled him half rotten – as his playboy behaviour showed. Z really went off the rails when she died. It took months for him to settle back down. Actually, it was the death of Uncle Yuri that seemed to snap him back into focus."

Sabre pursed her lips, refraining from saying anything. Brax was right and the death of the Queen over fifty years ago was unrelated. Needing time and space to process and develop a way forward, Sabre was about to say her goodbyes when Brax's pocket began to sing a popular Euro-trash pop song. Sabre eyed the demon in horror, "What the fuck is that?!"

Brax glared at her, "Don't pretend you don't like this song! It's the best!"

"If by the best you mean it makes me want to stab sharpened pencils in my ears, then yes. It's the best."

Abraxis merely rolled his eyes at her dry words, yanking his phone out of his pocket in apparent annoyance. He then promptly swore when he looked at the display. "Shit! It's the alarm from my calendar. Draven, we had that appointment with Hollis scheduled for an hour ago. Can you go soothe his ruffled feathers and go over his plans for the new building site?"

"Me? Why me?" Draven looked surprised, squinting at his liege.

"Because you and he speak the same language. You're both angels. Come on, Draven. You know Hollis doesn't like me at the best of times. And now that we've kept him waiting? I'm just not in the mood for his passive aggressive bullshit. I feel like I've been put through the wringer here, man. I'm on a hair-trigger and could very well end up punching Hollis in the face. I'm not finished with Sabre yet."

Sabre perked up at that, *he's not?*

Draven's posture softened and stepped close to Brax, laying a comforting hand on his arm, "I know you hate talking about all of this. But if it's all the same to you, I think I'll stay with you, Sir."

Sabre grinned at the angel, fiddling with the thigh holster and stroking the gun strapped to her waist, "Don't worry, there's no silencer. If I choose to shoot him, you'll hear it and you can come running to save the day like a good little angel."

"You are so annoying!" Draven suddenly yelled.

"Yeah? Well, so's your face!" Sabre was quick to shoot back.

"Why you –"

"Draven! Just go. Please. Or have you forgotten I have eighty years of fighting experience under my belt? I can take care of myself. I also happen to be the King," Brax said, drolly.

Draven looked at him in shock for a few seconds, and much to Sabre's surprise, dipped his head in a bow before striding off without saying another word.

"What was that all about?" she asked Brax, genuinely curious. Abraxis had said he wasn't finished with her yet and she was just silly enough to want to prolong their contact as well.

## CHAPTER SEVEN

Brax's sigh in response to Sabre's question was loud and long, causing Styx to stand up and pad over from where he had been chewing on a huge bone in the shade, "I surprised him is all. That's the first time I have called myself the King."

Sabre reeled back, "Say what now? You've been in charge for over a year."

"Yeah, well. I don't want to be. It was never supposed to be me," he said, the feelings of resentment and inadequacy that were always close to the surface began to quickly rise once more.

"Boo hoo, poor little princeling," Sabre mocked. She then knelt on the ground and began to stroke Styx's muzzle again – the most sensitive place on the hell hound's body. "Poor, poor daddy, isn't that right? Forced into a duty he wasn't born for and doesn't want." Sabre raised surprisingly serious eyes to his and dropped the mocking tone. "I might have an idea how that feels."

Brax stilled, mouth opening a little as he realised he and the fallen angel had more in common than he thought was possible.

In fact, Sabre might just be the one person in all of Purgatory who could understand his feelings. Considering her for a moment – and wondering if he was really going to have a D & M with a cold-blooded killer – he finally shrugged. *Why the hell not?*

Sitting down and folding his legs underneath him, he simply stared at Sabre until she slowly turned her head, the warm plum of her eyes shining brightly in the early morning sun and reminding him once again of his favourite fruit. *Forbidden fruit,* he reminded himself.

"Are we having a picnic?" Sabre asked, archly.

He shrugged, "Just thought we could chat some more."

"Chat?" Sabre looked positively horrified by the notion. "I don't chat."

"You do today," he responded cheerfully, wilfully ignoring her vicious scowl.

"If it's all the same to you, I think I'll just go and mutilate someone …"

Brax casually reached up and hooked a finger through her belt loops, dragging her back down again. "Sit. Mutilation can wait." Sabre scowled but didn't try to shoot him and he took it as a win. "What kind of king do you think I am? Do you think I'm a shitty one?" he asked in a rush, obviously surprising the hell out of the assassin.

"You want honesty? Or do you want me to stroke your royal arse like everyone else does?" Sabre finally said, raising a dark brow in challenge.

*Arse! Stroke the arse!* Brax promptly yelled within his own head. Keeping his face appropriately blank however, he responded blandly, "Let's go with honesty."

"Yes, you are a bit of a shitty king at the moment," Sabre stated.

"Wow. Brutal. I don't think I want this much honesty," he made to rise only to be yanked back down by Sabre.

"Don't be a baby," she chided. "Do you want to know why?"

Brax shook his head, "No. definitely not. I don't know why I thought this was a good idea," he grumbled, more to himself than to Sabre.

"Too bad. You asked for it," Sabre was unsympathetic.

"Fine. Hit me with it. It's not like I have a fragile ego or anything." Sabre seemed to think that was amusing if her twitching lips were anything to go by.

"Riiight," she drew the word out. "*All* men have fragile egos. But that's beside the point," she rushed on, allowing him nothing more than a glower. "You are currently a shitty king because your thirst for vengeance overrides your need for justice. Your hate, your grief, your pain – they are your priority. Not your people. A good king always puts his people first. There is no room for selfish endeavours."

"I ..." Brax couldn't form words if his life depended on it. Sabre had just successfully stripped him bare to his bones. Leaving him feeling raw and exposed ... more than a little ashamed. With a few short sentences, Sabre had achieved more than what anyone else had in a whole year.

"Now, if you had asked me what type of *man* I think you are ... I would have said ..." Sabre paused, her eyes running over his face and a thoughtful expression softening her features, giving them a friendly and decidedly feminine cast. "I would have said a good one. You know why?"

Brax swallowed, ducking his head, beyond grateful and humbled that the woman in front of him believed he was a good man. Why that was so, he had no idea. Brax remained silent, both wanting and dreading the answer to her question. Taking pity on him and not calling him out on his silence, Sabre continued on;

"Because only a good man would bother to ask the question in the first place."

Brax snapped his head back up at her simple statement, embarrassed to feel a blush heating his cheeks. The woman certainly had a way with words. *And a power,* he added. Sabre was giving off a distinctly righteous vibe, common with all angels, but one Brax hadn't thought to associate with her before then. And her words rang with a subtle hint of power, making the space around them feel intimate. Or perhaps that was just the atmosphere the two of them created together … Brax quickly stamped out the whimsical thoughts, clearing his throat; "I'm not sure if I should thank you or not," he admitted.

Sabre snorted, stretching her legs out in front of her and nudging a snoozing Styx with her toe. "Don't thank me, Brax. You can thank me when I hand over your family's killer."

"You still think I should do that? Hire you?" Brax asked, shocked.

Sabre narrowed her eyes, giving him a look that said he was daft. "You already hired me," she pointed out. "And why wouldn't I want you to do that?"

"Because you just said my need for vengeance made me a crap king!" Brax practically shouted.

"And so it does," Sabre acknowledged. "But it doesn't make you wrong. You're barking up the wrong tree if you think I'm going to tell you *not* to kill someone. Kill someone. Kill lots of someones! Killing is very cathartic."

Brax laughed over her exuberance, feeling his tense muscles relax, "Of course you think that way."

Sabre looked confused, cocking her head, "Is there another way to think?"

Brax snorted, "Yeah. Only like, a lot of other ways."

"Huh."

Brax shook his head, his smile staying on his face as he asked, "So ... is it my turn to tell you what I think of you?"

"Absolutely not! I'm not interested in what you think of me. I couldn't care less," was Sabre's immediate response, seemingly horrified.

Brax eyed her knowingly, "Oh, really? I think you're rather quick to protest there. I think –" His next words were muffled thanks to the hand Sabre had slapped over his mouth. The palm was predictably calloused as all working hands tended to be, but it was also warm and felt smaller than he had assumed it would be. Sabre came across as larger than life and gave off a superwoman vibe. But her murderous hands were surprisingly ... delicate. He moved his mouth a little when she appeared frozen in place, his lips lightly brushing her palm in a soft caress. Sabre shivered, goosebumps rising to the surface of the skin on her arms, and Brax watched the phenomenon, beyond intrigued.

"Shit! Sorry!" Sabre quickly removed her hand and wiped it on her pants.

An awkward silence descended and Brax struggled to think of a way to get the ease between them back. He kind of liked it. He cleared his throat, "So you think I should continue on this path? And what about staying King? Draven was correct when he said there are more than a few cousins about who are legally able to take the throne ..."

"You're thinking of abdicating?!" Sabre sounded genuinely upset.

"I've considered it," Brax admitted. "I mean, this was never supposed to be me! I was never supposed to be a king. Yes, I was the second born son, but my father was the oldest of his siblings. There were two others in line to the throne just in that generation. Then there was Mikhail. He wasn't just groomed from birth to be the next king – he was truly made for it. You never had the privilege of meeting him, but trust me, if ever there was a descendant of Cerberus worthy for the Crown, it was Mikhail." A look he couldn't recognise flashed across Sabre's face at the mention of Mikhail's name but it was gone before he could process what it was. "Like you said, I'm doing a piss-poor job, so –"

"Oh, fuck no! You are not going to throw that back in my face in order to justify your desire to shirk your duty. Does the blood of Cerberus run in your veins? Are you or are you not your father's son? Stop whining and get on with the job!"

And just like that, all the warm-fuzzies of moments ago evaporated, "How dare you speak to me like that!" he shouted.

"Oh, I dare. I dare a lot. You think you're the only one walking a path they weren't born to? You think you're the only one who has had to sacrifice to do their job? I'm a fucking angel! An *angel*! Born of the Heavens and tasked with good deeds and Grace and all that shit. But here I am – the best assassin and mercenary for hire in all of Purgatory. Do you hear me complaining?" Sabre poked him hard in the chest with her pointer finger, "Well, do you?"

Brax opened and closed his mouth silently a few times like a moron before he finally found his voice, "Actually, yes. It does sound like you're complaining. Rather vocally, in fact." Sabre narrowed her eyes dangerously and Brax quickly held up his hands, "Look, I'm sorry, okay? That escalated quickly. I guess I'm still a little touchy."

Sabre remained stiff for a few moments before letting out a breath and slumping a little, "What did I say about men and their fragile egos? That's a rhetorical question, Brax," she quickly tacked on. "Look … shit happens."

"Shit happens?" Brax laughed, but he couldn't say if it was in amusement or incredulity.

Sabre raised her chin, looking determined, "That's right; shit happens. You need to get over it. This may not have been the life I would have chosen, but it's *my* life. All mine. The same way yours belongs to you. It's up to me to make sure I do the best with it as I possibly can. It's up to me to make sure I don't waste it. The same applies to you."

Brax eyed her askance, "You really think killing people for money is doing the best you can?" Sabre's animated face went blank in an instant and Brax fought off a shiver from the abrupt change. Sabre really was a killer and he'd do well to remember that.

"Like I said; we all do the best with what we've been given. I've been given a whole bunch of fucked up shit. It's pretty hard to turn shit to rainbows. But every time I shank a bitch, I feel a little closer to that pot of gold, you know?" Sabre said, giving her ear an idle scratch.

*Annnd, I'm back to liking her again.* Brax was beginning to get whiplash from his flipflopping emotions. He liked her; he didn't. He respected her; he feared her. He admired her; he was ashamed of her. The list went on and on and he wondered what side of the coin he would finally settle on. Although, if he threw in his attraction to that smokin' hot body of hers, he figured the side of like and respect and admiration was going to win.

## CHAPTER EIGHT

Angels truly were a magnificent breed, Abraxis mused, watching as Sabre seemed content to wait out his silence and pat his great big stupid dog. He sometimes found it hard to believe that his kind – descendants from the first supernatural creature to crawl out of hell – were blessed with the Grace of the Heavens to watch over them and keep them safe. Cerberus had been the original gatekeeper of the veil between worlds. He had been a demon, a beast, and a man combined as one, and as the supernatural creatures began to evolve parallel with – yet vastly different to humans – Cerberus had decided to create a world just for beings like him. Thus, Purgatory sprang from the depths of Hell, whilst Earth was given life from the Heavens. It was why his lineage was so revered. He was a direct link back to their original creator and why – he assumed – his family was gifted with powerful angels created by the Gods.

Although, with practically only himself left, and all of his family's guardians falling with their charges, he couldn't help but wonder what was happening to all the pure blood angels. He knew

Draven wasn't the last heavenly angel left in all of Purgatory, but it must be close. He was certainly the last healer. Because his magic allowed him to heal almost any wound – even those that should be terminal – it meant he was regarded as one of the most powerful angels. That wasn't why Brax was proud to have Draven as his own though. No, first and foremost, Draven was his family. Although he must admit, Draven being a healer suited Brax perfectly. Despite his new title, he was a soldier and a General in the army. Having a loyal friend who could heal his brothers in arms was priceless. There were also the times when Brax had been poisoned or became ill. Yes – even a demon descended from the King of Hell Hounds could get the flu. And there was the other handy part of his abilities – the whole empathy and reading minds thing. All in all, despite his slightly uppity demeanour, Draven was pretty kickarse.

There were other angels created and born that had just as unique skill sets – as well as wing colours. Angels really did have the coolest powers. There were angels that could teleport. Angels that could open portals between the realms. Angels that were psychic and ones that could control the weather. Once upon a time, there were even angels who could bring back the dead. Those angels were created with the highest purpose, possessing wings the colour of rubies and were dubbed resurrection angels. Brax's great grandfather many times over – the very first King of Purgatory and Cerberus's first-born son was rumoured to have had a resurrection angel as his guardian. But they had never been seen since.

Glancing at the spunky, fallen angel beside him, he couldn't help but be curious about what her wing colour had been when she was born. Unfortunately, he had the feeling such a question would not just be unwelcome, but also lead to possible blood loss. Still, for some inexplicable reason, he was enjoying himself and felt more relaxed than he had in recent memory. "You're right about one thing," he confessed.

Sabre looked at him, "Just one?"

Brax's lips twitched, "Yeah. Just one. I *am* my father's son. And he would be damn disappointed in me if he could see me now. He was a remarkable man and a great king."

Sabre was silent for a moment, before looking at him from the corner of her eye, "I met him once," she then divulged.

That had him sitting up straighter, "What? Who? My father?"

"Yes."

"How?" Brax was beyond shocked.

"I was in the palace on an errand …" Sabre began.

"An errand. Yeah, right. You were there to assassinate someone," Brax interjected.

Sabre simply shrugged, not rising to the bait. "Whatever. Maliq was a nice guy," she offered.

"He was," Brax agreed quietly. "Wait … you spoke with him?"

Sabre nodded her head just once, still not looking at him fully, "I did. Briefly."

"Why didn't he arrest you? He had to have known who you are. Everyone knows about the angel assassin – even if it is mostly fairy tales," Brax allowed.

"Your father was fair and shrewder than he was given credit for. Maybe he saw something in me that nobody else could," Sabre said, voice soft.

"He gave you a chance." Brax made it a statement rather than a question, knowing it to be true. It was just like his father – trying to save everyone. Trying to help the helpless.

"He did," Sabre confirmed. "And I ran with it."

"Right," Brax huffed. "Ran with it all the way back to your assassin den." When Sabre didn't say anything, he decided to forge ahead and gather some more intel that *wasn't* fairy tale. "Did you meet your two partners through your assassinating?"

Sabre scrunched her nose up in surprised confusion, a cute look on her, before cocking her head to the side. "Partners? Who – oh, you mean Jinx and Gage. They are *not* my partners. I work alone. Always. Gage helps me out with somewhere to beat out my frustrations and I help Jinx out with a little self-defence. That's it."

Brax really thought she was protesting too much, but he let it slide. "What is the guy, anyway? I know the girl is a weretiger …"

"If you're so smart, you can figure Gage out yourself. And yes, Jinx is a weretiger – white Bengal shifter to be exact. They are both also none of your business," Sabre pointed out, looking like a momma bear protecting her cubs.

"I beg to differ. You work for me now. Anyone associated with you is a potential risk to me and mine." He didn't know why he continued to push her. But for some reason, he wanted as much information about Sabre as he could get.

Sabre eyed him in silence a moment, before asking, "Why so much interest in my sidekicks?"

"The interest isn't so much in your sidekicks as it is in you," Brax admitted, startling himself with his honesty almost as much as he apparently startled Sabre. Her mouth parted in a small 'o' and her eyes widened, even as she appeared to hold her breath. Then something truly delightful occurred. Sabre blushed. Her creamy skin turned to peach across her high cheekbones before deepening even further into rose. The effect was one of innocent beauty and Brax found himself transfixed, unable to look away.

"You're staring," Sabre accused, ducking her head. "Stop it."

"I can't seem to help myself," Brax admitted.

"Why? You know what? Don't answer that. You want to know about Jinx? I'll tell you," she quickly said.

Brax smirked, apparently she was willing to throw her pal under the bus in order to get the focus off her – and her rosy cheeks. Brax thought it was endearing as hell.

"I found Jinx five years ago in hell – not literal Hell – but a close second. She was a collared slave to a sex demon who used to share her around with his buddies. I slaughtered them and decided to keep her," Sabre ended her blunt explanation with a shrug.

"What?! Five years ago? But she would have been a child! Hell, she's still a child now!" Brax exclaimed, furious.

"I know," Sabre's voice turned flat and cold. "Hence, the slaughtering."

Brax shook his head, the depravity of some people knew no bounds. And it had nothing to do with whether they were demons, vampires, elves or humans. Wickedness and a lack of conscience crossed all races and species. Even angels. The corrupted woman sitting in front of him was proof of that. And for that reason, Sabre really should have been the last person to 'keep' a traumatised girl. "Let me get this straight, you rescued a young teen from a harem-slash-brothel where she was being held against her will by a filthy paedophile, and you promptly made her your protégé?" He remembered what she said about teaching Jinx self-defence. No doubt that was her way of saying 'training her to kill people for money'.

Sabre cocked her head, idly scratching her arm, "I hear the question in your tone but don't really understand it."

"You decided to turn an innocent young girl who had been the victim of a horrendous crime into a criminal and a murderer?" Brax questioned further, feeling more agitated by the minute.

"Firstly, Jinx is not now, nor has she ever been, a victim. Jinx is a survivor. Secondly, Jinx is *not* a criminal," Sabre's growl gave Brax's a run for its money.

Brax scoffed, "You just said you were training her! She seemed like a nice girl – if a little mouthy. Do you really want her to end up like you?"

Sabre's wine-coloured eyes narrowed and she stood up slowly, never taking her eyes off Brax. "You're starting to piss me off, Abraxis. This is why I don't chat with people. I always end up wanting to garrotte them. Jinx is nothing like me," she stated.

Brax stood up as well, slowly as to not cause the deadly, pissed off woman alarm. The last thing he wanted was to be garrotted. Still, he was alpha enough – and stubborn enough – to keep pushing his point. Thinking back to the previous evening, he thought of the lovely young werecreature in question. The white-and-black-haired teen – which now made a lot more sense knowing she was a white tiger shifter – had continued eyeing him and Draven from her position at the bar. Every time he looked back, she had been cleaning under her fingernails with one of the wickedest blades he had ever seen. When he and Draven rose to leave, Jinx, obviously having noticed his regard, gave him a jaunty wave with said blade, flashing a pointy canine for good measure. He regarded Sabre once more; "Uh huh. Yep. Sure. She's nothing like you at all. I bet she uses that knife I saw of hers to floss her teeth."

The assassin thawed a little, regarding him for a moment before surprising him with a question from left field; "What would you have done?"

"Excuse me?" Brax asked, confused by the sudden shift.

"What would you have done if you had found an innocent young girl, barely on the cusp of adulthood, beautiful and broken in one of the worst cesspools of humanity?"

"Notified the authorities. Gotten her help," was Brax's immediate reply.

Sabre nodded, absently patting Styx again who was once more leaning against her side like an overgrown golden Labrador. "Right. Help like killing her tormenters in front of her so she knew she would never be touched by their filthy hands again? Or perhaps teaching her how to defend herself so she no longer felt weak or powerless or like a victim? Perhaps educating her so she could be a confident, capable woman, so that she knew without a shadow of a doubt that she could slay her own demons in the future? Is that the kind of help you mean?"

Brax opened and closed his mouth a few times. Well, fuck, the fallen angel certainly had him there. There was no reply worthy, so he simply moved on; "What about her parents?"

"Her parents were the ones who sold her to that scum in the first place. Hype addicts," was Sabre's bland answer.

"I'm guessing they are no longer addicts?" Brax inquired, knowing it was because they were most likely no longer breathing rather than having cleaned up their acts.

"They met a slow and messy demise. Them …" she bent down to pick up Styx's bone and threw it for him to fetch before turning back to Brax, "… I did for free."

They stood in awkward silence for a few seconds before Brax cleared his throat. He had no idea what he was going to say. His mind was reeling with all his discoveries from their little chat. From Sabre's blunt assessment of life and its journeys, to the realisation that she had more depth than anyone he had ever encountered before. She was also fiercely protective and loyal. And righteous, he added, a trait that was a pre-requisite for any angel but one that he thought would be absent in the assassin. *If she's this awesome when doing evil, imagine how magnificent she would be if she used her powers for good?* Brax marvelled silently, staring at Sabre's face like she was the second-coming.

"Did you just say something was awesome?"

Sabre's confused voice broke into his reverie. *Fuck! Was I talking out loud?* "Huh? No! You must be hearing things."

Sabre eyed him warily, as if he were an escapee from an insane asylum. Brax couldn't blame her. His thoughts were certainly crazy. It was one thing to find the sexy woman attractive. But to find her mind just as enticing? That way madness lay.

"You know what? I don't even care. I'm outta here, Your Majesty. Off to find who has been murdering your family and stuff, you know?" Sabre turned and was almost out of sight before she abruptly turned back around, "But good chat!"

"Wait!" he yelled, not wanting her to have the last word. "I want you to take Draven with you when you make some of your rounds," he yelled after Sabre's rapidly retreating form. Her snort of derision could still be heard easily though, as well as her vocal response. She didn't stop or bother to turn back around as she screamed her reply; "Fuck no! No douches allowed."

Brax grinned, feeling somehow lighter than he had in months. Shaking his head over the absurdity of a murderous angel making him feel better about himself, the kingdom, and his grief, he didn't notice his guardian's return.

"Wipe that stupid smile off your face, my boy," Draven said, right before he slapped Brax up the back of the head. "You look like a love-sick fool."

Brax played his part, scoffing scornfully in response as if that was the last thing in all the realms that he was. But inside, where his heart was beating a frantic rhythm against his ribs, he wasn't so sure.

## CHAPTER NINE

The first seventy-two hours had predictably yielded sweet fuck-all. Sabre had spent her days – and nights – trolling the seedy underbelly of Purgatory and hassling her contacts in an effort to find some new leads. Unsurprisingly, she had discovered nothing new to further her cause. She had a trusted associate chasing up the whole dead angels angle but knew it would take time to yield any results in that direction. That was one area she couldn't look into personally because she wasn't exactly welcome in angelic circles. To say that she was *persona non grata* was a vast understatement. The only reason those stuck-up, feathered do-gooders didn't lock her up was because she had never hurt any of their kind. There were some lines even she wouldn't cross. Although, for Draven, she was sorely tempted.

She *had* made some subtle inquiries in the other directions though and had questioned her fellow assassins and mercenaries at the Blue Devil – garnering herself a few more enemies in the process. Sabre snorted into the beer she was currently drinking, *like I give a flying fuck*. There were two other assassin dens in

Purgatory but neither were close enough for her to go in person. Not unless she wanted to cash in some chips with a teleporter at least. It might well come to that and if it did, she figured she'd only get a one-way ticket and she would need at least a week or even more away. She didn't want to leave Jinx and Gage alone for that long now that she was stirring up trouble. The pair may not be her partners but there were supernaturals around who knew of their association. Knew, and currently respected, because they were more than aware of what Sabre would do to them if Jinx or Gage were touched in any way.

Her phone dinged and Sabre quickly snatched it up, assuring herself the sigh of disappointment to leave her lips was due to the message's content and not because it wasn't from a certain yellow-eyed demon. The message was from Hound – her angel investigator and simply read: *sweet FA*. "Great, sweet fuck-all," she murmured.

Jinx's sensitive ears picked up her muttered words and she raised a dark brow, "Is that from Hound? How is the sexy beast?"

Sabre smiled, shaking her head. Jinx had made no secret of the fact that she found the much older demon attractive and she wanted nothing more than to use him as her own personal scratching post. Hound was suitably horrified by the attention and had been dodging Jinx's wandering hands for two years. Of course, now that Jinx was nineteen and had reached the age of maturity more than eighteen months ago, Sabre and Gage had bets on how much longer the scruffy demon rebel could hide for. *If he even wanted to hide*, Sabre thought. She had seen his interested gaze following Jinx on more than one occasion. Fortunately, she hadn't had to kick his arse yet though and he was still a trustworthy tool to use.

"Yes, it was from Hound. I assume the sexy beast is fine – even though he has nothing of use to tell me." Jinx shrugged and

Sabre knew the tiger wasn't side-tracked. Tigers were singularly focused when on the hunt.

"He'll keep looking. In the meantime, send him a big kiss from me." When Sabre failed to move, Jinx motioned impatiently with her hand, "Go on: kiss, kiss, kiss, hug, hug, hug. Then add: hump, hump, hump."

Sabre laughed and Gage yelled, "Jinx!" before throwing a bottle cap at her from the other side of the table.

"What?" Jinx asked innocently, blinking her ridiculously long lashes. "Hounds love to hump."

Sabre couldn't argue with that. She had also spent the past three days wondering how another particular hound humped – and she wasn't referring to Styx. Sabre still didn't know what to make of her friendly little chat with Brax. It had been strange, basically giving the demon a verbal spanking. But to her eternal surprise, Brax had actually listened to her and seemed to take on board what she said. He was hurting – hurting bad. Sabre knew that to be true. He missed his father and his uncles, and perhaps his brothers the most. The three of them had been triplets, after all. The bond they had shared had no doubt been organic and strong in a way few things ever were these days. He had surprised her even further by sending her a constant stream of text messages – and even a few phone calls since then. Hence, her swift attention to her phone just minutes ago. Hardly any of them were related to her work and she was a little clueless what to do about it – other than reply back stoically and abruptly of course. But one thing Sabre did know; she liked him.

She had always had a thing for Brax's face … and his chest … and his arms … and his butt. His butt especially. Those glutes were a thing of beauty. All tight and muscled, they clenched appealingly when he walked. And when he bent over? May all the Gods have mercy. But this interest in Brax's brain? Yeah, that was new. It was also stupid. And a big fat waste of time and energy. Still, her own brain couldn't help mustering up a fantasy or two … dozen. Two dozen. Sighing, Sabre picked up her beer and drank it down in one go. She had dropped in on Jinx and Gage just to check in before she set about implementing the next step of her plan. It was a risky move and she had wanted them to be prepared for possible kickbacks. Of course, they had merely rolled their eyes at her and accused her of being a mother hen. Just because she had feathers, didn't mean she clucked. She –

"Wait …" Sabre cocked her head to the side. "What is that annoying buzzing sound?"

Jinx stifled a giggle, using her head to gesture to the side as her mis-matched eyes lit with mirth. Sabre followed Jinx's directions and turned to her left. Only to promptly scream and automatically reach for one of her many weapons. Thankfully, she was experienced enough and controlled enough not to immediately slice at the throat bared in front of her. "For fuck's sake, Draven! What the hell do you think you're doing? Are you trying to get your throat slit?"

"I've been standing here for two minutes, saying your name over and over again," Draven replied, sternly. "You have been wilfully ignoring me."

"You've been lurking there for two minutes?" she asked, surprised. "No wonder I've had a chill down my spine. That's just creepy, man. And was that what that annoying sound was? Your voice?"

Draven's look was full of disdain as he looked down his perfect nose at her, "You are maddening!"

"Yeah? Well so is your face," Sabre pointed out. She then sucked back her laughter like a champ, knowing the repetitive digs were getting to him. It was funny as fuck.

Draven yanked at his perfectly styled hair, "You could test the patience of a saint. Do you know that? Has anyone ever told you that?" he asked in quick succession.

"Yep," Sabre chirped. "Saint Julian. Right before I shanked him between the third and fourth ribs."

Draven's mouth fell open. "I do hope you're joking."

"I never joke about shanking," Sabre levelled her gaze on his.

"Why would you shank a saint? You know what? Don't answer that. I do not want to know. I do not want to know why you do any of the things you do. I'm only here because Abraxis wants me to go with you."

Sabre shook her head, "No."

Draven frowned fiercely, "Excuse me? What do you mean, no?"

Gage wandered over and leaned over the back of Jinx's chair, "She means there is no way the king wants that."

Gage quickly found himself the recipient of the golden angel's scowl, "And why is that? Not that I was talking to you in the first place," Draven added.

Sabre stood up slowly, keeping her eyes on Draven the whole time, "Watch your mouth, Draven. This is Gage's establishment –"

"Establishment?" Draven scoffed. "It's a dilapidated warehouse with dirty, blood-soaked cement floors, three tables, and six chairs. There looks to be a mini fridge over there behind the long table and one very large freezer. Why you require a freezer that big I have no idea, given you have inadequate seating and lighting. But that's irrelevant. This place –"

"Is my home," Gage broke in. "This place is my home. And you're standing in it. We don't all get to live in palaces, Guardian. I'd thank you to remember your manners when you're here."

Gage's softly spoken reprimand worked far better than Sabre's yelling would have and she was gratified to see shame wash over

Draven's features. Despite the shit she gave him, she knew he wasn't a bad guy. He couldn't be. Brax loved him. And if Brax loved him, there must be some hidden, redeemable qualities buried somewhere.

"I apologise," Draven said, looking Gage in the eye. "I am not usually so rude. I have no excuse other than this one," he stabbed a thumb at Sabre, "really gets to me. Please, accept my apologies," Draven held out a hand to Gage.

Gage eyed Draven for a moment before he smiled a little, offering his own hand so the two men could shake. "Don't worry, she has that effect on a lot of people."

"Hey!" Sabre yelled. "I'm standing right here."

"We know," all three of them said at the same time.

Sabre rocked back a step, "Okay. Never do that again. That was creepy and you three will not be bonding in any way, shape, or form. Understand?"

"Oh, I don't know. He is kind of cute …" Jinx winked at Draven, causing him to blush.

Sabre pushed a hand in Jinx's face. "No. There will be no flirting with the arsehole angel. Back to you coming with me," Sabre turned quickly to Draven, "I believe Gage's point was that Brax doesn't want you going with me because I'm sure he wants his guardian to remain unmaimed."

Draven crossed well-muscled arms across his chest, "I can look after myself, I assure you."

Sabre's voice was dry as she explained; "I wasn't referring to anyone else. I was talking about me. I'd be the one doing the maiming."

"Ha! I am not afraid of the likes of you. An angel with no Grace, no wings, and no morals," the perfect specimen of an angel in front of her taunted.

Sabre saw Gage palm his sawn-off shotgun and she quickly

shook her head at him. Not only would the lead not kill the angel, it would only serve to piss him off more and convince him how right he was about them. Sabre likewise placed a restraining hand on Jinx's arm, her protégé's hackles couldn't be seen in this shape, but they were well and truly raised. Instead of showing just how much those words cut her to the core – especially the part about her wings – Sabre plastered a practiced bored expression on her face. Spinning a small silver stake between her fingers, Sabre mused idly; "You know, Draven. I'd kick your arse, but I don't think Brax would appreciate a brain-damaged guardian."

It may not have been as satisfying as launching the stake through the air at the angel's eyeball, but Sabre still relished the thin scream to escape Draven's lips from her words. There was just something about pushing the other angel's buttons that really did it for her. It was probably because the man made it so damn easy with his by-the-rules mentality and holier-than-thou attitude. Still, there was a part of her that genuinely resented Draven. He was everything she could have been but was denied to her. She always stayed well away from what-ifs, but that rule was hard to follow when her antitheses kept getting all up in her grill. And flaunting his feathers at her. That shit was just plain unnecessary.

Draven eyed the three of them for a moment, taking in their dangerous postures before sighing abruptly, "Damnit! I've just done it again. I apologise," he spat out through gritted teeth, "I seem to have no patience today."

Sabre could have said any number of things, the first being she was sure Draven didn't have a lot of patience on any given day. But she kept her mouth shut and let the angel prostrate himself once again. Seeing him apologise twice in as many minutes was giving her a little rush.

"I am concerned for Brax. He has been on this path for a long time and now that he has hope that there is an end in sight, I just don't want to see him relapse. I want to help. It has been such a relief to see some of the old him these past few days. He has been more relaxed and smiling more. He even called up some of his old troops last night to catch up with them rather than ordering them to spy for him. It's a welcome change. I just want to ... help," Draven finished, a little helplessly.

"Brax has been happier these past few days you say?" Jinx asked, eyeing Draven shrewdly.

Sabre tensed. Jinx may have been young and she may come across as bratty or flighty to new acquaintances, but Sabre knew that was just an act. Jinx was highly intelligent, highly intuitive, and had a maturity well beyond her years. Sabre knew Jinx could take over the world if she put her mind to it. So she was more than a little concerned by the knowing look Jinx threw her way before turning back to Draven, apparently eager to hear his reply. Sabre was too.

Draven nodded, "Yes. He's been on his phone almost constantly. He must be talking to friends because he is always in a good mood afterward. It's wonderful to see."

Sabre suddenly found her small stake very interesting. She didn't dare make eye contact with Jinx or Gage.

"That's interesting," Gage mused, sharing an intrigued and decidedly mischievous look with Jinx. "Sabre has been receiving a lot more texts and calls than usual too. Must be something in the air."

Draven, completely oblivious to Gage's innuendo, nodded his head, "I would hope she is. I understand you have been making lots of inquiries."

"That's right! I have!" Sabre was quick to jump on the explanation and she shot a glare at the other two when they found her response so humorous. "And I was just about to go and make some more. So, if you'll excuse me ..."

Draven danced with death by stepping into her path, "Allow me to come with you."

"I already said no," Sabre returned, flatly.

"How about we all come?" Gage suggested, already grabbing his jacket and walking toward the door.

"Great idea!" Jinx clapped, joining him.

Sabre gritted her teeth, forcefully reminding herself that it was poor form to kill known associates. "This is not a school excursion. I am going to The Dungeon," she informed them.

The Dungeon was a local hangout for the baddies of Purgatory to drink, shoot the shit, and have sex. It was always filled with naughty supernaturals no matter the time of day or night and was exactly the type of place she needed to implement her new plan. It was also somewhere she didn't allow Jinx to go. With her history, Sabre didn't want her anywhere near sexual deviants and their very public sex acts. Gage, thankfully, was on the same page as her because he stopped walking. Jinx immediately opened her mouth to argue, knowing where the conversation was headed. Surprisingly it was Draven who spoke;

"The Dungeon? That is no place for the likes of you, young one."

Draven's voice was soft and it wasn't an order, but Jinx bristled nonetheless, "It's nothing I haven't seen before."

"That may be so," Draven allowed. "But I would feel decidedly uncomfortable if you joined us. Would you please do me this one small favour and stay here?"

Sabre's jaw dropped open. Firstly, since when was there an *'us'*? Secondly, Draven was actually being charming … and it was working! Jinx's eyes softened as she looked up at Draven as if he were her new best friend. "Fine. But you be nice to my assassin, you hear?" Jinx poked Draven in the stomach.

Draven smiled, "I will try my best."

"That's all anyone can do," Jinx conceded, before turning and trotting back into the warehouse.

"What just happened?" Sabre asked, staring after the feisty tiger suddenly turned sweet kitten. "Did you voodoo my weretiger? Maybe use your soft and squishy, pansy empath powers on her?" she accused Draven.

Draven's smiling face promptly scowled, "Of course I didn't use my powers on her without permission. And they are *not* pansy. My healing abilities are extremely powerful and highly sought after."

"Of course they are," Sabre soothed. "Everyone loves a good mood ring. Those things have great entertainment value."

"My empath abilities are more than just mood detectors. I –" Draven blew out a breath. "You really get to me. You know that, right?" Sabre shrugged even as he continued to eye her thoughtfully. "What colour were your wings, anyway?"

"Excuse me?" The abrupt – and extremely rude question to Sabre's reasoning – took her completely by surprise. Angels were highly protective of their wings. And though it wasn't a faux pas to have their wings out in public – it wasn't like walking around with your dick out or anything – wings were still highly personal as well as special. And very, very revealing. Because an angel's wings were a direct reflection of their powers. She knew Draven's would be white because he was a healer, but they could also have a mixture of silver feathers or even gold feathers if he were powerful enough. Angels born in Purgatory – or Earth, because that happened every so often – never grew feathers of silver or gold. But those created in Heaven, who performed their duties faithfully and righteously and whose powers were extreme were sometimes known to sprout the pretty, metallic primary feathers.

As for her own feathery situation, she knew Draven had used past tense to ask her about her wings because he assumed she no longer had them, what with her being fallen and no longer having any Grace. It didn't matter that Sabre had been off the angelic path since she was a child, questions about her wings still scraped her raw.

"Wow. Rude much?" Gage's snarky voice broke into Sabre's musings. "I haven't even asked about Sabre's wings. And I know her. And like her. And she likes me back. You – she hates."

"Thank you, Gage," Sabre patted him on the arm. It was good to have people in your life who understood you. She turned back to Draven, "That's kind of personal, don't you think?"

Draven rolled his shoulders as if uncomfortable, "It's not like I was going to ask you to show me, but …"

"You're lucky I can't do that. You might have been in for a shock," Sabre pointed out. Then she scoffed, "I mean, hell, why didn't you just go ahead and ask to see my vagina?"

Draven choked and turned an alarming purple colour, "Sick. So sick …" he mumbled.

Sabre wasn't sure if he was talking about her statement or the thought of her vagina, or that he was literally feeling sick – at the thought of her vagina. Either way, she was feeling better about the whole situation. A little violence over at The Dungeon would round out her mood and smooth away the last of the ragged edges, she knew.

"Don't listen to the angel, my love. You have a great vagina," Gage suddenly said, winking in her direction.

Then it was Sabre's turn to choke on her own spit.

Draven turned wide eyes to Gage, looking back and forth between him and Sabre, "You've had sex with …? What are you again?" he questioned Gage.

"None of your business," Gage and Sabre answered at the same time.

"Just know I'm something that eats flesh. So if I say Sabre has a nice vagina …" Gage leaned in close to Draven and whispered salaciously in his ear, "take my word for it."

Draven gagged, "Definitely going to be sick."

Gage laughed, turning back to Sabre, "If you and the rude-slash-charming angel here can handle it, I'll leave you to The Dungeon and I'll go check on Jinx."

"I can handle it," Sabre promised him. She shook her head at him in a scolding manner, knowing he would simply ignore her and continue to do and say what he liked. It was a trait she, Jinx, and Gage all shared and didn't seem so annoying when she acted on her own impulses. She had never had sex with Gage and never intended to. He was good-looking and also one of the best men she knew, but there was no sexual spark between them. Thankfully, Sabre added, because Gage had not been kidding. He really did eat flesh and although he was fucking around, she didn't want him anywhere near her goodies.

## CHAPTER TEN

As soon as she walked into the room, the entire atmosphere became tense for a whole different reason other than the large number of supernaturals currently fighting, gambling or having sex. It was because Sabre had a habit of spilling blood whenever she made an appearance at The Dungeon. She just couldn't seem to help herself. The clientele were always so mouthy, and she always had a hard time ignoring their words. Besides, why would she bother to ignore them when it was simply easier to cut out a few tongues? On this particular occasion though, she had vowed to herself to behave – despite her need for a good fight. She was there for one reason and one reason only; to stir some shit up on behalf of the King. Although, with her wingman in tow, she wasn't sure if violence was going to be avoided, because if there was one thing the riffraff hated more than her, it was a goody-two-shoes angel.

"You're not welcome here, angel-bitch," a gravelly voice said from behind her.

Looking over her shoulder, Sabre saw that it was Ox. Ox was

a troll – a very smelly troll – and the owner of the establishment. He was also scared of her and Sabre knew it. "Now, is that any way to talk about my new friend?" she asked, sternly.

Ox's beady eyes darted to Draven for a split second before returning to her, "I was talking to you."

"Oh, my mistake. That's what I call him, so I got confused for a second there," Sabre explained.

Beside her, Draven huffed but remained silent. She really had no idea why he was intent on following her around. Sure, Brax had said he wanted Draven to help multiple times during their correspondence over the last few days. But he had also said he wanted to chat with Sabre in person again too. She had taken both statements with a grain of salt because both were just as ridiculous as each other. Yet, here she was, with a plus one. Did that mean the other wasn't outside the realm of possibility too? Shaking off the strangely appealing notion, she addressed Ox once more;

"I just need two minutes, then I'll be out of here. I won't even break any bones or set anything on fire this time. Pinky swear …" Sabre held up her little finger, but Ox rudely ignored it, wordlessly snarling at her before retreating to a dark corner.

"Do you piss off everyone you meet?"

The sardonic question came from next to her and Sabre turned to Draven, "Most of the time," Sabre admitted. "It's a gift."

"Some gift," Draven muttered, eyes scanning the room but face remaining surprisingly neutral.

"Not your usual haunt, huh?" Sabre guessed.

"No. A fact I'm ever grateful for. Is it yours?" he then asked, blue eyes latching onto hers and seeming to search for something.

Sabre had no idea what the angel could possibly be looking to find but he wouldn't find it in her eyes. She had learned to shut down her expressions long ago and knew she now no longer had any tells. *Thank you, Carlisle's training.* As for Draven's question, establishments like The Dungeon were a necessary and inevitable part of her job and Sabre found herself frequenting them enough that she was on a first name basis with the owners like Ox. But did she like it? That would be a resounding *fuck no!* If she had a choice, she would burn the place to the ground. Still, her answer was; "I have my own table reserved. What does that tell you?"

Draven's mouth tightened and he looked less than pleased. Still he followed her to the table she had been gesturing to and watched impassively as she tipped the fornicating pair of nymphs onto the floor. Eyeing the dirty tabletop, Sabre idly wondered how much DNA was permanently ingrained into the wood before stepping onto it. "I hope I don't get pregnant from this," she muttered. Then she whistled loudly between her teeth; "Right! Listen up, fuckers! King Abraxis has officially hired me to identify and hunt down the tosser – or toss*ers* – who have been picking off his fam-fam. I am very invested in this and you all know what that means …" Sabre scanned the room, taking note of expressions and body language and storing it all away in her brain to process later. "It means when I find the culprit, Imma cut a bitch. So if any of you have any information for me, I kindly suggest you offer it up willingly." The room was dangerously quiet and she didn't so much as get a *'fuck you'* in response. Sabre looked down at Draven, "Wow. Tough crowd."

Draven looked appalled as Sabre jumped down from the table and dusted off her hands. She then strolled through the silent room and out the door as if nothing were amiss. Studying her hands, she scrunched up her nose; "Ick. I feel dirty in all the non-fun ways. You don't happen to have any hand sanitiser on you, do you?"

Her innocent question was met with a very big, angry frown,

"That's it? You walk in, threaten to … cut a bitch … and then walk out? What did that achieve?"

Sabre stopped walking, giving half her attention to Draven but keeping vigil on The Dungeon as well. They were only about twenty metres away – not nearly far enough to be having a chat. Still, Sabre replied; "That just achieved more than years and years of subterfuge and quietly seeking answers under the table, I promise you. Look," she motioned with her chin at the handful of supernatural beings slowly making their way out of the dingy interior of the bar. "Like rats fleeing a sinking ship," she murmured, feeling excited to see the results of her loud and public statement in the coming days. She had no doubt word would spread that she was working for the king. She also had no doubt that fact would piss off a lot of people. And pissed off people were her favourite kind. Because pissed off people made mistakes. She would glean new information from today's brief outing, Sabre was sure of it. The angel next to her though, clearly didn't think so.

"You're certifiable!"

"I'm really not," Sabre countered. Draven didn't fire anything back, which she found odd and she looked at his handsome face only to find him shaking his head and looking disappointed of all things. "What's with the look?" And then it hit her – the whole 'wanting to help her deal'? It had been about him the entire time. "Why did you come with me today?" she asked, icily.

Draven shook his head, "Truthfully? I wanted to see who you really were. I know what you do for a living but I wanted to see if there was more to you. If perhaps there was more than a sarcastic killing machine, intent on adding to the crime statistics of Purgatory," Draven admitted. "Because I have this insane speculation that Brax, *my Brax*, believes there is a decent, genuine person under all the leather and he's somehow getting sucked in."

Sabre lifted her chin, ignoring the pitty-pat of her heart over the last part of info, "And what did you determine?"

"That you are irredeemable."

Draven's flat assessment of her made her flinch and Sabre actually took a step back. "Wow. And you've come to that conclusion after just three meetings with me." Sabre shook her head, "You really hate me, don't you?"

"I'm an angel. We don't hate anyone," was Draven's prompt reply.

"Please," Sabre sneered. "Don't give me that holier-than-thou bullshit. You're talking to another angel here. We can hate. Very easily."

"Fine. Yes, I hate you," Draven finally hissed. "I hate everything you stand for because it is against everything *I* stand for. Angels are good. We are *good* beings, Sabre. You are a betrayal to everything we are and it's shameful and *embarrassing*. I find you embarrassing. And the last thing – the very last thing in all the realms I want is you in close proximity to my charge. Brax is everything that is good and right in the world. He is strong and capable and so very noble – though he doesn't see it. But he is vulnerable at the moment and I won't see him taken advantage of. I see the way he looks at you and I see the way you watch him. You can't have him, Sabre."

Sabre had a hard time wrapping her head around everything Draven was saying. Her gut clutched hearing his words of hate – nobody liked hearing that. But it was the promise of taking Brax away that really made her sweat. Not that he was with her at the moment or anything, but the hope growing in her heart was a small blessing she never thought she would have – even if it was useless. Sabre was sure Draven was the only person in the entire world whom Brax would never deny anything. Including her. Sabre opened her mouth to respond but nothing came out on the first try. Trying again, she was annoyed to find her voice weak and thin;

"I have no intention of taking advantage of Abraxis. Despite what you think of me – which is to say less than nothing – I can assure you I am no threat to the King. As for the rest …" Sabre raised her chin, eyes suddenly blazing, "I'm a betrayal against our kind? Easy for you to say, you weren't raised in an assassin den. You fell to Purgatory and fell into the royal house of Cerberus. A hundred odd years of daily torture from the age of eight and I'd like to see how quickly you changed your tune."

"There is no amount of torture that would cause me to betray my duty. None," Draven snapped his reply.

Sabre snorted, knowing how very wrong he was but unable to prove it unless they swapped places. "Well, luckily for me I didn't have a duty to betray," she said instead.

"That just makes you even more pathetic," Draven shook his head once again. "Never. Never would I do what you do."

Sabre squeezed the bridge of her nose, suddenly feeling exhausted. "I know you think you really mean that, Draven. But you don't. You see, when you say never, you actually mean *until*."

"What?" he asked, looking confused.

"People always say never but what they really mean is until. You would never cheat on your wife *until* you have ten shots of bourbon at the work Christmas party and Mary shakes her stockinged arse at you. You would never steal anything *until* you're starving and cold and have nowhere else to go." Sabre cocked an eyebrow at Draven, "You would never betray your birthright *until* …"

"No," the stubborn angel shook his head hard. "I don't believe that."

"Believe what you want," Sabre told him. "But I used to say never a lot too and look at me now. Are we done?"

Draven watched her in silence for a moment and Sabre met his stare levelly, "Yes. We're done," he finally agreed.

"Thank fuck for that," she muttered, turning away. Luckily she did because a swish of movement caught her eye. She didn't have time to yell a warning, instead palming the small silver stake she had been playing with that morning, she launched it a mere centimetre over Draven's left shoulder.

Draven gasped and swore, grabbing her wrist in a punishing grip but Sabre quickly shook him off. She strode over to the fallen vampire, giving him a kick, and was satisfied when he didn't move. Her aim had been true.

"What did you do?" Draven yelled, disbelief on his face and in his voice.

Sabre eyed the fallen vampire dispassionately, "Killed a vampire."

"Killed a vampire?" Draven wheezed.

"Uh huh. Killed him dead," she confirmed. Draven seemed to be having a hard time breathing, so Sabre cut him some slack, hoping to get on with her earlier plan of getting the fuck away from his judgemental arse. "You're welcome," she said.

Draven's crystal blue eyes widened further – a feat Sabre didn't believe should have been physically possible. "You're welcome? You're welcome?!" he repeated, looking between her and the ever-increasing pool of red spreading from beneath the vamp's chest. "You are the most disturbing person I have ever met."

"Really?" Sabre felt a smile light her face, taking it as the compliment she genuinely believed it was. "That is the nicest thing you've ever said to me. Are you going soft on me?" she asked, wondering if perhaps they were having a bonding moment despite Draven being a hater just minutes before.

"Soft?" Draven's voice was incredulous.

*So, maybe not bonding,* Sabre admitted with an internal shrug.

"You're sick!" Draven continued, the hard, cold tone of his voice snapping Sabre out of her good humour. "You just killed an innocent man!"

"Innocent?" she burst out laughing. "There was nothing innocent about that vamp," she assured the other angel.

"He was just standing there. Unarmed. You didn't even give him a warning. You truly have fallen from all Graces, haven't you?"

Sabre felt the familiar ice flood her system, and she scolded herself for forgetting for one moment who exactly Draven was. And who she was. She strode over to the fallen body and kicked him over. A thin, shiny blade cleverly concealed between his fingers could barely be seen in the mid-morning light, but she knew Draven's eyes would be able to see it. "This is a skeleton blade," she informed him. "It is the weapon of choice from the Memnar Guild. He was about to launch it into your eyeball. Like I said …" she knocked her shoulder against his on her way back past, "you're welcome."

"Sabre … wait!"

But Sabre's patience was at an all-time low and all she could manage was a snarled, "Get fucked!"

## CHAPTER ELEVEN

Sabre was laying prone on her bed at the Blue Devil when her phone began to ring beside her. Her fingers twitched to snatch it up immediately – she recognised the ring tone she had set for Brax – but she stopped herself and let it ring out. When *'Carry On My Wayward Son'* began to play for the fourth time in as many minutes, she finally stabbed the little green button. "What?!" she yelled in lieu of a hello.

"And hello to you too," Brax's voice drawled from the other end of their connection. "I see you're in a good mood this evening, Sabre. Could that have anything to do with a certain trip to a certain bar earlier today?"

Sabre mimed his royal tone, pulling funny faces because he couldn't see. "Let me guess …" she finally drawled, "Draven tattled on me."

"He said you walked into a bar, yelled that you were hired by me as my personal assassin and then killed a vampire in front of him."

"Concise," she acknowledged. "I have nothing to add."

"Sabre …"

Rubbing her temple, Sabre squeezed her eyes shut. She was terrified to learn what else Draven had said to Brax after their heated conversation. Somehow, she doubted Draven had changed his tune about her having contact with Brax just because she had saved his sanctimonious arse. "Look, I know you don't understand the logic, but I assure you –"

"Oh, I understand. You're hoping some of the super-secret evil-doers get pissed enough to fuck up and start blabbing. Maybe a little, *'Did you hear Sabre is working for the monarchy and is chasing her own arse? Well, I once got one over on her you know? I am a super awesome baddie with balls of steel,'* yada, yada, yada. Am I right?"

Sabre pulled the phone from her ear and looked at it in surprise. Though she would like to see the expression on his face right then, she was glad he couldn't see hers. She was shocked he was able to read her so well and more than a little turned on that they apparently thought along the same wavelength. Abraxis was a man of many talents. Clearing her throat, she muttered, "Maybe a little …"

"Then how about this; you're even hoping that the person behind the killings gets pissed enough and bold enough that he comes after you next. Am I getting warmer?"

Sabre sat up. Brax wasn't just getting warmer, he was scorching. That had been the next stage of her plan, but one she hadn't given more than a passing thought to, even in her own head yet. How did Brax understand her so well?

"I don't approve of your actions," Brax informed her, sounding every inch the King he proclaimed he didn't want to be.

"Are you firing me?" she held her breath.

"What? Firing you? Of course not!" Brax sounded genuinely

surprised over the notion. "But I don't want you getting hurt because of me."

Sabre felt herself melt back against the mattress. Other than a small handful of people, there had been very little concern over whether she was hurt or not. Sabre relished the warmth that spread through her system for a few precious seconds, knowing a few simple words from Draven could take that concern away. Why the angel hadn't used his influence to get Brax to dump her like a tonne of bricks she didn't know. But for now, she could only assume Draven had kept his feelings of hate and embarrassment to himself because Brax's voice was tinged with warmth.

"Don't worry about me. I can take care of myself," she finally responded.

"Oh, I don't doubt that. But just because you can doesn't mean you should always have to."

Sabre bit her lip, remaining silent until she trusted herself to speak, "I have to go. It's late and I have things to kill and stuff."

Brax's sigh held a note of disappointment, "Fine. Go kill. But, Sabre? Thank you for saving Draven today. And thank you for not killing him yourself."

A dial tone met her ear and Sabre clutched the phone to her chest. The man understood her, that was for sure. How did someone – who had only heard the worst of her by reputation – and was raised in such an opposing environment, possibly understand her on such a fundamental level? *Especially the not killing the angel part,* Sabre thought, because it had definitely been touch and go. Maybe it was because he was so sexy? Yeah, that had to be it. Because he was –

A tentative knock on her door interrupted her crazy, lustful thoughts. Jumping from the bed and palming her favourite sig sauer, Sabre flattened her back against the wall next to the door before flicking the safety off with her thumb. Aiming the muzzle of the gun through the drafty crack in the door, knowing from experience she would hit some part of the person standing on the other side, she looked through the peep hole. Sabre immediately relaxed, putting the safety back on and tucking the gun away in the rear waistband of her leather pants. Undoing the series of locks – which were largely useless given who she lived with – she was pleasantly surprised to see Phaedra on the other side.

Phaedra was a pixie – tiny in stature but mighty in nature, she had a delicate constitution at direct odds with where she lived. She was in Carlisle's mansion as an indentured servant, paying off family debts for the next seventy years. She had already been there close to two hundred. The pixie was also one of two people in the entire den who Sabre trusted implicitly, so she didn't hesitate to usher her inside.

"Phaedra, how are you?" Sabre immediately asked, running critical eyes over the small, pretty woman. It wasn't uncommon for Phaedra to visit her covered in bruises from where other residents had gotten too handsy. In those instances, Sabre paid them a visit and taught them a lesson they didn't soon forget. She may not be able to physically harm Carlisle, but the same rule did not apply to the other assassins and mercenaries.

Phaedra smiled, straight white teeth flashing in her dark, pretty face, "I'm good."

"Uh huh," Sabre moved closer and lifted the pixie's pointy chin, "Are you hurt?" Phaedra shook her head. "Are you in trouble?"

This time Phaedra rolled her eyes, moving out of Sabre's grip, "No, Sabre. I'm not in trouble. I've just been minding my own business and doing my job. Same old, same old."

Sabre merely grunted, causing Phaedra to smile wider – and Sabre to roll her eyes. Pixie's were a cute, mischievous bunch. They were non-violent and their magic was delightfully playful.

But they were also sneaky and they could do a lot of harm if they were cornered.

"I came because I heard the new king hired you for some merc work," Phaedra announced.

"You heard that, huh?" Even if Sabre hadn't just announced it to the world Phaedra would still have known. She heard nearly every damn thing. Not only was she a cook in the kitchen but she also served food in the dining hall, allowing her to hear all kinds of useful – and dangerous – things.

The pixie nodded her head, sending her dark curls bouncing everywhere. "Yep. I also heard you're looking for information about the deaths of anyone from the royal line."

"That's right. Our esteemed king wants to find those responsible for killing his family. Which is probably fair enough, I guess. I hear they were nice," Sabre conceded.

"Yes. Most people take exception to their entire family being systematically wiped out," Phaedra acknowledged.

Hearing a tone in the other woman's voice, Sabre eyed her suspiciously. Sure enough, Phaedra's hazel eyes were twinkling and she was fighting heroically to hold back a smile. "Yeah, yeah, laugh it up. Mock my social ineptitude why don't you?" Phaedra finally released a giggle, the sound tinkling in the room and turning up the corners of Sabre's mouth as well.

"Sorry, but Sabre … you crack me up," Phaedra laughed one more time.

Sabre shook her head at that. She thought she was the least funny person on the planet. Scratch that; on all four planets, well, planes. There was nothing funny about gutting people for a living. Okay, *she* thought gutting people was often funny as fuck. But Sabre knew most people didn't. And they certainly didn't laugh when she did it to them, or when they saw her do it to others. They usually cried. Or screamed. Or ran away crying and screaming. *Annnd, I'm monologuing,* Sabre thought in annoyance. It was a bad habit of hers, and one that had gotten her cut more than once because she hadn't been paying attention like she should have been.

"Sabre? You talking to yourself again or what?" Phaedra broke the silence – and the monologuing.

She managed to restrain her pout. There was nothing appealing about a pouting assassin. "I was planning strategies. Death strategies."

"Uh huh," Phaedra sounded sceptical but thankfully chose not to tease. "Anyway, I came to talk to you because I may or may not have some information about the assassination of King Maliq."

Now that had Sabre focusing in on the pixie with laser focus, "What sort of information?"

Phaedra bit her bottom lip in an uncharacteristic display of nerves. It had been a long time since she had feared Sabre in any way, shape, or form. "Well … I was the spotter."

"What?!" Sabre hadn't meant to yell, but that was just about the last thing she had expected to hear.

In the world of snipers, spotters were the teammate who made sure the shooter had the greatest chance for making a successful shot by calculating distance, tracking the trajectory of the bullet, and making the wind call. In the world of assassins, however, a spotter was a witness. It may be seen as counterproductive to have a witness to a murder, but there were some contracts where it was unavoidable. Like when the assassin holding the contract employed a third party to help fulfil the mission. Or if a slow acting poison was used. A spotter would be used to witness the actual death and then report back in order to attest to the validity of the assassination. A spotter was always secret, with the contract holder not knowing who would be following and watching. Carlisle was the only one who could send out a spotter and the only one they then reported to. Sabre knew the controlling, distrustful incubus often sent spotters to spy on regular contracts randomly as well – even if they didn't meet the criteria. Carlisle was a real arsehole.

Learning Phaedra was used as a spotter was new. Sabre had never considered it before and she cursed herself for being ignorant and naïve. After all, the little pixie with earthen magic and the ability to shrink in size would be the perfect spy. Couple that with her sweet disposition and guileless eyes and no one would suspect the strong, independent, intelligent woman that lurked within. Sabre knew Phaedra was simply biding her time and paying off her family's debt so she could one day raze the Blue Devil to the ground. And when that day came, Sabre was going to be there to strike the match.

"Did you witness the death of King Maliq?" Sabre asked, getting right to the point.

Phaedra nodded quickly, "Yes. BUT –" she quickly raised her voice when Sabre began cursing and asking who it was. "But I didn't see who it was. Or rather, *what* it was behind the scenes."

"Third party?" Sabre guessed.

"Yes. And I never knew who was hired to take the hit in the first place," Phaedra quickly added.

Sabre grunted. That wasn't unexpected. The person – or persons – behind the death of several members of the royal family, including King Maliq, were the best kept secret in Purgatory. Well, almost, Sabre amended, knowing full well *her* secrets were the best kept. And possibly the most toxic. "Maliq was killed with poison," Sabre stated. "So, not only was it a long-distance kill, a third party was hired as well? Damn, this guy is a real fucking coward."

Sabre, herself, had never once killed a single soul with poison. When she killed, she killed face to face. Or face to back. Or face to side. Whatever. The point was, she never took the easy way out and she never hired someone else to do the dirty work for her. She might have a fucked-up job description, but she took pride in it.

"Right," Phaedra agreed. "Whoever this guy is, they wanted double the protection from possible detection."

Sabre scrubbed a hand over her face, expelling a harsh breath, "Okay. You said you didn't see who or *what* killed Maliq. What did you mean by that?"

Phaedra walked over and sat on the end of Sabre's bed, tucking her small feet underneath her. Sabre very deliberately had no chairs in the room because she didn't want visitors to think they could stay and chat. Usually, they rarely made it through the door. Unless you were a pervy incubus den master or a rare trusted companion of course. Sabre remained standing so she could pace off some nervous energy should she need to, but she gestured toward the pixie to start talking.

"I think Maliq knew he was dying," Phaedra revealed. "I mean, more than just feeling like shit because he thought he was sick or something. I think he knew. He had this … resigned look about him. Like he knew his death was inevitable, so he didn't bother trying to call his guards or anything."

Sabre closed her eyes briefly, remaining silent and not agreeing one way or the other. She had no doubt the former king did know. He was rumoured to be clairvoyant – a gift from his maternal side way back when one of Delphi's Oracles had married into the royal line thousands of years ago. It wasn't common knowledge and Sabre only knew because of the stalking she did of all things royal. And then there was that one day when … She quickly halted her thoughts. That was something she didn't dare replay even in the safety of her own mind. She was highly adept at blocking those with mental powers, but she wouldn't put it past Carlisle to try to tap into the minds of his assassins regularly.

"Anyway, I was only there for ten minutes max. Just long enough to see the look of resigned sadness on the king's face before he started to convulse. But ... I wasn't the only one there. There was something else. I couldn't make out what it was but it was low to the ground and it had red eyes," Phaedra announced in a rush.

Sabre froze in mid-step, "Red eyes?"

"Yes. Red, glowing eyes from the shadows," Phaedra described further.

Despite what the humans on the Earth plane liked to think, there were an extremely limited number of supernatural beings who could boast having red irises. And vampires weren't one of them. The only creatures with red eyes came straight out of Hell. Literally. Sabre felt her heart begin to pound as endorphins flooded her system. She had a lead. She finally had a solid lead she could start investigating. "Phaedra, why didn't you tell me this before?"

Phaedra looked contrite, "I'm sorry, Sabre. But I didn't even consider it. Why would I? I didn't know you had any interest in who killed the King from two successions ago. I mean, why would you?"

The other female had a point. All of Sabre's previous investigations had been on the down-low so as to not arouse suspicion. As such, she had effectively tied her own hands and limited how much she could find. Exactly nothing, as it turned out. But not now. Now she had something. Maybe even more than something. She walked over to the bed and gave Phaedra a big smackaroo right on her forehead.

Phaedra's eyes twinkled, "Please tell me that wasn't the kiss of death?"

Sabre laughed, "Never. Thank you. You may have just helped crack the case."

Phaedra looked pleased, jumping agilely from the bed. "Yay! You're welcome. What are you going to do now?"

"Now?" Sabre rubbed her hands together and began to mentally catalogue the weapons she would need for her surprise trip. "Now I'm going straight to Hell."

## CHAPTER TWELVE

"Do you think I like hurting you? That I do this for fun?" Sabre's silky voice whispered against her target's neck, causing a rush of goosebumps to prickle over his skin. She moved up a little, nipping at the shell of his ear and delighting in his shudder of revulsion. "Because if you do …" she continued, "then you'd be right! I fuckin' love this shit!"

Sabre chuckled darkly when the wendigo beneath her whimpered in fear. She wasn't a sadist by nature and didn't get off on pain if truth be told. But there was a certain satisfaction to be gained when watching a putrid excuse for a heartbeat sweat bullets and shit his pants. It had taken her two days and five speeding tickets to travel by car to her destination. It wasn't really a hardship – she loved her car. Even though Carlisle took a huge percentage of her pay, killing for a living still made her a lot of money and she wasn't afraid to indulge in a few luxuries. Namely full body massages by a six-armed Gegenees and her silver Maserati Alfieri. She loved the exceedingly expensive car with the supple leather seats and automatic butt warming. And boy, could her baby fly! Hence, all the speeding fines. Still, driving had been the most expedient way to get to the veil she needed to. Sure, there was a veil into Hell a lot closer, but it would have taken her into the fifth circle of Hell and she would have had to have travelled even longer within Hell itself in order to reach the inner most circle. *No thanks.* She would happily pay her speeding tickets if it meant she didn't have to spend days smelling nothing but sulphur. Besides that, the smell lingered in her hair for weeks and even sometimes seeped into her leathers.

So, here she was, outside the hidden entrance to the veil that opened up almost on Lucifer's doorstep, straddling a wendigo who looked about ready to piss his pants any second. She'd had a few run-ins with Alba in the past and the Keeper of this particular veil was well within his rights to piss himself. Sabre didn't have a problem with wendigos in principal, and she didn't even have a problem with a little cannibalism under the right circumstances. How could she when Gage was one of her favourite people in the world? But she was a firm believer that a person's meal should be dead first and not left hanging by their armpits, alive for days as they were eaten from the feet up. Alba had a particularly nasty habit of doing just that. The only reason he was still breathing right now was because he'd promised to go on the straight and narrow for his children's sakes.

"Open the veil, Alba," Sabre crooned, running the tip of a blade down his sternum.

Alba shook his head, grey eyes wide, "I can't! You know I can't! He'll kill me!"

Sabre sighed in disappointment, "Alba, Alba, Alba … *I'm going to kill you.*" She raised her knife and gripped the handle with both hands, making a show of bringing it close to her quarry's heart. Alba shrieked, the sound incredibly high-pitch and sure to set off all the dogs in nearby neighbourhoods.

"Wait! Wait, wait, wait," Alba cried, tears streaming from his face and snot leaking from his nose.

Sabre leaned back a little, not wanting any of the mess to touch her. Blood and organs she was okay with. Snot? Not so much. "Are you going to say something I want to hear?"

The wendigo gulped and nodded, "I can't let you in. Like, I literally can't. I don't have those kinds of powers. You know that. It was why I was given this gig in the first place. BUT –" he screamed as Sabre lifted the knife once more. "I can contact the King and ask him to let you in."

"Huh," Sabre lowered the blade. "You know what? I didn't even think of that. I was just going to cut you up into teeny tiny pieces until I got what I wanted." Her casual comment was met with a bug-eyed stare and Sabre grunted, squeezing her knees together and squashing the air from Alba's lungs. "Now, Alba. Don't make me go back to Plan A."

Alba nodded quickly, slowly digging in his pockets for his phone. Sabre narrowed her eyes but didn't question how the mobile phone was able to dial between realms. No doubt it had been magicked by a wizard. Alba stuttered a few pathetic words before Sabre lost her patience and snatched the phone, "Lucifer. It's me. I need in for a chat."

Silence was all that could be heard for a few heartbeats before a deep voice replied; "Fine. But leave the wendigo in one piece. He's proving useful."

Lucifer hung up before she could say anything else and she handed the phone back to Alba along with a sharp slap to his face. "Have you been good, Alba?"

"Yes!" Alba screamed. "I haven't eaten anyone alive in years. I promise!"

Sabre eyed him for a few more seconds before moving off him. "You better be telling me the truth. If I found out you've eaten someone against their will while their heart is still beating, not even Lucifer will be able to save you," she warned, meaning every word.

Alba nodded frantically and Sabre turned her back on him. The wendigo was no threat to her. Almost immediately, the air around her began to turn electric, causing the hair on her arms to stick up. No doubt, the hair on her head was likewise standing at attention, but she chose to pretend otherwise. A blurry doorway began to appear in front of her, the veil looking almost like a lace curtain waving gently in a non-existent breeze. Stepping through the doorway between different planes of existence was always extremely underwhelming. It was just like stepping through any old door, except it was accompanied by a happy little tingle. The stone path she found herself on led to a trendy red door attached to a two-storey stone house. The door opened just as she stepped onto the welcome mat. Yes, the Devil had a welcome mat.

"Sabre, to what do I owe the pleasure?" the man himself asked.

Sabre looked up in awe at the hottest being in Hell. Lucifer was one very sexy angel; dark hair, ivory eyes, and a body any pro swimmer would be proud of. Why then, did his sexiness seem a little less than the last time she had seen him? For some reason, she found herself comparing Lucifer's white eyes to the incredible yellow of Brax's – and finding them lacking. Shaking off her crazy thoughts, Sabre boldly stated her mission; "I came to ask if you have a personal stake in the downfall of the line of Cerberus. Did you kill King Maliq?"

Lucifer looked genuinely surprised and Sabre breathed out in relief. She had known the other angel for years and had always liked him. They had a lot in common – what with being angels perceived as fallen from Grace – as well as being handed a couple of shitty deals in life. After nearly fighting each other to the death in an epic battle fit for tomes, they had fallen into an easy truce and a genuine friendship. Sabre had stressed during her entire journey here over the possibility that Lucifer was behind the hits. But despite her instincts to the contrary, she was still duty-bound to seek out answers from the man himself. For more than one reason.

"What the actual fuck, Sabre?" Lucifer growled, blocking the entrance into his home.

He was the only angel she knew who could growl like a shifter and Lucifer didn't need to say more in order for her to know she was standing on shaky ground. They might have been friends, but he was still the freakin' devil. Taking a deep breath, she humbled herself a little, "I'm sorry, Lucifer. But I just had to be sure. I didn't really think you were involved but my intel led me here, and, well ..."

Lucifer stared at her for a moment, his white eyes staring right through her. And they could, Sabre knew. Lucifer's unusual – and a little disconcerting – pearl-like irises were able to peer into any being's soul and judge the goodness in their hearts as well as any wickedness they may have lived throughout their lifetime. Hell's angel was judge, jury and executioner. *Hell's angel was really fucking cool,* Sabre thought. Thinking of his powers, Sabre felt a small flicker of envy which she ruthlessly squashed. Her latent abilities also held dominion over the soul and being in the other angel's presence was a stark reminder of that.

Seemingly satisfied with whatever he found lurking beneath her surface, Lucifer gestured for Sabre to enter his humble abode and to take a seat in the comfy-looking brown leather chair in his living room. Lucifer curled himself up like a damn kitten into the corner of the matching three-seater lounge. "Why would I want to kill King Maliq? He was a good man and an even greater King," Lucifer stated. "We were always on friendly terms. I admit, I was quite disappointed when he took a one-way ticket up top instead of joining me here. I don't think we'll have the same problem though will we, my pretty little killing machine?" Lucifer cooed in her direction.

Sabre shook her head. The angel and King of Hell was an incurable flirt. Still, he was an honest one and she had no doubt where she would be spending eternity when her time came. Looking around her at the casual elegance of Lucifer's living room, she couldn't say she was disappointed. She was certain Hell knew how to throw a party unlike the feathery team of snobs upstairs. Lucifer chuckled and she glared at him, "Stop checking out my soul. It's creepy as fuck. Makes me feel naked."

Lucifer's smile revealed even white teeth and cute as pie dimples in his cheeks. He waggled his black eyebrows, "Do you want to be naked?"

Sabre laughed, picking up a pillow from the chair and throwing it at him. "No! Will you quit trying to get into my pants? I'm on a serious mission here."

Lucifer lounged back, at ease in his own domain. "Ah, yes. You're working for the new king now. The middle brother isn't it? Abraxis? Can you imagine marrying into that royal line and having to birth triplets?" Lucifer shuddered.

Sabre wasn't too proud to admit that she shuddered a little too. The line of Cerberus always bred true, with the King in power producing triplet sons no matter who the Queen was, or which brother happened to be ruling at the time. Sabre couldn't imagine carrying around one parasite for twelve months, let alone three at the same time. Considering it was a moot point, Sabre pushed the gruesome thoughts from her mind and addressed Lucifer's last question; "Yes, Abraxis currently sits on the throne. He hired me to seek out the hidden threat who is slowly wiping out his family one at a time. I'm starting with Maliq and it led me straight to Hell."

"How so?" Lucifer asked, bluntly.

"I found a witness if you can believe that. A spotter. It seems the person that took out the hit hired a third party to do their dirty work. A being with red eyes," Sabre divulged, keeping her own eyes on the lethal man in front of her.

"Minions have red eyes," Lucifer grunted.

"I know. Hence, my presence in your humble abode," Sabre said.

Minions were strange little creatures. They weren't demons, couldn't shapeshift, didn't sprout wings, and were completely carnivorous. They were only about one metre tall, completely hairless with red eyes and extremely sharp, pointy little teeth. Their teeth also happened to be in multiple rows, just like a great white shark. They came in all different shapes and orientations with some standing on two legs, while others ran on four. Some had tails and some had forked tongues, while others had webbed hands and feet instead of opposable thumbs. In Sabre's expert opinion; they were creepy as fuck. Lucifer seemed to hold a strange affection for the little critters. They couldn't speak in any language she knew but they *chittered* quite well. Lucifer had no problem understanding them. He was also the only being in existence who could command them. They would literally walk off a cliff if Lucifer snapped his fingers in their direction, which was why Sabre had to check it out.

"It wasn't a minion," Lucifer finally stated. His words were firm and held no hint of a lie.

Picking up yet another pillow – *and why did the man have so many throw pillows?!* – Sabre placed it over her head and proceeded to scream into it. She finally got her first break and now she was staring back at a brick wall. She had no idea what she was going to do now. She –

"Are you going to keep smothering yourself or do you want to pull up those big girl panties I know you're wearing?"

Lucifer's voice snapped her out of her self-flagellation, and she lowered the pillow only to glare at him, "I'll have you know, nothing but silk will work underneath these leather pants. Too much butt sweat." Sabre really shouldn't give him any ammunition but she couldn't seem to help herself. Lucifer brought out the playful side of everyone.

"Silk? What colour?" Lucifer leered. Thankfully, he quickly moved on, "There is one other being in Hell that has red eyes," Lucifer pointed out.

Sabre frowned, her brain working overtime before it hit her, "Oh, come on." Lucifer snickered, his hair as glossy and as black as a raven's wing, ruffled appealingly with the movement. "I hate those things," Sabre whined.

That caused Lucifer to laugh outright, "I know! Remember that time it –"

"I remember!" Sabre snarled, "And don't push our friendship by bringing it up again." Lucifer continued to chuckle a little but mercifully kept his trap shut. Sabre took a precious few moments to relax back into her chair, knowing such opportunities were few and far between. "Who would be able to control one?" she finally asked.

Lucifer's response was prompt, "Only their master."

Sabre rolled her eyes. She knew that. She had been angling for a list of names but Lucifer couldn't help but be obtuse at times. "And who might that be?"

"I'll make some enquiries. But Sabre, I honestly don't believe anyone in Hell has a personal stake in wanting to dethrone the Cerberus line. Especially the higher-ups. Why would they? Any demon who commands such a creature is already a ruler in their own right."

"The individual rulers of the Seven Circles of Hell, right?" Sabre sought clarification.

"That's right. As well as their second in commands. And although I am one of them, I am most definitely not it!" Lucifer threw his hand up in the air like a goof before continuing on, "And nor is Alexis," he added, mentioning his second by name. "Abaddon wouldn't either. The man hates them even more than you. I'll check with the others. But Sabre … I honestly think you're looking at an internal problem," Lucifer's white eyes were earnest on hers.

Sabre sighed, "Yeah. I think that too. But my intel led me here, so … Besides, someone somehow managed to wrangle one of those slippery beasts to do their dirty work. Looks like Purgatory isn't the only realm with internal issues."

Lucifer's handsome visage darkened into planes of anger, "Solid burn, Sabre," he acknowledged. "And something that will be rectified. I assure you."

"Thanks, Luca," Sabre fell back on his nickname, reminding him of their shared history and friendship. The sardonic quirk of his lips let her know he was well aware of her intentions.

Still, he rose when she did and held out a hand, "I'll update you as soon as I can. And you'll do the same for me, won't you Sabre?"

Sabre squeezed the hand in hers, feeling the thrum of power, "You have my word." Lucifer's white irises glowed bright and blinding for a split second before fading away. Sabre didn't bother saying anything else as she stepped back through the veil between their two worlds. After all, what more was there to say? She had just made a deal with the Devil.

## CHAPTER THIRTEEN

Brax gave the magically concealed door in front of him a solid knock with his closed fist. The glamour work was good, he acknowledged. He doubted he would have seen the hidden entrance if he hadn't been told what to look for. But then again, now that he looked at the building, he realised the scale was a bit off. It was smaller than it should have been on the upper level and there was a distinct lack of windows. However, given the derelict appearance of the rundown warehouse, and also what the ground floor area was used for, he didn't think there were too many people who would come looking for a non-door. He couldn't hear any sounds from the interior and figured there was likely a sound barrier in place in addition to the false façade. Which was why he was so startled when the flat, concrete wall in front of him suddenly swung inward.

Sabre was standing in the now open doorway. And she was holding a freakin' machete. He really shouldn't have been surprised. He may have only known the woman for ten days now, and though she was perhaps the biggest conundrum he had ever met, one thing he knew with certainty was that violence ran through her veins. Once upon a time she may have been destined for different things – for *softer* things. But that angel was long gone and he couldn't say he really cared. For some reason, the woman standing in front of him with the ten-inch blade, fierce frown, and tight leather really did it for him.

"Brax?" Sabre asked, machete lowering even as her fabulous plum eyes narrowed. "What the fuck are you doing here?"

Brax snorted out a laugh. Sabre's welcome left a lot to be desired, but he found himself smiling and relaxing against the door jamb, "Looking for you."

She narrowed her eyes, glancing behind him suspiciously, "How did you find my secret lair?"

"Secret lair?" Brax shook his head, "Sabre, you live above the place where you partake in illegal cage fights. Plus, it's owned by your best friend. Not exactly secret."

Sabre huffed, "He's not my friend. I am an assassin. A killing machine. I don't have friends."

Brax barely refrained from rolling his eyes, "Of course you don't. Family then," he offered.

Sabre's eyes narrowed, "I don't have family either."

"Oh? So what is Jinx?" he challenged.

Sabre huffed, the sound decidedly derisive, "A pain in my butt is what she is."

Brax found himself grinning, "Yeah, that sounds like family to me."

A small, genuine smile escaped Sabre's stoic facade and Brax found himself mesmerised by the tiny crack in the assassin's armour. He cleared his throat, "Can I come in?"

"No," came the prompt reply.

Brax raised his eyebrows, "Just no?"

"Would *fuck no* work better?" The smile that lit Sabre's face this time was full of sarcasm and challenge – but no less appealing.

Brax sighed and shook his head, asking without thinking; "Why do you make me feel so good?" The startled look on Sabre's face would have matched his own had he not quickly regained control of his motor functions.

*What the hell?!* He thought, silently. Why was he admitting such things out loud? Why was he even *feeling* such things? He hadn't even seen Sabre since that day in the gardens at the palace but his physical attraction to her certainly hadn't waned. And thanks to his daily phone calls, he was quickly coming to the realisation that he found Sabre's personality just as appealing as her tits. And shit – now he was thinking of Sabre's tits. Clearing his throat and keeping his eyes locked on hers, he simply waited.

It took mere seconds for Sabre to regain her own equilibrium and she responded with her usual offhanded sarcasm; "Huh, usually the only time I make someone feel good is when I deliver the final blow to their brain stems. You know – put them out of their misery."

"Uh huh, sure. Big, bad, scary assassin. I get it," Brax acknowledged.

"I am scary," Sabre stated. "Grown men piss their pants when they see me."

"Kinky," Brax waggled his eyebrows at the fallen angel in front of him, wondering for the umpteenth time how she seemed to bring out the playful side of him. Nobody had been able to do that since his brothers had died. He and his brothers had always been close, despite the complete dichotomies of their natures. Mikhail, as future King, had been the most serious of the bunch. And Z as the baby with the least responsibilities, had been the most spoiled and easy-going. Brax liked to believe he didn't suffer from 'middle child' syndrome and instead was a good balance between the two. He was known to be serious but as the General of the biggest army in Purgatory, a little stern was needed. And before the shit storm of the last year, he had been known to have fun a time or two.

He realised he had been standing in the doorway, lost in thought for more minutes than was strictly polite – or wise. Especially given who he was letting his guard down with. Draven would have kicked his arse. *And he still will,* Brax thought to himself, acknowledging the argument to come once his guardian learned where he was. It wasn't often he could strike out on his own – Brax understood the need for the constant hovering. He really did. But that didn't mean he had to like it. Given Draven had a special kind of dislike for Sabre, Brax knew he was in for a decent nagging when he finally went home.

"Where's your guard dog?" Sabre asked, peering around him, seeming to pluck the thoughts of Draven from Brax's mind.

"Are you referring to Styx or Draven?" Brax asked.

Sabre smirked, tapping the machete against her leather-clad thigh, effectively drawing his attention to the shapely muscle beneath. "Draven," she sneered the other angel's name. "He know you're here?"

Brax crossed his arms over his chest, "He's not the boss of me."

"So, no then," Sabre surmised.

Brax narrowed his eyes again, standing to his full height of six-foot-three, "I am the King. As well as a fully-grown demon. I come and go as I please."

"Uh huh. You keep telling yourself that. Just don't come crying to me when you get your arse spanked for hanging out with the wrong company," she told him.

"Whatever. You disappeared on me," Brax tried to keep the accusation out of his voice. It had been ten days since the day at the palace and although he had been texting and calling every day, Sabre had been gallivanting around the rest of the time. "I'm here for an update. Let me in."

Sabre hesitated one more second, before sighing in resignation and swinging the door open. What he saw the moment he entered had his eyes widening in shock and his feet cementing to the floor. "What kind of fucked up place is this?" He turned to Sabre, knowing his eyes were probably as wide as saucers, "Hell, Sabre. I knew there was something seriously wrong with you, but I never imagined this kind of ... *wrong*."

CHAPTER FOURTEEN

Sabre winced, Brax's words echoing around the room. She knew he would react this way, which was exactly why she didn't want him inside her studio apartment. Still, she didn't let it show, slamming the door behind his fine arse when he finally entered. "How did you get here anyway?" Sabre demanded, feeling defensive and exposed. The only other people to ever enter her inner sanctum were Jinx and Gage. And they knew better than to laugh or question her. Judging by the incredulous and slightly horrified look on Brax's face, Sabre was going to have to perform some serious badarsery in order to gain back respect.

"I walked," came the demon's flippant, off-handed reply. He appeared too engrossed in taking in his surroundings than to be really listening to her.

Stalking around until she was directly in his path, she stopped his wide-eyed wonder and pacing with the tip of her favourite machete against the dark material of his t-shirt. "That's not what I meant and you know it. This is my secret lair. My *evil*, secret lair. How did you find it?"

Brax didn't even bother looking down at the instrument of death resting directly over his heart, he simply pushed it away and snorted, "Your evil lair has fairy lights."

Sabre growled, she just knew this would happen if anyone saw the inside of what she considered to be her home. She may have been required to have the room back at the Blue Devil den and though she did stay there more often than not, this place was her hideaway. It was her sanctuary. The one place she could relax her rigid control and just be herself for a few precious hours at a time. But if the King knew where it was – and *what* it was – then she was likely going to have to burn the whole thing to the ground. She couldn't allow herself to appear vulnerable to anyone. Especially the demon standing in front of her.

"And?" Sabre challenged, responding to Brax's earlier comment. "Fairies are the personification of evil," she pointed out.

Abraxis nodded his head, his gaze still a little wide-eyed and crazed as it took in the room. "You'll get no arguments from me there. Those little motherfuckers are vindictive. And they have really sharp teeth."

The serious look on his face as he divulged that last part almost had her laughing out loud. She could only imagine how he came to know that fairies had needle-like teeth that could pierce just about anything. She managed to hold herself back, knowing she couldn't afford to let down her guard any more than she already had to the pretty man. It was bad enough he was standing in her private place, looking just about perfect in a tight t-shirt, combat cargo pants and boots.

"Nice place you have here," Brax told her. "Though, I have to say, it's … pinker than I thought it would be." Sabre narrowed her eyes dangerously, offering him a look that was hot enough to flay skin from bone. The look didn't seem to bother Abraxis as he choked on a laugh, squinting at her refrigerator. "Is that a puppy calendar?"

Sabre slapped his hand away from the A4 sized, glossy calendar featuring Finnish Lapphund puppies. It had been a gift from the Earth realm and she adored the tiny, teddy bear-looking baby dogs. "This is where I keep my weapons of murder and mass destruction," she informed him, her tone chilly.

Brax said one word; "Glitter."

Sabre leaned in close enough to hear the catch in his breath as she whispered in his ear, "Have you ever been glitter bombed?"

"Can't say that I have," Brax admitted, after clearing his throat.

"Then you have no real understanding of what torture truly is," Sabre stated, her hand clenching on the machete she was still holding. She really felt the need to slaughter something – just to prove a point. A girl could like puppies, glitter, and fairy lights and still know how to disembowel someone … couldn't she?

Brax focused his eyes on hers and Sabre was gratified to find the mocking light gone, "Sabre, seriously. What is all this?"

It was on the tip of Sabre's tongue to say; *this is me*. But that would have been a lie. It wasn't her. Not really. She may have kept this place as her sanctuary. Her private oasis away from the blood and the death and the killing. But this place with its fluffy pillows, scented candles and sparkling lights was not her real life. It was a lie she allowed herself – a mirage – so she could keep doing what she did and still maintain a tiny piece of her soul. She had responsibilities and loyalties the same way Abraxis did to his people. Though, she knew neither he nor Draven – or anyone else for that matter – would see it as the same thing. But she had a code she lived by. Yes, she hated herself for some of the things she had done. But would that stop her from doing it in the future? No. Because she was also a soldier at heart and she followed orders well. She would never, ever betray her true employer. No matter what.

In the end, Sabre placed her weapon on the small round table, "This is just a place to be away from the assassin den. I like my privacy. Now, what exactly do you want from me that you couldn't have asked me in one of your many phone calls?" And they were many, Sabre thought. And she just happened to love them.

Brax widened his stance, long legs eating up the tiny space in the studio, "Like I said; you disappeared for a few days and all you've said about it was that you had to go on a road trip and how you were pursuing leads. Have you learned anything useful at all? What leads?"

Sabre pursed her lips, "Can I just point out, you've been trying to get information for over a year. I've been on the case less than two weeks. You're lucky I have any leads to pursue at all."

Brax huffed, "Two weeks should be plenty of time for someone with your reputation."

Sabre told herself not to preen, that it wasn't a compliment, still she raised her chin, "Actually, I have found something. A witness."

"A what? A witness to one of the assassinations?" Brax's fists clenched and Sabre saw the muscles in his forearms stand out in stark relief. "Whose? And you're only telling me this now? We talk every day!"

That was true, Sabre allowed. But they mostly talked about inconsequential things like food and sports, what their favourite season was and who would win in a fight; Buffy or Sabre. Sabre firmly believed it would be her of course, but Brax was on Team Buffy, stating he would have to witness it in order to know conclusively. And he would have to witness it in the rain when their clothes would be wet and torn and muddy. Who knew Brax was such a pervert? Sabre had been biding her time, hoping to have a full report and some real answers before taking her new information to Brax. But it seemed the time was now to reveal her new findings.

"A witness to your father's death," Sabre admitted.

Brax's knees must have weakened because he grabbed harshly at the chair in front of him, "Dad?" His usual strong, gruff voice was thin and had Sabre's stomach pinching uncomfortably for some reason. "That was forty years ago."

"I know."

"How could there be a witness from back then? How did we not find them? Mikhail, Zagan, and I searched extensively," Brax looked and sounded so confused.

"Well, you know my little trip with Draven? My not-so subtle revelation to the masses that I was working for you and hunting down the royal killer? Paid off," she tried not to sound smug. But if the droll look on Brax's face was anything to go by, she hadn't succeeded.

"Tell me," Brax demanded.

Sabre nodded, "Okay. But I want you to bear with me a little first, okay? For starters, I don't think your father was poisoned –" Brax interrupted her before she could get any further and reveal she knew it to be venom rather than poison being the cause of death. The two were very different, with hugely different implications and was probably why they had been roadblocked in the first place. They had the wrong cause of death.

"It *was* poison. It had to be," Brax's voice brooked no room for argument. "There are things I can't divulge but trust me when I say any other means of death would have been nearly impossible. Poison was one of the only ways to ensure my father was killed."

Sabre stared at Brax for a moment, not relishing the upcoming conversation but knowing she would have to broach it if she was going to get Brax to believe her and change his mind. Figuring it was best to rip off the bandaid, she abruptly asked; "What was your father's ability from Cerberus?"

Brax gaped at her, "Excuse me?"

"You heard me. You're father's attribute – his legacy. Oh, don't look so surprised. I know all about how the line of Cerberus works. The royal line breeds triplet males – always. And each of you receive a different legacy from the genetic pool. It's like a biological lucky dip. The original Cerberus could open portals between realms, as well as command the veils – handy when he wanted to get out of Hell. His skin was also completely impervious to damage – it was like a hide made from vibranium and adamantium combined."

"Wait," Brax looked to be having a hard time keeping up and he rubbed the bridge of his nose, asking; "Vib-what?"

"You know, the material that makes up Captain America's shield and Wolverine's claws? Imagine if they were melded together – that shit would be completely indestructible," Sabre informed him, feeling clever and wise at the same time. Brax didn't respond to that, just continued to watch her with an indecipherable look on his face, so Sabre ploughed ahead; "Anyway, the third ability is the ability to skinwalk – literally shed your skin and become someone else. Entirely different to shapeshifters who share their bodies with the souls of an animal and can shift into their animals. What I want to know is what ability your father inherited."

Where one second Brax looked shell-shocked and confused, the next he was in her face and clutching her upper arms in an iron grip. Sabre snarled up at him, barely stopping her reflex to draw one of her blades and gut the man where he stood for manhandling her. She allowed no one to touch her uninvited. No one.

Giving her a small shake, Brax demanded, "How do you know that? That is the most guarded secret in all of Purgatory."

Sabre snorted, "Hardly the most guarded secret." She would know; she held those. Sabre looked at the hands that were still gripping her harshly and then back up into that handsome face with the tortured eyes. "Let go of me," she enunciated carefully.

Brax's inner beast flexed at her growled words, she could see it in his eyes. Yes, she knew a lot about the royal family. Everything there was to know in fact. And although only one triplet was born with the ability to skinwalk, all of them were born with their own inner beast. She knew it wasn't quite like a shapeshifter, sharing a spirit with their animals. No, the beast *was* them. It was a part of their makeup. It was the blood that pumped through their veins. She knew the beast wouldn't be pushed. It was an alpha – Brax was an alpha. And he may be new to the whole king thing and also reluctant – but he was a General. A leader to hundreds of demon soldiers. He wouldn't back down simply because she asked. Sabre felt a flare of something entirely different in her stomach at the thought and braced herself for his reaction.

Brax's upper lip lifted in a tiny snarl – as if he was holding himself back. "Where did you learn that information? I won't ask you again."

"And I said; Let. Me. Go. I won't ask *you* again," Sabre fired back.

Brax's nostrils flared, the beast taking in her scent. His hands gripped her more tightly for a heartbeat before he let out a huff and stepped back abruptly. To her surprise, he spun away from her, showing her his back. "Only the royal family and their guardian angels are privy to that information," Brax informed her quietly.

"I'm aware," Sabre admitted, just as quietly.

Abraxis turned around, "Then how did you find out? Is there a traitor in the royal line?"

Sabre forced her face to remain impassive in the light of Brax's clear concern. To him, betrayal was obviously one of the things he hadn't counted on – and perhaps couldn't survive. The lovely little spark of heat and *want* died a quick death in a fizzle on the heels of that realisation. There was no way the demon could possibly want someone like her. She made her living betraying everyone around her.

Including the throne.

But she didn't admit any of that. Instead, she lied, "I've looked into your cousins and extended family. There's no traitor. I'm an assassin, Abraxis. The best assassin in all four realms. I have ways of gaining information. It's why you hired me. I've told you this before."

Brax seemed to mull over her words but his defensive stance and the suspicious look in his eyes didn't abate, "Why do you want to know about my father's legacy?"

Sabre sighed, "Because it will help me determine if I'm right about the cause of death and if I'm right to continue to follow my new lead. As well as whether or not you're also in danger," she added.

Brax snorted a mirthless laugh at that. "Me? Oh, I pray I am the next target from that gutless piece of filth. Sneaking around, hiring rodents to stab my family in the back. Coward!" he spat the word out. "I long for the day he comes for me so I can rip his spine out with my bare hands."

Sabre could appreciate the sentiment – and the imagery. But was worried over his blasé attitude. She stepped closer, "You have to be careful. Don't get cocky. This person – or persons – have picked off five members of your family."

Brax snarled, "I'm well aware of that. Why do you think I stooped so low as to hire you?"

Sabre winced, "Ouch."

Brax ran his hands over his head and through his dark hair, making an enticing mess of the thick strands. "Shit, I'm sorry. I just … I don't need a reminder of how much family I've lost. Okay? I'm well aware."

The angel that was left within her wanted nothing more than to gather the lost and hurting demon close and soothe his pain. But the assassin who had spent more than a human lifetime at the hands of some of the cruellest mercenaries smirked at her. So, instead, she simply arched a disdainful brow, "Apology accepted. Now, your father's legacy, it was the armour? Right? The same as you?"

Brax's golden eyes narrowed dangerously again, "What makes you think that?"

Sabre sighed, "Can we please not play this game? As you just reminded me, you hired me. You can be assured that any and all information I have – or require – is directly related to fulfilling my job requirements." She ploughed ahead, suddenly impatient with the back and forth banter, "The witness said they saw red eyes glowing in the darkness right after your father's body was discovered. Red eyes," she stressed again.

That had Brax pausing and straightening, "Red? There are no creatures in Purgatory with red eyes."

"I'm aware," Sabre stated.

Brax's eyes narrowed, "How reliable is your witness?"

"Reliable," was all she said.

"What has red eyes? One of Hell's minions?" Brax guessed.

Sabre shrugged, "A minion from Hell certainly would, but

they are controlled completely by Lucifer. And he hasn't had a hand in this. I checked."

Brax reeled back a little, "Wait, what? You checked? Checked how?"

Sabre raised an eyebrow, "I asked him. He's heard of the troubles here of course but assures me he has had nothing to do with them personally. I believe him."

"You asked him? You talked to Lucifer?" Brax wheezed.

Sabre frowned at him, "That's what I said. That's where I was the past few days. I had to drive a little to get to the correct veil. What's your problem?"

"My problem? You tell me you spoke to the King of Hell, as easy as you please and you ask me what my problem is? Woman, *you're* the one with a problem. Lots of them," Brax stated.

"I happen to be talking to the King of Purgatory right now. No biggie. How is talking to the King of Hell any different?" And it wasn't really. Not to her at least. Other than the fact that Lucifer happened to be her friend, when you dissected enough people like she did, you began to realise that everyone was the same on the inside. Everyone was made up of blood and bone. Everyone bled. And everyone died. Even if some were harder to kill than others – everyone still died.

Shaking off the macabre thoughts, Sabre said, "Lucifer's a cool guy. If he says he and his minions didn't have anything to do with it, they didn't. But there are a few other creatures in hell with red eyes that could have made the journey here. A basilisk for example."

"A ... basilisk ..."

Sabre saw the moment the implications of that settled into Brax's frontal lobe. She knew exactly what he was thinking. Basilisk were indigenous to Hell and their venom was one of the only things in all the four realms that could kill absolutely anything – angels and demons included. And Sabre suspected that its venom would also be enough to erode through an otherwise impenetrable armour. Which was why she wanted to know about Maliq's legacy – as well as Brax's.

"That ... that makes a terrible kind of sense," Brax acknowledged. "We always assumed poison because it was one of the only things that could kill him. Dad's skin automatically became impenetrable whenever it came into contact with a weapon or something that would do him harm. But we never found a wound on him."

"I'm thinking it would have healed very quickly, given your father's genetics. But the venom would still have been fatal. I'm sorry," Sabre added, knowing the conversation was opening old wounds.

Brax was silent for a moment before shaking his head, "No, this is good news. I mean, it's always good to know the truth and this could help, right? What now?" he asked.

Sabre nodded, "It does help. Now we know the real cause of death, I can hunt for the real killer. I have a lead on who could control a basilisk. I'm just waiting to hear back." Sabre didn't say that lead was Lucifer. Brax had already acted like that was weird, so she stayed as vague as possible, "And once I know who ordered that basilisk to kill your father ..."

"You might have solved who is behind all this," Brax finished, looking shocked and more than a little impressed.

Sabre shrugged like it was no big deal, warning, "Don't get your hopes up. Things are rarely that easy."

"Yeah," Brax snorted, "No shit."

When the silence stretched out, Sabre started to get a little twitchy – which resulted in her blurting out the first thing that came to her head, "Can I try to stab you or something?"

Brax turned to her slowly, honey irises wide and reflecting the light, "Excuse me?"

He was looking at her like he thought she was crazy and she stopped to consider the appropriateness of her question for a moment. Jinx was always telling her to do that. Apparently, sometimes she was clueless about socially acceptable conversations. Like, apparently discussing the entrails of her recent victims was not good manners when out to dinner. Who knew? Judging by the look on Brax's face right now, she figured asking to stab someone was probably not socially acceptable either. She sighed, "Sorry. Sometimes I forget not everyone wants to be stabbed."

Brax started to laugh and then must have realised she was being serious for his laughter cut off abruptly. He eyed her curiously instead, "Really?" he asked.

She shrugged, "Yeah. I mean, it doesn't seem like a big deal to me. Your skin is impervious to all forms of weaponry, right? Other than basilisk venom and I don't happen to have any handy." Which was true. Her one vial was secured in her secret vault.

Brax continued to watch her in silence for a moment before finally gesturing to his chest, "Okay. Go ahead."

But Sabre felt like the moment had passed, "No," she pouted. "I don't want to anymore."

Brax rolled his eyes, "Oh, please. Yes you do. Come on. Stab me."

Sabre crossed her arms over her chest, watching as his eyes tracked the movement and seemed to linger on the vee between her breasts created by her arms. "I said no. I'm over it. You've taken all the fun out of it with your prolonged silence and overthinking."

He huffed out a laugh, "I can't believe we're arguing about you stabbing me. Come on," he took a few measured steps closer to her before leaning down and whispering against her ear, "I dare you."

"A dare?" Sabre immediately perked up.

Brax nodded, lips twitching, "That's right."

Sabre tried hard not to skip when she went over to her knife rack. Never having encountered such a protective armour before, let alone skin, Sabre chose a blade that was her least favourite. It was unbalanced and nicked, and she rarely used it for killing anymore, so she didn't care if it ended up breaking. Making her way back over to Brax, she smoothed her hand over the bronzed skin on Brax's arm and ignored his sharply indrawn breath, figuring he took exception to her touch. *Too bad*, she thought. She might not get another chance to indulge her fantasies and she was going to take it. His skin was warm and covered in fine hairs that were surprisingly soft, yet masculine. Giving his arm a prod, she grunted. It looked and felt exactly like normal skin. Looking up, she caught him staring down at her with the oddest look on his face.

"You sure you want me to get stabby with you? Because I gotta say, you look and feel like normal flesh and blood to me," Sabre confessed.

His eyes lit up, male cockiness shining through, "I'm sure." He leaned down, his breath teasing her ear as he whispered, "Do your worst."

Fighting back a shiver, Sabre told her runaway pulse to calm the fuck down. She quickly spun the blade between her fingers and jammed it deeply into the pristine forearm in front of her. At least, she tried to. Her blade made a loud pinging noise even as it snapped off fair to the hilt.

"What the fuck …" she murmured, leaning in to get a better look. Where once was warm, tanned skin just seconds before, a dull grey hardened exoskeleton now appeared. It overlapped almost like fish scales and shone a little in the low light. It rippled over Brax's skin for a moment before fading out of sight once more. "No way!" she exclaimed, running her hand over where the scaled armour had been. "That is so wicked! Can I do it again?" Not bothering to wait for him to answer, Sabre grabbed an arrowhead made of titanium and sliced it over his arm this time. She watched, completely entranced as the scaled skin, stronger than any element in all the realms – including Heaven and Hell – rushed to the surface to protect its charge.

"Wow," she breathed. "That really is something. Is it like that everywhere? What if I aim for your heart?" She quickly cut his shirt down the centre with the arrow clutched in her hand and stabbed at his chest. His entire torso lit up with grey, opalescent scales and she squealed her excitement, clapping her hands together. "This is seriously the best thing I have ever seen! I could do this all day," she laughed, a little breathless in her happiness.

As the legacy from Cerberus settled back into flesh, Sabre suddenly became aware of what she had just done. Dear Gods! She had just literally cut the shirt off the King's back and stabbed him in the heart! Feeling her face heat, Sabre cleared her throat and took a hasty step back. At least, she tried to. But she found herself securely ensconced in a pair of sturdy demon arms. Chancing a glance up, Sabre stilled, her breath catching in her throat. She may be an angel, but she recognised that look well.

Lust.

Clearing her throat, she said, "I'm sorry. I can't believe I did that. If you'll just …" she gave a wiggle, trying to dislodge his arms to no avail. Of course, she could have escaped within seconds had she really wanted to. But apparently she didn't want to – despite the voice inside her head screaming; *Abort! Danger!*

"You …" Brax began.

"Me ... what?" she asked, transfixed by his honeyed stare, barely breathing.

"You really are beautiful," he revealed.

Sabre sucked in a breath. That wasn't what she expected him to say. She was expecting a joke or perhaps some kind of male, horny comment. Unfortunately, such a comment was the one thing that could successfully douse her humour and cool her own growing lust. Stiffening and ducking under his arms, she was across the room before he could even blink. "I'm not beautiful," she informed him, voice flat. "I'm deadly. You'd do well to remember that."

CHAPTER FIFTEEN

Brax eyed the frosty woman standing in front of him, so at odds with the playful, laughing woman of mere moments ago. He hadn't meant to reveal his thoughts but he couldn't seem to help himself. Sabre had just been so vibrant and full of life, like a kid in a candy store. *Or an assassin who just discovered impenetrable armour,* he laughed silently. Who knew stabbing him and watching his skin flare could bring so much joy? And it had been joy, Brax thought. Nothing else could light a face like that. *And, oh, what a face ...* with her eyes warm and shiny, her high cheekbones flushed, lips curved up so that her dimples flashed ... Sabre had been breathtaking. Too bad his words had the opposite effect to what he intended. Most woman would be thrilled to be called beautiful. But Sabre was terrified of it. For some reason, that just made her all the more appealing to him.

He didn't think it was all that brave to step up to the feisty assassin. After all, his butt was impervious to anything she might try to attack him with. It tickled him when she took a hasty step back, and he felt his beast stir like a predator on the hunt.

"Because I believe in full disclosure, I'm going to tell you something, Sabre," he murmured, watching her eyelashes flutter.

"What?" Her voice was hostile but also held an almost pleading note too as she looked pointedly at the floor.

"I'm going to strip you naked, pick you up, throw you on that sparkly bed in the corner, and then fuck you until we both forget our names." He heard Sabre's breath catch, but the stubborn woman still didn't look up at him. Bending down, he bit her earlobe none too gently, relishing in the sound of Sabre's excited gasp. "How does that sound, my deadly little angel?"

"It sounds ..." Sabre broke off, lifting her head, plum eyes locking onto his, "It sounds like the best idea I've heard in forever."

"Fuckin' A," Brax agreed, swooping down to capture her lips with his in an aggressive kiss before she could change her mind.

Brax's world tilted on its axis when Sabre's tongue met his for the first time. Electricity sparked along his skin and his heart galloped as if he had been struck by lightning. Groaning, he angled his head forcing Sabre to follow his lead and was more than satisfied when she gave as good as she got. Her hands gripped him by the ears, fingernails digging into the sensitive skin as their breaths mingled and their bodies set alight. Although Brax wanted to bask in the willing heat of Sabre's lips against his own, he wanted to feel her naked skin writhing against his more. Pulling back, he rested his forehead against hers for a few moments, each of them panting for breath. Bending his knees enough so they were eye to eye, he reached behind Sabre and began to undo the buckles on her leather corset.

"Your clothes are sexy as fuck, you know that?" Brax asked, peeling the leather top off, hardly containing his excitement when it revealed a form-fitting, pale pink sports bra and acres of creamy skin.

"They're practical," Sabre countered. "Leather is much harder to penetrate than cotton."

"Uh huh," Brax ignored her denial, instead focusing on undoing her pants and peeling the black leather down and off her endless legs. Sabre obligingly lifted her feet, allowing him to fling the pants over his shoulder. Remaining on his haunches, he looked up, finding silk cream underwear that almost camouflaged with the milky perfection of her skin. It was surprisingly scar-free given her occupation. But then, angels were able to heal from just about anything so he knew even though her skin didn't tell tales of past hurts, there still must be plenty.

The thought of Sabre hurting caused a rush of adrenaline to flood his system and he forced his clawed hands to unclench. Why he was feeling so protective, he had no clue. But he was willing to go with it. Running his hands from her calves to her thighs, he revelled in the heat and smoothness of Sabre's skin, indulging in a few nibbles with his mouth here and there. His rewards were the soft catches of Sabre's breath and the rapidly pounding pulse he could feel when he kissed the inside of her wrist.

"Are you going to get to the good bits anytime soon? Because I think you're drastically overestimating my attention span here," Sabre suddenly grumbled from above him.

Choking on a laugh, Brax raised his head, "It's called foreplay, Sabre."

"Yeah, well. Less *fore* and more *play* I say."

Because he could appreciate where the woman was coming from – he was about ready to burst and he wasn't even undressed yet – Brax stood up and made good on his promise. He quickly divested the fallen angel of her underwear, picked her up and threw her on the bed a mere two metres away. Delighting in her feminine squeal, he prowled closer to her, toeing off his boots and unzipping his pants. Seeing the look of dazed lust in Sabre's eyes, Brax slowed his roll once more, peeling back his pants and slowly revealing the hard length of his confined cock. Sabre made a sound that was suspiciously like a whimper, licking her lips and causing his dick to jerk. Groaning, Brax quickly shucked his pants, giving his dick a few strokes under the hungry gaze of the perfect woman on the bed.

Sabre raised her arms, the only invitation he needed and Brax found himself on top of her, aligning their bodies within a second. They both groaned when his hard flesh met her wet softness and Brax gave a few experimental slides of his cock between her slick folds. Sabre gasped, back arching and pebbled nipples raking against his chest. Placing a series of wet kisses and nibbling bites from her ear, down her neck and across the top of her chest, Brax finally made it to her breasts. They were round and high with the palest pink nipples he had ever seen. A little less than a handful but that suited Brax just fine and he swooped down, taking a hardened peak into his mouth. Sabre screamed a little, her hands clutching his back and legs rising to lock around his waist. For someone who didn't like foreplay, Sabre sure seemed to be enjoying it, he thought, smugly.

After giving her other breast the same level of attention, Brax raised his head, taking in the flushed face of the woman beneath him. "Sexy as sin," he muttered, lowering his head for another kiss. He felt Sabre's lips curve against his even as they opened up, allowing him entrance.

"Well, you got the sin part right anyway," Sabre told him, her breath coming in gasps when they parted.

Brax leered down at her, allowing his hands to map the contours of her disciplined body. Testing her readiness with his fingers, Brax groaned when he was met with delicious wetness. Promising himself he and his inner beast would get a taste of that later, he lined himself up at her entrance now, not willing to wait another second to be in her perfect body. He was just about to push himself in, when a thought hit him, "You've done this before, right?"

Sabre looked a little dazed and very crazed as she shook her head, "What?"

He cleared his throat, feeling heat climbing up his neck. Something he didn't think was possible. "I mean, you're an angel. They don't have much of a sex drive. I just wanted to check that, you know, you weren't …"

"A virgin?" Sabre smirked at him and he nodded quickly.

"You keep forgetting – I may have been born an angel but I'm not living like one and I sure won't be dying as one. You can relax, great King. I'm no virgin." Then she pulled him down on top of her once more, her fingernails raking down his back, and the last vestiges of hesitation crumbled like dust under her skilled hands.

Brax reached down and gripped his shaft, pushing Sabre's thighs wide with his other hand. Pushing with his hips, Brax gritted his teeth at the view of his cock being swallowed so perfectly by Sabre's body. "Gods … Sabre!" Brax grunted, pushing in until their pelvis were flush against each other.

"Yes! More!" Sabre urged him on with her words and her body, her hands grabbing at his arse and hauling him even closer.

Groaning, Brax bit down on Sabre's exposed neck, using his lower fangs to keep her in place as he shoved his cock in deep, as deep as he could go. Sabre keened, the sound high and wild as she met him thrust for thrust. Releasing her neck, Brax sought out her mouth for a kiss full of passion and heat and dominance. Sabre gave as much as she took and Brax was so turned on by the strength of the woman beneath him that he knew he wasn't going to last long. Cupping her buttocks in both hands, he reared back onto his knees, opening Sabre up to his gaze – and his cock – even more. Sabre arched her back – the assassin toned and flexible – pulling on her own nipples as she writhed and gasped still meeting the pounding of his hips with her own.

He felt the rippling release of Sabre's inner muscles a second before she cried out, the sound loud and long, and almost rupturing his eardrums. The tight clenching of her body had him cursing and his rhythm faltering. But he gave a few more solid thrusts before his own body erupted in ecstasy, his dick exploding and filling Sabre to the brim. Gasping for breath, he had the presence of mind to lower Sabre's legs and fall to the side next to her instead of crushing her beneath his considerable bulk. He was panting and sweaty and his body was still twitching with small aftershocks. Brax had just had the best sex of his entire life and it was with the last person he would have expected.

Looking to his left, he saw that Sabre had rolled to her stomach and was splayed out like a starfish. *A very satisfied starfish*, Brax thought, none too smugly. Eyeing the long lines of her back, he was more than a little surprised to see that Sabre wasn't as blemish-free as he had assumed earlier. In a straight line down the centre of her back was a tattoo in black cursive. Pushing himself onto an elbow, he ran a hand down the Latin letters, translating them as he went. Sabre arched into his touch like a cat, the contented sound she made in the back of her throat sounding much like a purr as well. He smoothed his hand down her ink once more, following the curve of her wonderful arse, before eyeing the space between her shoulder blades with interest.

"What should you have been?" he asked, curiosity getting the better of him.

"Excuse me?" Sabre immediately stiffened beneath his questing hands.

"When you were giving me your pep talk – 'rah rah, shit happens, go team!'" He shook his hands like he was holding imaginary pom poms, eliciting a small giggle from her – the uncommon sound making him feel ten-feet tall. "You said this wasn't the path you were born to. You're an angel, clearly you were supposed to do something else. I'm just wondering what you should have been? What colour are your wings? Or, rather; what colour *were* your wings?"

"Firstly, I'm a fallen angel," Sabre corrected, pulling out of his arms and sitting up with her back to him. "Secondly, the colour of my wings is none of your business. Jeez, what is it with you and your stupid fucking angel, thinking you can just ask to see my vagina any time you want," Sabre continued to grumble, incoherently.

Brax had absolutely no clue what Sabre was talking about. Her vagina? What the fuck? "Umm, why are you mumbling about your vagina? And what does Draven have to do with it? I mean, you just showed me your vagina – it's very pleasant. You haven't shown him too, have you?"

Sabre quickly dropped the clothes she had only just picked up, her mouth hanging open in shock. "That's foul! I wouldn't piss on Draven if he was on fire!"

Brax chuckled, stretching himself out on the bed, "Lovely imagery."

"Get up. Put your clothes on," Sabre demanded, launching said clothes at Brax's face. "And I was referring to you two being nosey and asking about my wings. Draven seemed to think he was entitled to ask as well."

Brax ignored the pile of clothes in his hand in favour of watching Sabre hastily don her own. Her fair skin bore the evidence of their recent escapades, with beard-burn, hickeys, and even a set of indentations from where his fangs had pierced her skin ever so slightly. The sight caused male satisfaction to swell in his chest – and other places. Smirking at his rapidly hardening cock, Brax figured his chances for a repeat performance were probably somewhere between zero and never. Still, he wasn't going to be rushed, so he propped himself on his elbows, "I just figured that you know my secret. Vibramantium," he reminded her, joining the words together. "Don't you think it's only fair I know yours?"

Sabre, now fully dressed and looking casual in black leggings and a loose t-shirt, put her hands on her hips, practically spitting, "If you knew half of my secrets, your head would explode!"

Brax laughed, it probably wasn't wise but he was feeling all kinds of awesome thanks to his recent orgasm. And it turned out a grumpy, pouty Sabre wearing old cotton instead of leather was just plain delightful. The pillow thrown at his head would have had more effect if it weren't covered in rainbow sequins and featured a pug saying; *'Pugs, not drugs.'* Brax simply caught it and raised an eyebrow, "Really?"

Sabre screamed in frustration, "Out! You've had your fun and now you can leave. And don't be thinking this epic mistake will be repeated, because it won't," Sabre promised him.

Brax moved slowly, making a show of pulling on his pants and tucking his new erection away. He noted the way Sabre's eyes followed the movement and how she licked her lips unconsciously. She may say she wasn't interested in more, but her body was telling a whole different story. Dragging on his shirt, Brax made his way around the room at a leisurely pace, locating his socks and boots. Sabre watched him in silence the entire time, her laser-sharp eyes never leaving him. He felt like he was being stalked by a predator. Usually, such a sensation would have his blood boiling and the alpha in him issuing a challenge for dominance. Strangely though, his inner beast – in other words *him* – simply purred. Once his boots were laced, he stood up, keeping his eyes on Sabre's, "That tattoo on your back …"

Sabre cocked her head to the side, surprise lighting her features from the abrupt topic change, "What about it?"

"It's from *Dante's Inferno*, right?" he asked. Remembering the passage inked in Latin in a line down her back, Brax translated; "*'The path to Paradise begins in Hell.'*"

"That's right," Sabre admitted, shifting a little as if uncomfortable.

"Fitting," Brax acknowledged, finally making his way to the door. "Because Sabre, baby, I have a feeling we're both trapped in our own personal hells. And you know what that means? Paradise here we come."

Shutting the door behind him, Brax couldn't help but think Sabre was his perfect kind of paradise.

## CHAPTER SIXTEEN

Sabre forced her mind on the task at hand rather than what had transpired three days ago in her studio. She couldn't believe she had slept with Brax! Out of all of the stupid, stupid things she could have done, that had to be at the top of the list. And to make matters worse, her once dormant sex drive had decided to spark to life. It had been a long, horrified three days. Sabre had been forced to stay at the Blue Devil for the past couple of nights because her secret lair was now all sexified and echoed with the groans and shouts of shared pleasure. Not to mention, Sabre had not been willing to risk Jinx or Gage getting a good look at her. The pair would sniff out her broken celibacy and grill her until she cried for mercy. *Stupid, stupid, stupid,* she continued her self-flagellation.

"I mean, what was I thinking? As if my life wasn't complicated enough, you know?" she asked the demon lord currently tied to a chair in front of her. Dra'mon quickly nodded his head as if he understood what she was talking about. She didn't blame him – Sabre knew she looked a little deranged.

"Have you ever had sex with the wrong person?" she asked Dra'mon

The demon nodded enthusiastically, "Sure I have. All the time."

Sabre narrowed her eyes at him, "You a slut or what?"

"Huh? No! I just –"

"You just, what? Thought we were going to be all buddy-buddy and maybe I wouldn't keep torturing you for information?" Sabre knew she was acting like a bi-polar pageant queen but she couldn't seem to stop the madness.

Dra'mon was a demon lord, second in command to the demon ruler of the third circle of hell. He was also the only demon lord who had been unable to provide an acceptable alibi as to his whereabouts in the few days preceding and post assassination of Mikhail. And because he was one of the few who could command a basilisk to do their bidding, Sabre had been getting chop-happy with a few of his fingers. She hadn't yet felt the need to move up to any other appendages, but she was feeling just unstable enough to do so. Lucifer had come through and handed over Dra'mon along with all that information just that morning thanks to his ability to not only open and close the veils, but also to teleport anywhere. And that included between realms. Yeah, Lucifer was really fucking powerful.

Sabre stood up to pace once again, feeling as if ants were crawling under her skin. She scratched at her arm, "What is this?!" she screamed in frustration, "Supernaturals aren't supposed to spread STDs, right? I swear, if I didn't know better that's what I'd think this is! Ever since I fucked the King, I can't concentrate, my mind wanders, I get goosebumps every time I think about him. I get butterflies in my stomach at random times of the day and night. I feel hot and flushed and I swear my heart is beating to a different rhythm than before." She turned to Dra'mon, pointing a mace at him, "What do you think?"

Dra'mon looked like a stunned mullet, "You ... you slept with the King?"

Sabre stilled, *damnit, Sabre! Now you're going to have to kill him,* she chided. But that just proved her point. She would never normally run her mouth that way. Something was very wrong with her. "Pretend you didn't hear that and answer my question," she ordered the dead-man-walking.

Dra'mon cleared his throat, "Well, it sounds kind of like ... you're in love."

"In love?" Sabre laughed so hard she was concerned she was going to rupture something. Bent over at the waist, she gasped for breath, hastily wiping the tears of hilarity off her cheeks. "Oh, Dra'mon, you're funny. I'll give you that." She walked over to him and pushed the sharp points of the mace against the bare skin of his chest, "Lucifer didn't tell me you were a comedian. But comic relief isn't going to save you."

Cringing away from the mace, Dra'mon pleaded, "Please! I told you, I don't know anything about the death of King Maliq!"

"Hmmm," Sabre mused, applying pressure and seeing a few beads of blood drip from beneath the spikes. "So you never commanded a basilisk to bite King Malik?"

"No! Why the fuck would I?" The demon snarled, all pretences of their chummy banter disappearing.

"Well, you see, that's what I'm trying to find out." Sabre stepped back and swung, the mace coming down and crushing the demon's hand. Sabre smirked when Dra'mon screamed like the little bitch he was. "Why is your basilisk the only one to have died in the last five hundred years? And why did it die just a week after Maliq was killed?"

Spittle ran down Dra'mon's chin as he shook and shuddered, looking at his hand in horror. "It just died! I don't know why."

Sabre tsked, "I'm gonna need more than that, Dra'mon. How about I go ahead and take this out," she yanked with all her might, the spikes pulling free of his hand but unfortunately taking a lot of skin and bone with it. "Oops, my bad."

"Fuck you, you crazy bitch!" Dra'mon panted.

Sabre snorted, "Not even on your best day. Now, I really don't want to have to get my blowtorch out. I hate the smell of burnt flesh. That shit really stays in your sinuses, you know?" Even as she spoke, Sabre rifled through her bag of tricks.

"Okay, okay! Listen, I do remember the basilisk you're referring to. It went missing for one night – just one fucking night, I swear! I didn't think much of it, but then when it came back its fangs were broken. That's pretty much lethal for those types of creatures. Anyway, it died within a few days."

Sabre frowned at the sweating demon. She was inclined to believe him. Still, *someone* had ordered that big-arse snake to bite Maliq. "Did you or did you not command the basilisk to bite and kill King Maliq?"

"Not. Not, not, not!" Dra'mon screamed, eyeing the samurai sword Sabre now held.

"Then, you're less than useless to me," Sabre concluded, stabbing the sooky demon in the heart. Dra'mon let out one more thin scream, eyes bulging with awareness of his imminent demise, before they went glassy.

Sabre sighed, stepping back. She eyed the mess in front of her for a moment before giving the dead demon a solid kick to the shin. "And I am *not* in love! Stupid jerk."

## CHAPTER SEVENTEEN

The second Brax entered her field of view Sabre felt her pulse race and her skin become clammy. Dra'mon's words were on repeat in her head and she couldn't turn them off no matter how hard she tried. She didn't believe them for a second, Sabre assured herself, still she gave the object she was holding a hard squeeze for good measure. Blood dripped down her fingers, hitting the ground in soft splats and she felt a little better already. Walking further into the gardens of the palace, Sabre refused to make eye contact with Brax because if she did, all she would think about was how his yellow eyes glowed like fire when he orgasmed and how wonderful his big, demon-sized dick felt inside of her.

*Stop thinking about demon dicks!* Sabre cautioned herself. But it was so hard not to when Brax was striding toward her with stubble on his cheeks and his hair a little wild. He was wearing all black again, something they had in common and something she could appreciate. She liked wearing black because it hid blood so much better than any other colour. She didn't know if Brax did it for the same reason, but it really worked for him. Slapping herself around a little mentally, Sabre stayed in place and waited for Brax to come to her.

"You disappeared again," Brax accused as soon as he and his angel sidekick were within speaking range.

"I didn't disappear. I've been working," Sabre fired back.

"Wait ... what is that?" The look of horror on Draven's face as he pointed to her bloody hand and its contents was the best thing Sabre had seen in years.

"This?" Sabre held up the piece of flesh, still fresh and covered in blood and gore. "It's a trachea."

Draven's blue eyes widened impossibly further, "A trachea?"

Sabre nodded casually, "Yeah. Sorry, I forgot I was holding it."

Draven sputtered for a moment, looking from Sabre to Brax and back again. Brax merely shook his head, remaining silent, but Sabre was sure she could detect a hint of amusement in his amber irises.

"How do you forget you're holding a trachea?!" Draven demanded, voice a little shrill.

Sabre shrugged, "I dunno. I hold a lot of tracheas, I guess."

Draven took a step forward, thrusting his finger in her face, "You –" he began, only to be brought up short by Brax's restraining hand to his chest.

"Draven, relax."

"Relax?" Draven turned to his charge, "You want me to relax? This crazy woman skips around clutching dead-men's flesh and you want me to relax?!"

Sabre suppressed the undignified giggle threatening to burst forth and instead rolled her eyes, "I am sorry if I upset your delicate sensibilities but –"

"Delicate sensibilities? Any sane person would take issue with you clutching a trachea!" Draven yelled, interrupting her. He turned to Brax, "I'm sorry, Brax. I know you think we need her but she is so far more than deranged." The straight-laced angel threw his hands up in the air, "I don't even know what more than deranged is!"

"Psychotic?" Sabre suggested, helpfully. The frustrated and disbelieving gurgle she received in response was music to her ears.

Brax shook his head, "Sabre, do you care to explain why you have a trachea in your hand? And how did you get in here with that anyway?!"

Sabre smiled, "I can get into Hell. You think your gardens can hold me out? Don't worry, your boy, Hugo, is just taking a nap," she mentioned the soldier who she had just placed a sleeper-hold on.

"You injured a royal soldier? A member of the Demon Horde?" Draven looked fit to be tied – something Sabre would love to do.

"I didn't injure him," Sabre said, exasperated by the angel's drama. "He's simply sleeping, like I said. Go and check on him if you don't believe me."

"Brax?" Draven asked his charge.

Brax nodded, not appearing too concerned for the safety of his soldier, "Go ahead. See how he is and heal him if he needs it."

"You are more trouble than you're worth," Draven sniped at her as he walked past.

"Yeah? Well, so's your face!" Sabre yelled to his retreating form, snickering when she saw the angel's shoulders stiffen.

When Draven was out of sight, Abraxis levelled his canary-yellow peepers on her, "Stop fucking with my angel."

Sabre pursed her lips, "I have no idea what you're talking about."

Brax snorted, crossing his arms over his chest and inadvertently flexing his biceps and the corded muscles in his forearms at the same time. Sabre barely swallowed her whimper of need – which was both pitiful and embarrassing. Her sex drive – which had been non-existent for, well, forever – had definitely decided to wake itself up. Yes, she may have drooled over the hunky demon from a distance for years. But now that she knew what he was packing under his clothes, Sabre was doomed. But she still wasn't in love, Sabre assured herself. Dra'mon was a pathetic excuse for a demon lord and had no clue whatsoever what he had been talking about. Sabre realised Brax was still talking and she forced herself to listen to his words and not just watch his lips move.

"I know he looks and sounds like your typical stuffy angel. But I assure you, the man is a warrior. He's been by my side, fighting on the front lines with my Demon Horde for years – as well as patching everyone up once the fighting was done. There's more to him than meets the eye. You keep pushing him, and you'll find that out personally," Brax promised.

"I'm not worried," Sabre assured him. "After all, he'd have to take that stick out of his arse first before he could do any real damage to me. And I'm sure that would take a lot of time. And a lot of lube." Brax's laugh brought a smile to her own face and she found herself sighing like a fucking schoolgirl with a crush.

"Do you want to tell me the real reason why you're holding some poor sap's windpipe?" he finally asked.

"He lied to me," Sabre revealed. "And then he told the truth. But he lied first. So I killed him."

Brax took the news like a pro, merely raising an eyebrow, "Uh huh. And just who was the poor schmuck?"

"Dra'mon, demon lord and second in command of the third ring of Hell."

Brax had been nodding his head but froze when he heard that, "What?"

"Yeah, Lucifer was kind enough to drop him off this morning. He was the only one who didn't pass the King of Hell's questioning about the basilisk. I've already informed Lucifer of my findings. That's a part of the deal we made," she informed Brax.

Brax pointed to Sabre's bloody hand, "That is the trachea of the guy who owned the basilisk?"

Sabre nodded, "It is. He told me the basilisk died because its fangs were broken."

"Because it hurt itself piercing my father's skin-armour," Brax stated.

"Correct."

"Why did he order it to?" Brax began to pace, looking more and more agitated.

Sabre felt bad for him but told him the truth, "He maintained that he didn't."

Brax stopped moving, "And you believed him?"

Sabre waggled her head from side to side, "Not really, no. But he seemed to believe himself and trust me, there's no point trying to get blood out of that stone."

"So you ripped out his trachea?" Brax stated, trying to follow along.

"Among other things," Sabre agreed.

"So you have nothing," Brax's voice was flat and disappointed, bordering on bitter. "Again."

"Hey! I managed to find a witness, the real cause of death for your father, made a trip to Hell to talk with Lucifer himself, have ruled out your cousins, and have now ruled out one of the beings capable of controlling a basilisk. I've accomplished more in the past two weeks than you have in a whole year!" Sabre yelled the words, feeling insulted and unappreciated. And considering she was hearing Dra'mon's suggestion of love over and over again in her brain, Sabre was also not surprised to feel a little bit hurt, "Oh, and I also think Carlisle has something to do with something," Sabre revealed, thinking of her den master.

Just the evening prior, she had updated Carlisle with how her work for the king was going. She had, of course, lied her arse off and told Carlisle exactly nothing. Especially about the basilisk and her trip to Hell. The incubus had been particularly shifty and closed-mouth. It was definitely making her suspicious and she vowed to put Hound on his trail as soon as he finished his angel research for her. Hound was damn good at sniffing things out that didn't want to be sniffed out because he was so damn charming.

"Who the fuck is Carlisle?" Brax snarled, sounding surly and put-out.

"He's the owner of the Blue Devil," Sabre spoke slowly. *What does Brax have to feel put out about?* she wondered.

"Your assassin den? Does that make him your Master?" Brax pushed.

She nodded once, "Yes."

Brax stared at her for a moment, jaw clenched but working rigidly as if he were chewing broken glass. "What makes you think he knows something?" he finally asked.

Sabre explained about the comment Carlisle had made about wanting to keep close tabs on her because he knew someone who wanted to destroy the throne. The longer she talked, the more Brax's eyes seemed to glow until finally they looked like iridescent fireflies, shining angrily in his sexy demon face. *Yep, he was definitely good and pissed*, Sabre marvelled, feeling a tingle begin between her legs. Angry demon equalled sexy demon.

"And you're just telling me this now?!" Brax yelled.

"Why are you mad?" Sabre didn't understand men at all.

"Because you've been keeping something pretty integral from

me, that's why," Brax exclaimed. "What else have you been keeping from me?"

"Hey, now," Sabre's voice lowered in anger. "I haven't been keeping anything from you." She quickly crossed her fingers behind her back because it was totally okay to lie as long as one's fingers were crossed. Jinx had assured her of that. "I'm telling you things as soon as they become pertinent. What more do you want from me?"

Brax stared at her for a few seconds before dropping his head back on his neck, "I'm sorry, okay? I just –" He raked his fingers through his hair in agitation. "I just feel like we take one step forward and two steps back. None of this makes sense. We're no closer to finding the killer than when we started. I'm just ... tired. I'm tired, Sabre."

Sabre's anger deflated in an instant and she stepped up to him. Reaching out her non-organ-holding hand, she rested it on his chest. "I know you are. I'm sorry. I'm trying the best I can."

Brax gripped her hand with his own, holding it against his chest so she could feel his heart beating beneath her palm. "I know you are. And I appreciate it. Thank you."

Becoming steadily lost in the heat of his eyes, Sabre cleared her throat, yanking her hand with more force than necessary from his, "Anyway, dead demon lord could still prove useful."

"Useful, huh? Too bad he can't talk anymore, what with having no throat and all," Brax said, drolly.

"Hey hey, the King has a sense of humour. Who knew?" Sabre fired back. "I don't need him," she then said. "If I did, he would still have a pulse. All I need is this," she held up the somewhat macerated trachea.

"I don't understand," Brax admitted.

"Gage," she replied in one word.

"Gage? Warehouse owner, cage fight organiser and secret evil lair landlord?" Brax questioned, clearly very curious about Gage's origins.

Sabre nodded, "That's right."

"How can he help? And what is he? If I didn't know better, I would say he was human. But he doesn't smell right. And those black eyes of his ... definitely not human," Brax decided.

"You're mostly right," Sabre admitted. Wondering if Gage was going to kick her arse for revealing his secret to Brax. "Gage is a zombie."

Brax did a double take, "A what?"

"A zombie," Sabre helpfully repeated.

"That's not possible. Zombies are nothing but animated corpses. They don't talk or laugh or smile. They certainly don't have friends," Brax pointed out.

"Yeah, well, Gage is special."

And he was, Sabre thought. Brax was correct when he said zombies were little more than walking dead bodies. They retained no memories of their previous lives and only maintained gross motor function due to their primitive hind brain. It also meant their desires were based purely on survival, and that meant food. Yep, zombies craved and ate flesh. The human movies from the Earth plane had gotten something right when they portrayed rotten, decaying flesh, moaning mouths, and stumbling corpses seeking out brains. Zombies were what happened to humans who entered Purgatory – and died here – when they had no magic or any kind of supernatural-ness about them. A human who died in Purgatory and not on their own plane, meant their souls weren't looped into the death planes of Heaven and Hell. Thus, their soul's kind of went walkabout causing their bodies to do the same. Purgatory really wasn't a fun place to die if you were fully human. It didn't have too many zombies because non-magical humans were few and far between. But sometimes, one slipped through.

Which is exactly what happened to Gage some fifty years ago. But Gage wasn't your typical zombie. In fact, he was more of an akuji – a name Sabre herself had coined in reference to Gage because he was just so unique. Akuji was a name of African origins that literally meant 'dead and awake'. Kind of like a zombie but not. Just like Gage. Because although Gage was technically dead and did in fact need to eat flesh to keep his body animated, he was still in possession of his soul. Gage had been killed in Purgatory, therefore his soul had left his body, unable to find rest or solace in either Heaven or Hell. But fortunately for him, Sabre had contacts and had been able to place his soul back into his body. Unfortunately for Gage, his body had been left to decompose for too long and rigor mortis had set in. His resurrection had been incomplete. It was a phenomenon Sabre had never come across before and at first, she had considered killing the man all over again. But Gage had acted surprisingly like the human he had once been, and she had given him the benefit of the doubt. She was beyond glad she had. Not only had she owed him a debt – the life of one she held dear – but he had also become a true friend to her. She sometimes thought he was the only reason she had any humanity left in her at all.

"Gage is really a zombie? And that means he can get memories from the flesh he consumes?"

Brax's incredulous question brought Sabre back to the moment and she refocused her attention. "He *kind of* is a zombie, and yes, he can access the life and memories of the person he eats. I'm hoping he can tell us a little more about Dra'mon and his fangy friend. Gage prefers to be called an akuji," Sabre admitted. "But I still like to call him a zombie just to fuck with him."

"Of course you do. Fucking with people is your hobby or

something," Brax said, dryly before leering at her. "And I would know. You fucked me after all."

"Shh!" Sabre hissed, looking around frantically. Draven still wasn't back and there was no one else within ear shot, but Sabre didn't want to run the risk of anyone hearing that. "We are never speaking of that again! Just like we are never doing that again!"

"Are you sure?" Brax purred, getting all up in her personal space, "Because you don't sound so sure. And those pretty little nipples of yours, poking against your shirt certainly don't look so sure. They look aroused to me," he pointed out, reaching out a hand and gently brushing it over the erect tips.

Sabre gasped, her traitorous body instinctively gravitating toward his touch. She allowed her body to hum with pleasure for all of two seconds before she swept out her foot and knocked Brax to his back. Quickly moving her booted heel over his manjunk, Sabre sneered down at him, "You're awful easy to take down for a demon General."

Brax breathed in a shocked breath, eyes darting down to his very vulnerable balls, "You fight dirty. Why am I not surprised?"

"There's no such thing as fighting dirty when you're fighting for your life," Sabre promptly replied.

Brax relaxed back against the ground, searching her face. Looking for what, Sabre had no clue, but the focused scrutiny was making her uncomfortable and she shifted her foot, intending to remove it. But large, warm hands on her calf halted her movement and she raised her eyebrows in silent query.

"And is that what you think you're doing? Fighting for your life?" Brax asked.

"That's what I'm always doing. That's what I've always done," she informed him. Only this time, she knew she wasn't just fighting for her life. No, she was fighting for something much more important; her heart. The thought made her want to flee and she was turning to do just that when Brax surprised her by toppling her to the ground and quickly rolling them over so that his heavy weight pinned her beneath him.

"You know, if our clothes fell off right now, we could accidentally have sex again," the sexy demon above her stated, a purr rumbling in his chest.

Sabre looked up at him, but it was hard to keep a straight face when Brax's own face had taken on a playful, almost boyish look. The man above her was relaxed and happy in a way she hadn't seen him before and she felt pride surge within her knowing she had contributed to that. For some reason, she had the ability to make him happy … And he did the same to her.

"We agreed we weren't going to do that again," Sabre finally said, trying to sound stern.

"I don't remember agreeing to any such thing. If I remember correctly, in the last phone conversation we had yesterday you yelled something about it being the 'best worst mistake' of your entire life before you stuttered, dropped your phone and then finally hung up on me."

Sabre felt her face flame. Even though she had been doing her best to hide from seeing Brax face to face, the man had been persistent with his phone calls and texts. Only now they were worse. The demon was sexting her. Sabre had no idea how to flirt and certainly no idea how to talk dirty or have phone sex – as Brax had been trying to cajole her into the previous evening. She remembered muttering something like Brax just said before panicking and dropping her phone, only to have a night filled with erotic dreams. "Yeah, well. It was true then and it's true now. Now get off me. No more hanky panky for you, Your Majesty."

"Hmm," Brax hummed as he sniffed at her neck. "Okay, no more hanky panky. How about just some panky then?"

Sabre stifled a laugh – the man was incorrigible. "No! No sex of any kind. If Draven comes out and finds us like this, he'll try to kill me you know? And then I'll have to spank his perfect angel arse and he'll get all bloody. There will be tears and snot. And that is something I can't handle. The snot, not the blood. Tears are touch and go depending on who they belong to. Draven's would actually be fine. I would relish those tears. I would dance naked in those tears. I would –"

Sabre's inane chatter was cut off by a mouth slamming down on hers. She put up a token fight, she really did, but in the end she melted into the ground, her arms and legs raising to wrap around Brax in a cocoon of heat and desire. Brax's hard length rubbed against her and even through the combined thickness of their clothes it felt amazing. Sabre moaned into the king's mouth, lifting her hips to aid in the friction and wondered how she had gone so long without this feeling. Lust, desire, *need* … it felt amazing. Brax pulled away, his lips immediately going to her throat, sucking up stinging marks then laying soothing kisses in their wake. Gripping his hair she – *shrieked*. There was no other word for it and it definitely wasn't her proudest moment. But when a hell hound the size of a pony decides to get in on the action and lick inside your ear, shrieking is a justifiable reaction.

Styx followed up his statement of affection with a headbutt to Brax's shoulder. Brax grunted, cursed and put up a feeble struggle but ultimately found himself on the ground next to her. Styx, clearly happy with his work and thinking it was playtime, pounced on Brax's chest. It was Brax's turn to shriek as one of Styx's paws came dangerously close to the bulge in his pants. Brax let out a sharp command, cupping his junk, and Sabre fell into hysterics when both males went unnaturally still and stared at each other. Her laughter was all the permission Styx needed to switch his attention to her. This time when he pounced, all four legs landed on the ground outside her body, effectively caging her in as he tried to nuzzle his giant head against hers. It was like the hell-dog was trying to mimic his master and Sabre cooed at the sweet boy;

"Aww, what a good boy. You're so sweet. Good boy, Styx. Yes, I love you too," she promised him, patting him roughly and using her fingernails behind his ears just the way he liked.

"Styx, off!" Brax demanded, sitting up and frowning in their direction.

Styx cast his master a side-eyed look that clearly said; *yeah, not gonna happen.* Before he literally laid down on top of her. Sabre grunted at the weight but was still able to breathe, so she indulged the overgrown puppy, smirking at Brax. "Looks like I have a new favourite man. And his name is Styx."

Brax cursed, "Damnit, Styx. I would never cock-block you like this," Brax grumbled, pushing and pulling on the beast to get him off Sabre.

Brax's disgruntled words only caused Sabre to laugh once more, hence fuelling the beast's excitement and the whole shenanigans of the last five minutes hit the replay button. By the time Styx was peacefully sitting next to Sabre – because she had asked him nicely – Brax was pouting next to her. Sabre withheld her laughter, belatedly realising that she had laughed more in the last ten minutes than she had in the last one hundred years. Looking at Brax under her lashes she swept her gaze over him from head to toe. What was it about the gorgeous demon that seemed to reach inside of her and squeeze her heart? She liked him, Sabre realised. Liked everything about him; his loyalty and love for his family, his determination to see his job through, the way he made eye contact with her when she spoke as if he was really listening. And his face – man, that beautiful face of his with the hard angles and the couple of days' worth of beard growth because he was too lazy to shave it off. A curious flutter began in her belly that had nothing to do with lust and Sabre found she couldn't swallow due to the sudden dryness of her throat. Had Dra'mon been right? Could she be in love with Abraxis? Damn that fucking demon lord! She really wished she could kill him all over again.

And that reminded her … she had a trachea and several other body parts to deliver to Gage. It was a great excuse for her to flee the scene of domesticity; the whole happy, relaxed man and his loyal hound thing was beginning to get under her skin. Standing up, she found herself unable to move when Brax grabbed her ankle.

Looking down, she merely raised an eyebrow, "I really don't want to have to get my pickaxe out, Brax. Let me go," she warned him. Why the threat of death by pickaxe made the crazy demon smile, Sabre didn't know. But the mischievous look in his eyes was very becoming. His large, warm hand began to make its way over her ankle and up her calf muscle. It finally came to rest just under her butt cheek at the top of her thigh, causing a delicious tingle to spread upward directly between her legs.

"Come to me tonight," Brax whispered, and it was a command rather than a question.

Sabre quickly shook her head, giving her racing heart a silent *fuck you*, "No."

Brax's brows lowered, creating a network of frown lines on his forehead. Eyes glowing and reflecting the light, he pulled her in close by her legs, invading her personal space. "Sabre, if you don't come to me, I'm going to think you're a coward."

Sabre shoved against his shoulders, cursing when the muscled behemoth barely moved. "I'm no coward. I just have things to do tonight."

Brax's eyes roved over her face, seemingly satisfied with what he saw because he nodded, relaxing a little. "Okay. Tomorrow night."

"Busy then too," Sabre fired back.

"Sabre ..."

Brax's words were more of a growl than anything else, and a little distorted because his lower incisors had elongated. Sabre shivered a little, remembering the feel of those unique lower fangs digging into her shoulder and holding her still for mutual pleasure. She wanted to feel that way again more than anything but Dra'mon's taunt of her being in love, coupled with her own growing self-awareness over the matter made her reluctant to agree. If she were standing on the cusp of love, another night in the passionate and tender arms of her lover would surely send her tumbling over the cliff. And Sabre knew what awaited her at the bottom of that cliff; jagged rocks, broken glass, and probably a grenade or two. There would be no warm arms or tender words to break her fall. She would just be ... broken.

"Brax, this isn't wise ..." she began.

Brax shifted to his knees, straightening his torso, and making him a few inches shorter than her. Looking up as he grasped her waist, he murmured, "I'm not the wise king; that was my father. I'm not the good king; that was my brother. I'm the king who's been kicked in the teeth by life and is struggling to do what's right. And this, *you Sabre*, you feel right."

Sabre swallowed audibly, "How's a girl supposed to argue with that?"

"She's not. And if she says she feels differently, then I would say she's a liar," Brax stroked her back as he spoke casually.

Thinking quickly, Sabre decided there was something she had to do first before she gave herself to Brax again. It was a contingency plan in case there was nothing left of her afterwards. Because she had no doubt only one of them would be walking away from the encounter with a still beating heart. Here's a spoiler; it wouldn't be her. Because she would have handed it over to Brax in post-orgasmic bliss. "Okay. I'll come to you. But I have some things to do first. I need two days."

Brax searched her face for a moment, "You have yourself a deal." He quickly gained his feet, "Do I even need to bother to let you in?"

Sabre patted his dimpled cheek, "Sweetheart, I could take a bath in that huge marble tub of yours with the onyx dragon tap fixtures and you wouldn't even know it." That said, she turned and strode away, laughing out loud when a disbelieving voice yelled from behind her;

"Wait a minute! How did you know my taps have dragons on them? Sabre! Sabre!"

## CHAPTER EIGHTEEN

"What is that disturbing look on your face?" Gage asked, startling Sabre out of her inner musings.

"Huh? What look?" She asked, scowling at the zombie-man when he pushed her feet off the table where they had been resting.

"Feet off the table, you heathen," he scolded.

Sabre rolled her eyes, "This table regularly has dead bodies on it but you're worried about my feet?"

Gage levelled his black eyes on her, "It's not polite."

"Whatever," Sabre grumbled, but she kept her feet firmly on the ground. Gage may be something different now, but the human he was born as continued to shine through. He was perpetually badgering her or admonishing her over the smallest things. She could show up holding a trachea like she had a few minutes ago and the man didn't so much as blink. But if she tried to eat dinner without a napkin? All hell broke loose. Sabre didn't mind. In fact, she secretly loved it and hoped the akuji never changed. Not only was Gage determined to cling to his humanity, but he was determined to drag Sabre and Jinx along with him. On the days when she was covered in blood and drowning in lies and violence, Sabre was beyond grateful.

"Now ... back to that look," Gage prompted, redrawing her attention.

"What look?" A feminine voice spoke from behind her.

Sabre nudged out a chair for Jinx, not even bothering to look because she would recognise her voice anywhere.

"Sabre has a look on her face that on anyone else I would say was happiness. But on Sabre's face it kind of just makes her look constipated," Gage informed Jinx.

"Hey! I can do happiness!" Sabre's affronted tone caused Jinx and Gage to snap to attention. Sabre sniffed, "What? I can."

"Well, sure," Jinx allowed. "But it's usually because you've gutted something. Have you recently gutted something?" Jinx inquired, thoughtfully.

"Yes. A demon lord as a matter of fact!" Sabre hastily replied. "I just gave Gage his trachea, plus a few fingers, an ear, and even some brains."

"She did," Gage acknowledged. "But I must say, the trachea looks somewhat *handled*."

"Yeah, sorry about that. I wanted to push a few of Draven's buttons." Sabre grinned a little evilly, "It worked."

Gage rolled his eyes, continuing to prod at the contents of the Esky Sabre had provided, "I swear, messing with that angel's Zen is your new hobby. Can't say I blame you, he makes it very easy. Still, I kind of like him. Brax too. He comes around here a bit you know," he raised his eyes to Sabre. "It was kind of weird at first. I thought he was trying to shut this place down or something. But he just comes to shoot the shit. Has some funny stories from his time as General," Gage added.

Sabre knew that would be something Gage could appreciate because he had been in the military on Earth. He had been SAS –

the elite soldiers of the Australian Army. But Sabre was reeling over that revelation for another reason; Brax visited Gage and Jinx to talk with them? Sabre hadn't known that. Why would he be talking to her friends? Was he trying to get intel on her? The thought made her feel a little sick.

"Brax comes here when I'm not here? Does he ask questions about me?" she demanded.

Gage's dark irises passed over her face once more, lingering on her eyes before he slowly shook his head, "I just told you; he comes to talk. People like talking to me, you know that. It's my charm." Gage made it a statement – and it was true. There weren't many supernaturals who Gage couldn't talk to. Eventually, *everyone* fell for the dead-but-awake man. "And you know I would never talk about you behind your back, Sabre. He asked a few questions the first time but soon found out his inquiries would get him nowhere. He has since respected those boundaries." Gage shrugged, "I think he's lonely. I like him."

"I agree," Jinx chimed in. "He's a good guy. And definitely not hard on the eyes."

Sabre's mind was reeling. Not only was Brax worming his way into her heart, but he was also charming her friends! She'd had no idea. Brax had never mentioned it once before – nor had the pair in front of her. It could mean only two things; they had all been hiding it from her because they feared her reaction. That was unlikely because Jinx didn't fear anything, least of all Sabre. Or none of them mentioned it because they didn't think it was a big deal – because they all genuinely liked each other and it wasn't related to her at all. *Huh, my friends like my lover,* Sabre thought. And then had to force herself not to hyperventilate. Shit just kept getting realer.

"Sabre? You okay?" Jinx asked.

"Fine," Sabre croaked out.

Jinx's nose twitched and her eyes narrowed but she didn't question Sabre further, instead coming out with; "And I don't mind Draven either. That is one gorgeous male! But he sure is stuck up. I know just what he needs – a good rogering."

Sabre didn't know what the sound was that left her throat. Maybe a gurgle? Or perhaps the sound a goat makes when it gets startled? Either way, it wasn't attractive. But what was she expected to do when her nineteen-year-old ward used the word rogering and Draven in the same sentence? "Nope," Sabre said. "Nope, nope, nope. There will be no rogering with Draven. Ever! Don't make me cut off his dick, Jinx, I'm begging you. Because you know I'll do it."

Jinx burst into laughter, "The look on your face! I was talking in general terms. I have no intention of sexing the angel up – no matter how beautiful his face and body are. I'm just saying; sex would help with his overall ... ambience." Jinx eyed Sabre curiously then, "You know, if I didn't know any better, I'd say you've gotten some action. You are very relaxed, and as Gage pointed out, kind of happy – in a constipated way."

Sabre avoided eye contact with the young feline, not willing to touch that comment with a ten-foot pole. "Gage, you think you can consume some demon lord now?" she pointed to the Esky.

Gage nodded his head, picking up the cooler and moving away, "I'll chow down and let you know what I see."

"You know you don't have to hide from us when you eat, Gage," Sabre reminded him. He often felt the need to go into another room whenever he consumed organs or flesh, as if he were embarrassed or ashamed. But it was something Sabre wouldn't stand for. It was a part of Gage and therefore a part of their lives too. She accepted the zombie-man just as he was and didn't want him to feel uncomfortable or feel the need to apologise simply for being himself. "We're family," Sabre followed up softly. The looks of shock on Jinx's and Gage's face would have been comical if Sabre weren't so embarrassed. She had never said that out loud before. Maybe Brax was making her soft.

Gage stopped walking away and turned back around. He slowly placed the Esky back onto the long bench table and opened the lid, "I ... okay," he said, reaching inside.

Sabre smiled at him before turning back and asking Jinx about how her studies were going. Sure, she wanted Gage to feel comfortable enough to be himself around them, but she didn't want to stare at him while he ate. That would be just as weird as if someone stared at her when she ate. She'd probably have to throat-punch them, Sabre thought. Jinx caught her up on how her tertiary courses were going and Sabre explained what had gone down with Lucifer and Dra'mon while Gage ate the demon in question quietly in the corner. It was probably weird to most people, but Sabre wasn't most people and she thought the entire scene was very domestic.

"Demon lord from one of the inner circles is rather tasty," Gage offered, making his way over to take a seat with Sabre and Jinx at the small, round table.

Sabre grinned at him, "Good to know. What did you find out?"

Gage leaned back in his chair, regarding her seriously, "Well, he wasn't lying to you; Dra'mon did not order the basilisk to kill King Maliq. He had memories of the super snake returning after going missing, having a broken fang, and then perishing several days later. The timeline coincides with the murder of the old king and I have no doubts that it was the same basilisk."

"Damnit! I didn't think he was lying to me – I was rather persuasive," Sabre added. "But I was hopeful. Brax was right; we're back to square one. If he didn't order the basilisk, who did? Maybe it was charmed?"

"I didn't think it was possible to charm a basilisk?" Gage asked,

Sabre groaned, banging her head against the table, "It's not. I'm just grasping at straws."

"What if the basilisk *thought* it was commanded by Dra'mon?" Jinx offered, her brow furrowed in thought.

Sabre sat up straight again, "What do you mean?"

"Well, what if someone who looked and sounded exactly like Dra'mon ordered the basilisk? It wouldn't know the difference, right?" Jinx explained further.

Sabre's internal antennae started pinging. "Like if someone was using a glamour?"

Jinx shrugged, "Yeah. Or a skinwalker maybe?"

Sabre tapped out an unconscious beat on the tabletop with her fingers, mulling over Jinx's suggestion. It was a damn good one. The girl really did have the devious mind of an assassin. Too bad for her Sabre had expressly forbidden that particular career path. No matter what, Sabre was determined Jinx would end up nothing like her, the weretiger was much too good for that. "It's a good theory. One well worth exploring," Sabre admitted. "Thank you."

Jinx smiled, looking pleased, "I'm glad."

"In fact, I might even discuss it with Hound tomorrow," Sabre mused, thinking of her upcoming meeting with the rebel.

"You're meeting with Hound?" Jinx's dual eyes sparkled with keen interest. "Oh, can I come?"

"No."

"But –"

"No," Sabre repeated. "You'll only flirt and make his words all stuttery and then I'll have to box him over the ears to get him to think straight again. Just no." Jinx's crush on the demon rebel would have been cute if it weren't so pointless. Sabre knew Hound would never allow anything to happen with Jinx for too many reasons to count – despite the fact his brain turned to mush whenever the weretiger was around. On top of that, Hound had a very intricate and powerful glamour in place, so Jinx didn't even know what his real face looked like. In typical male fashion though, Hound had chosen a face that was superbly attractive. Still, Sabre knew it wasn't his real one and it just made her want to punch him in his perfect nose every time she saw him. Which wasn't often these days. Circumstances didn't allow for it.

"Okay, well, thanks team. I'll be off and –"

"Wait. I'm not done."

Sabre was halfway out of her chair but she sank back down upon hearing Gage's words. "There was something else?" Sabre asked.

Gage looked at her very seriously, "You could say that. Like the fact that you've been having sex with Abraxis and are in love with him." Gage crossed his arms over his chest, daring Sabre to deny it.

*Fuck, fuck, fuck!* Sabre raged. She had completely forgotten that that part of her conversation with Dra'mon would also be accessible to Gage. Gage had no doubt seen and heard it all verbatim. And as her friend, he would be able to read the look on her face and see the truth in her eyes, no matter the words of denial she had spoken to the dead demon lord via his memories. Sabre quickly shook her head, saying nothing, wondering if she could kill one of her best friends and live with it. Considering the gleam in their eyes, Sabre figured it would be worth it and was just palming a knife when Jinx spoke.

"You're in love?" Jinx's pupils expanded as her tiger chimed in, before she gasped, hands covering her mouth, "Dear Gods! You're in love!"

Sabre slammed her closed fist down on the table, snarling, "I am not in love!"

Jinx completely ignored her outburst, eyes sparkling with fervour, "In love. With the king. Of course you are, he's clearly the love of your life. It makes sense. Think about it," Jinx urged. "It explains why you've been stalking him all these years and lusting after him from afar."

"I wasn't stalking him! And there has been no lust!" Sabre fervently denied.

Jinx stared at her, "You are so in love with him."

"Am not," Sabre returned.

"Are too!" Jinx fired back.

"Am not!" Sabre hurled one of her throwing knives at Jinx, who simply moved an inch in order to avoid a blade to the face. The knife stuck into the back of Gage's chair instead. Sabre ignored his annoyed growl, forging ahead, "Enough! I am not in love with Abraxis and the next person to say so will get their tongue cut out."

"You are soul mates! Destined to be together!" Jinx howled, completely ignoring Sabre and her hollow threats. "I mean, I've seen his biceps. I can only imagine what his dick must be like," Jinx sighed, eyes turning dreamy, "You can't fight fate, Sabre. He's yours."

Sabre tossed a helpless look in Gage's direction, begging for help but he simply shook his head, humour lighting his eyes, "All I can say is that he must have a magic dick if you're spouting words of love and destiny after only a couple of weeks."

Sabre screamed in frustration, standing up so fast she knocked her chair over, "I am not spouting words of love and destiny. That is jerk-face Jinx over there," Sabre pointed an accusing finger at her. "Although, I will admit one thing; Brax's dick is pretty magic." Sabre felt like it would be sacrilege to deny that at least.

That comment seemed to give them all pause and after a solid thirty seconds of silence, the three of them burst into laughter.

Jinx rose from her chair to wrap an arm around Sabre's shoulder, "Oh, Sabre. Do you really love him?"

"I –" Sabre shook her head. "I'm not allowed to. I can't afford to."

Jinx's eyes held sympathy as they looked into Sabre's and she patted Sabre's hair, "I'm sorry. I won't tease you anymore. But … did you really have sex with him?"

Sabre moaned, dropping her head into her hands, "Yes. I really did. I really, really did."

Gage stood up as well, coming to a stop on Sabre's other side, "Let me get this straight; you had sex with the man whose brother you were hired to assassinate? The same man who happens to be the King of Purgatory and who hired you to find said assassin – among other things. Do I have that right?"

Sabre scrunched up her nose, "Well, when you put it like that, it sounds kind of like a poor life choice."

And perhaps it had been, Sabre admitted silently. Because everything Gage said was true; Sabre had indeed been hired – and ordered – to kill Mikhail. Looking down at her calloused hands, she sometimes imagined she could still see the red from the previous king's blood staining them. It had been a hard job to take – and to execute. Perhaps the hardest of her life. But she had done it anyway. Because of her impeccable reputation. And because of loyalty. And love. Not that she could ever explain that. Jinx and Gage knew the truth and they knew how hard it had been on her at the time. It was why they had been so against her taking the job from Brax in the first place.

"You think maybe I overstepped a little?" Sabre eventually asked.

Gage held up his finger and thumb about a centimetre apart, "Maybe just a little."

Sabre slumped, "I don't know if it's love. What do I know

about love? But I do know I like him. And … and he likes me too. I can see it in his eyes."

"What are you going to do when he finds out you killed his brother?" Gage asked, eyes direct but endlessly kind.

Sabre's own eyes were dry as she answered the only way she could; "Watch that like turn to hate."

## CHAPTER NINETEEN

"Hound," Sabre breathed, relief and something else flooding her system the moment she laid eyes on her contact.

"Sabre," Hound returned the greeting, sounding likewise a little breathless. "It's been too long."

Sabre quickly nodded her head in agreement. It had indeed been too long since she had seen Hound in the flesh. They kept in touch as much as they could via email and phone but it wasn't always possible given how often Hound was in another realm. Sabre liked to think of herself as an island, but in actual fact, she had rather a lot of people in her periphery and a large number of resources. Most of them were because they owed her a debt of some kind, but some, like Lucifer and Hound were just because they had good intentions. If there was one thing Sabre believed with all her heart, it was that Hound was dedicated to the preservation of the royal line. He worked in secret behind the scenes to ensure the line went on. He had been hunting for the mysterious foe for years, unbeknownst to Brax and every other royal out there. And she knew he had helped Brax out with intel and resources in the past year too. Sabre had stumbled upon the demon rebel years ago and she trusted his intentions without hesitation. Which was why she had asked him to look into the angel angle for her.

"Anything about the angels?" Sabre got right to the point – one of them, anyway. They didn't have a lot of time. They never did. "What does Heaven have to say about so many pureblood angel deaths?" Hound was one of the only people in all the realms able to make the trip up to Heaven without being dead. Lucifer was also capable but circumstances for him were tricky with the Gods and Sabre would never ask him to do so.

Hound shook his head, bald head gleaming in the low light of the alleyway. "I've made a couple of trips topside but haven't learned much of anything. The angels aren't saying much, only to acknowledge the fact that guardians of the Cerberus descendants are being picked off like flies. So much so, that none of the created angels want to get saddled with one as their charge."

Sabre curled her lip, "Douches."

Hound smirked at her, "Most of them are rather uptight, I'll give you that."

"What about the Gods? Or maybe an oracle or two?" Sabre pressed, hoping Hound had used some of that infamous charm of his to schmooze a goddess.

Hound went to tug on a strand of hair, only to curse when he came up empty. Hound was used to having hair but his chosen glamour didn't cater to his habitual gesture. "The Gods are avoiding me – other than Loki. And I can take what that cheeky fucker says with a grain of salt. The only oracle I could speak with simply spouted some crap about the royal line needing its guardians for the same purpose it always had. When I pointed out there wasn't many of the royal line left, nor their angels, the oracle intoned that the ones left were more than enough."

Sabre snorted, thinking of Draven, "I highly doubt that."

"Oh, I don't know. I think the royal guardians are perfect," Hound murmured, a small smile playing around his lips.

Sabre shifted uncomfortably, saying nothing and moving right along, "Can't you just talk with one of the dead guys when you're up there?" Sabre asked, already knowing the answer but feeling frustrated as fuck.

Hound levelled a look at her, "It doesn't work that way. You know that. I can't talk with the dead – only the living. No matter what plane of existence I visit."

She did know that. Hound had explained it to her time and time again. But it seemed like a really stupid rule to her. She opened her mouth only to be stopped by Hound before she could speak.

"Whining about it won't achieve anything, so don't do it," he warned.

Sabre sniffed disdainfully, "I don't whine."

Hound laughed, "Oh, you do. Quite spectacularly."

"What is it with everyone hassling me lately? It's like there's no fear anymore. Have I lost my edge? My homicidal touch? I swear, if it isn't Jinx or Gage giving me shit, it's Brax," Sabre shook her head.

"Brax?" Hound's eyebrows elevated in surprise, "You call the King, Brax? I didn't realise you were so familiar with him."

Hound's voice sounded curious and Sabre winced. He was a perceptive man and could easily pick up on nuances in tone and body language. Thankfully, Sabre was a pro at resting bitch-face. The conversation with Jinx and Gage from the previous evening had rocked her to her core. Sabre had always been good at compartmentalising – it was the only way she had been able to survive as both an angel and an assassin. And up until that conversation, Sabre had been able to place Brax in one very pretty, shiny box, while she shoved the fact she had assassinated his brother into another dark, endlessly deep box. Unfortunately, that box had now popped its rusty hinges and Sabre was left staring at a dead Mikhail with a cross bolt through his heart every time she closed her eyes.

"Sabre? What's going on?"

She hadn't realised she had closed her eyes until Hound's voice brought her back to the present. Looking into his familiar green eyes, untouched by the glamour spell work, she prepared herself to address the other reason she had wanted to meet up with Hound in person. "I need to tell you something," she confessed. "You see, ah, something has happened with the king …"

"King Abraxis? Is it the killer? Did they make a move? Is the king hurt?" Hound fired off the questions.

"No, no. It's nothing like that," she was quick to put those fears to rest. "It might be something worse though."

"Worse than the last official royal being injured or killed?" Hound asked doubtfully.

"I guess it depends on your perspective," Sabre muttered, feeling her palms begin to sweat. "You see, I kind of … slept with him. Because I like him. And he likes me too. I think. I mean, he says he does. And I believe him. Which is just insane I know. But —"

"Stop," Hound ordered, causing Sabre to shut her mouth with a snap. "You slept with Abraxis? And you *like* him?"

"Yes," Sabre chewed on her lower lip and moved from foot to foot, anxiously awaiting Hound's reaction.

"That's …" Hound shook his head in disbelief. Gripping her shoulders, he forced her to look into his eyes, "Wait … what is that look? Are you – are you in love with him?!" Hound asked, looking and sounding stunned.

Unlike with Jinx and Gage, Sabre couldn't lie to the man. She had been unable to from the moment she had met him, so she answered as truthfully as she could, "It's complicated."

Hound eyed her in deafening silence for a minute before a small smile graced his lips. "Sabre, my dear assassin. Love isn't complicated. It's either there or it isn't. So, is it there?" he asked once again.

She wasn't sure why, but Sabre felt like it would be the ultimate betrayal to deny her love for Brax out loud again. Like, if she were to say no to the universe just one more time it would somehow be taken away from her. And for once in her life she wanted to be selfish and keep something that was just wholly hers. So she answered the only way her heart would allow; "Yes. Yes, there is love there. From my end at least."

For a moment she could have sworn Hound's eyes shined with unshed tears but the glistening green of his eyes was gone in an instant and she passed it off as a trick of light. Instead he laughed outright, dragging her in for a bear hug that practically cracked her bones. Sabre was both shocked and pleased by the uncommon affectionate display and indulged herself by leaning into the large man's strength for a precious moment. When Hound pulled back his look of happiness and wonder had been replaced by a more serious look.

"When the time comes, you know you're going to have to make a choice," he pointed out seriously, though not unkindly.

Sabre sucked in a deep breath, the oxygen feeling like ice in her lungs. Still she nodded, keeping her eyes on the demon's as she answered, "I know."

"I'm sorry," Hound whispered.

But Sabre simply shook her head, "Hound, even when faced

with terrible choices, my actions are still my own. That has ever been true in my past and will always be true in my future. Your feelings of guilt are misplaced."

His lips twitched, "Oh yeah? Well, you can't tell me how to feel. You're not the boss of me."

Sabre sighed; he had her there. *She* definitely wasn't the boss of *him*.

## CHAPTER TWENTY

"Out!" Brax pointed to the living area of his suite. "I mean it, Styx. Tonight is my time with Sabre. You can have her tomorrow. I'm capable of sharing her attentions – probably. But only with you!" Brax told his hell hound. Styx, looking highly dejected, slowly slinked from the bedroom and into the living room, curling up on his huge bed by the door. If looks could kill, Brax would be six feet under. Still, he wasn't going to pander to a huge hell-dog when he was finally going to see Sabre naked again.

It was almost midnight and Sabre still hadn't shown up. He had given her the two days she had asked for and he hoped she had come to some semblance of resolution when it came to the pair of them. Because Brax very much wanted them to be a pair. He had no idea how such a thing would work let alone how he would tell Draven. But it was useless to pretend otherwise. He thought about Sabre all the time like a lovesick fool and he wanted more than just thoughts of her to keep him warm at night. He wanted the angel herself to keep him warm.

A pressure in his back caused him to grunt and drop swiftly into a fighting stance. He felt his skin rippling to protect him against the projectile, even as he reached for a weapon of his own. A humour-filled chuckle had him cursing and standing back up. Rolling his shoulders, he glared across the room, "Did you just stab me in the back?!"

"It was a slingshot," Sabre corrected, holding up a piece of leather. "And you're lucky you have super cool skin because you didn't even hear me climb in your window. What if I had been an assassin?" Sabre scolded him from where she stood negligently against the wall by his open balcony window.

"You *are* an assassin," Brax's response was dry as he took in the woman decked out in black leather. She was a sight to behold with her short hair, trim but curvy body and lethal lips twisted into a hint of a grin.

"Oh, yeah," Sabre smiled and it damn near took Brax's breath away.

"You came," was all he said.

"I told you I would," Sabre pointed out, just as softly.

"And you always keep your word?" he challenged.

"Not always," Sabre admitted, pushing off from the wall and sauntering around the room. "But I will always keep my word to you." Sabre used her head to gesture to the bathroom. "Mind if I wash up a little?" she held up her hands, "I have dead things on my hands."

Brax shook his head, "Go right ahead. I'm not into necrophilia." He certainly didn't want dead-thing-hands anywhere near his cock.

"What the actual fuck?!" Sabre yelled from the depths of the bathroom, her voice echoing loudly.

"What?" Brax asked, quickly running across the room to look inside. "What is it?"

"It looks like Chewbacca died in here!" Sabre exclaimed, her reddish-purple eyes wide in disbelief as she looked in his shower. "What's with all the hair in your drain?"

Brax felt an embarrassed flush rise up his neck and over his cheekbones. In preparation for the rendezvous, he had cut and styled his hair into something less swamp monster and more male model. Glancing into the shower, he cringed when he realised he had made the unfortunate mistake of not cleaning up all the hair. "Umm … I kinda cut my hair," he mumbled, beyond embarrassed.

"No shit," Sabre agreed. "Seriously, all this came from your head? Do you feel lighter? Maybe your brain will work better now that it isn't so weighed down."

"My brain works just fine," Brax assured her, before leering, "Besides, that's not the brain I'm hoping will see some action tonight."

"Oh, really? I gotta say dick-brains don't tend to be real smart. They kind of only know how to point in two directions; north and south," Sabre fired back, scrubbing her hands almost raw in his sink.

"Well, lucky for you, my dick-brain is telling my dick to point due north."

"It is?" Sabre's eyes widened comically in the mirror, "That's a happy coincidence."

"Yes, I think so too," Brax grinned. He couldn't believe how much fun he was having. He always ensured his sexual encounters in the past were pleasurable for both parties. Otherwise, what was the point? But the banter and the casual fun that Sabre brought into his bedroom was a novelty. It had been a long time since he had enjoyed the company of another as much as Sabre. He was willing to admit – if only to himself just then – that he was rapidly falling in love. He manfully withheld the giggle forming in his throat, *I'm falling in love with an assassin!* Regaining his composure, he saw that Sabre was watching him curiously in the mirror, her own hair nicely styled, though he was positive that was pure luck rather than any doing on her part.

"What about your hair?" he ended up asking.

Sabre gave her head a shake, "What about it?"

"Do you always keep it so short?"

Sabre looked at herself in the mirror, carding her fingers through the dark strands. "Why? You don't like it?"

"Of course I like it," Brax was quick to assure her. "It highlights those amazing cheekbones of yours and makes your eyes look like sugarplums."

Sabre gaped at him, "Sugarplums?"

Brax grinned, crossing his arms over his chest and leaning back against the marble wall. "I think that's a great pet name for you, Sugarplum. Really suits your personality." Sabre's look of disgust was one to rival even Draven's and Brax couldn't contain his laughter.

"Yeah, yeah. Laugh it up. And to answer your question: yes. I always keep it this short." Sabre surprised him by continuing on, "During training when I was a kid, my Master grabbed my ponytail, damn near yanking my head off its shoulders before almost gutting me. I shaved my head that very night. This is actually the longest it's been in a long time," Sabre revealed.

Brax straightened from the wall slowly, "When you were a kid? How old were you?"

Sabre pondered for a moment, revealing, "Ten."

"Ten? You've been in the assassin guild since you were ten years old?" Brax tried not to sound as horrified as he felt but it was damn hard. He had a feeling Sabre never talked about this kind of stuff and he didn't want to scare her off. But damn, hearing about it spoken so casually was lighting a slow burning rage in his gut.

"I've been a part of the Blue Devil Den since I was eight," Sabre corrected.

"Eight? But …" Brax shut his mouth.

"What?" Sabre prompted, leaning back against the sink.

Brax shook his head, "Nothing. Eight years old. It just explains a lot." He looked into eyes that by some miracle weren't haunted, and said, "You never really stood a chance, did you?"

The comment was made with just enough pity and understanding to piss Sabre right off. She straightened up, her eyes glaring daggers at him, "Don't pity me, Abraxis. I may have been a child once but I haven't been for a long time. My life may have been stolen from me or it might be just how it was supposed to be. Did you ever think of that? That maybe this was my purpose? Maybe this life was the task asked of me from the Powers That Be?"

"No," Brax's response was quick and sharp. "That's not possible. That would be too cruel."

Sabre arched a sardonic brow in Brax's direction, "And who ever said the Gods were kind?"

"Hmpf. True. That's why I much prefer it here – or even Earth. No meddlesome Gods to worry about. Just your run of the mill supernaturals. Or humans, in the case of Earth." And that much was true at least. Heaven and Hell might sound evocative but they came with a whole shitstorm of unique problems that Brax wanted no part of. He watched Sabre watching him and figured he may as well keep digging into what made her tick. The more he learned, the more enamoured he became. She had been eight years old when she had been stolen to be trained as an assassin? The woman was a walking miracle.

"What happened to your parents?"

"My what? I don't have –" Sabre quickly slammed her mouth shut.

"You don't have?" Brax prompted her.

"I don't have many memories of them. I was too young. Too traumatised I guess," she tacked on, shrugging negligently.

Brax couldn't help thinking she was hiding something from him, but he liked his ribcage where it was so he didn't call her out on it. "You say that as if it's no big deal. Being traumatised as a child."

"It is what it is. I am what I am. It was a long time ago," Sabre brushed him off. "Are we going to keep walking down memory lane or are we going to fuck?"

Abraxis eyed her, a tiny smile quirking one corner of his mouth. "You're a complicated creature, aren't you?"

"You better believe it, baby," Sabre jabbed him hard in the stomach as she walked past him into the bedroom.

Watching the sway of her hips as she walked, another thought hit him like a lightning bolt, "How old are you anyway?"

Sabre spun around. She ran her tongue along her teeth before she answered, "Old enough that I want to pull out your fingernails for asking me that."

"Ah," Brax's eyes twinkled, "older than me then, huh?"

Sabre snorted, "I've been an assassin since before you were born. I thought you said you knew my reputation?"

"I do. But I'm not interested in the reputation of Sabre, the notorious assassin. I'm interested in the Sabre who is going to be sharing my bed." *And my life,* he tacked on silently. It must have been the right thing to say because she answered him;

"I'm one-hundred and eighteen. I've been doing this job for one hundred and ten years, three months, and six days," came Sabre's very exact response.

That made her twelve years older than him. Who knew older

women could be so sexy? "Not that you're counting or anything," he offered in response to her specific reply.

"Right. Not that I'm counting. You know, all this talk of my fucked-up childhood and my dwindling ovarian reserve is really getting me in the mood," Sabre informed him, beginning to prowl around the room again.

"Really?" Brax asked, surprised.

"No. Not really, you moron!" Sabre rolled her eyes dramatically and she started stripping off her clothing in economical movements. "Those are perhaps the worst topics you could choose to talk about if you're looking to get laid."

He watched as Sabre did a kind of shimmy thing to get out of her tight leather pants, gratified to see silk between her legs once again. "Ah, but I'm not just looking to get laid, am I?" He said, moving closer slowly, "I'm looking to get to know you."

Sabre reached out, grabbed a fistful of his t-shirt and hauled him in close, "Brax, we talk every day. You send me dick-pics. I know it's only been a couple of weeks, but trust me, you know me better than almost anyone else in the whole world," she murmured into his throat.

Pulling back so he could see her face, he asked, "Is that true?"

Sabre met his eyes, the reddish-mauve irises alive with warmth, "Yes. It's true."

The simple confirmation nearly felled him to his knees and he grabbed onto her slender hips for dear life as he ravaged the perfection of her mouth, mapping her body with his hands. Before he knew it, they were both standing naked in the middle of the room and Sabre had dropped to her knees in front of him. His eyes widened and he felt his claws extend out past his fingernails when Sabre gripped the base of his cock and licked it around the tip.

"Tell me if I do something you don't like," Sabre murmured, looking like pure fucking sin.

"Baby, you're about to put my dick in your mouth. There isn't anything you could do that I won't like," he promised her, forcing his hips to remain still when all he really wanted to do was paint her pretty lips with his pre-cum.

"Yeah, well, I've never done this before, so you might change your tune."

It took a few seconds for Sabre's words to penetrate his brain because she had started to blow warm air against his balls. "Wait, wait, wait. You've never given a blowjob before?"

Sabre pulled back and sat on her feet, cocking an eyebrow at him, "Angel, remember?"

"You told me you weren't a virgin!" Brax's voice was laced with accusation.

"And I'm not. I've had sex. I just haven't done much of anything else," Sabre shrugged like it was no big deal.

"Just how much sex have you had?" Why Brax felt the need to ask, he had no idea. Because he really didn't want to know. Once was more than enough as far as he was concerned.

Sabre sighed, as if bored with the conversation, "Not much ... like an hour's worth maybe."

"An hour?!"

Sabre nodded like it was no big deal, "I gave it whirl once but it didn't really live up to expectations, so I just didn't bother with it again."

Brax tapped his long nails against his thighs, "Well, now I feel a little whore-ish," he finally said out loud.

"Whore-ish?" Sabre laughed.

"Yeah. I mean in comparison, I –" Sabre gave his dick a tight squeeze, cutting off his words.

"Do you really want to be telling me about your past lovers

when I'm kneeling naked in front of your erection?" she asked, sweetly.

He cleared his throat, "Ah, yeah, no. Sorry."

Sabre smirked, "I didn't think so. Now, as I was saying. I haven't done this before. But I've seen it a lot and I've done some research. I'm supposed to use my teeth ... right?"

Brax moved backward so fast he almost tripped over his own feet. "What? No! No teeth, no teeth!" he screamed, cupping his goods with his hands.

Sabre began laughing hysterically and Brax realised he'd been had. And not in the way he wanted to be had. He growled as he prowled back over to the kneeling assassin, tapping her lips with his still-hard length. "Open up, my smiling assassin."

## CHAPTER TWENTY-ONE

Well, if the trembling thighs and quivering muscles were anything to go by, then Sabre figured her inaugural blowjob had been a success. She had been pleasantly surprised to learn she had enjoyed the feeling of Brax's hard flesh against her tongue, the rounded head pressing excitingly against the back of her throat, almost cutting off her airway with every shallow thrust of his hips. She had been a little unprepared for his orgasm and things had gotten a little messy, but for some reason, Brax seemed to enjoy the sight of her with the evidence of his pleasure all over her face and breasts. *Go figure,* Sabre thought.

"You really are incredible," Brax panted, lifting Sabre to her feet.

Sabre shook her head; the demon was delusional. Maybe it was a man thing? After they orgasmed they lost a certain amount of brain cells through their dicks and were rendered stupid for a length of time before said cells could regenerate. Still, Sabre decided to accept the compliment and not argue. After all, she was feeling pretty incredible. The only thing that could make her feel better? Her own orgasm.

As they moved closer to the bed, Sabre halted abruptly, eyeing the vast expanse of the mattress. "This is an orgy bed," she pointed to the massive bed in the centre of the room. "There can be no other purpose for this bed other than orgies. No wonder you feel like a whore."

Beside her, Brax choked and sputtered, "I'm not a whore! Whore-ish – I said *whore-ish!*"

"Whatever," Sabre crawled onto the bed, flashing her arse at the man-whore behind her. "You're lucky I get to reap the rewards of all your skanky ways." She yelped when a palm landed a resounding smack against her butt. Flipping over, she glared at Brax, "Do you have a death wish?"

Brax smirked at her, his beautiful cock already making a valiant effort to rise again. "Please! Don't pretend you didn't like that."

Sabre narrowed her eyes at him. The warmth she could feel radiating from her right butt cheek was rather intriguing, but she wasn't going to tell him that. "I tell you what; you can spank me if I can spank you."

Brax's tawny eyes lit up, "Deal!" he yelled, before jumping on the bed and smothering her with his mouth and hands.

Sabre laughed, mock fighting him off, "Of course you like the idea. You're such a pervert! Get off me!"

Brax rumbled, biting at her neck and shoulders, "I thought you liked me on you?"

Running a palm over the broad width of his shoulder and down his flank, Sabre settled her hand in the crease where thigh met butt. Giving him a squeeze, she whispered in his ear; "I do like that. But I thought this time …" she gave his ear a little nip, "I would be on top."

Brax's breath sawed from his chest harshly and he quickly flipped them both over so that Sabre straddled his waist. "I like how you think, woman."

Sabre smiled, aiming for sexy and seductive, "Then you're going to love this."

Swooping down, she took his mouth in a brutal kiss that spun quickly out of control. Sinking her teeth into his bottom lip, Sabre was rewarded when his lower fangs elongated and pushed up through his lips. They were incredibly sexy and she carefully ran her tongue along the sharp points. "I want to feel these in me again when I come," she told him.

"Fuuuuck …" came the panting reply.

Smiling in satisfaction, Sabre sat up straight, smoothing her hands over Brax's collarbones and pecs where the demon had a light sprinkling of hair in a trail that arrowed straight to his groin. Having followed that particular treasure trail earlier, Sabre instead pulled at the nipples that were directly in front of her. Her nipples were incredibly sensitive and she wondered if the same was true for men. The harsh moan and stuttered breath assured her that, yes, Brax's nipples were indeed an erogenous zone for him. So, Sabre spent the next five minutes going to town on the stiff peaks until Brax was thrusting helplessly beneath her and begging for mercy.

"Your nipples are an erogenous zone," she cackled wickedly, "Good to know."

"Sabre, my whole body is an erogenous zone when it comes to you," Brax panted, muscles straining and shining with a light layer of sweat.

"Hmm," Sabre leant down and pecked his lips, "That's good to know too," she said, right before she reached back and grabbed his meaty member with her fist. Jacking his length a couple of times, Sabre marvelled at the satiny feel of Brax and decided it was time to put them both out of their misery.

Lining herself up, Sabre braced her other hand on Brax's chest, before feeding his dick into her core. She gritted her teeth against the feeling of being impaled, staring between them where her body seemed to swallow Brax's cock so perfectly. And he certainly felt perfect, Sabre thought. *Too perfect.* She closed her eyes, hoping to beat back the emotions rushing to the surface from the feeling of being so *taken* and so *cherished.* She had never believed anything could feel so incredible as the way the two of them fit together. The pleasure coursing through her system was akin to ecstasy and she hadn't even started moving yet. But she didn't need to rock her hips to know that she had been correct in her assumption; she was in love with Brax and there was no safety net to catch her. Knowing this could be her one shot to make love to her demon, Sabre opened her eyes and let Brax see the truth that was in her heart. She didn't know whether to be grateful or rage against the universe when she saw that his eyes were squeezed tightly shut, his face a mask of pleasure-pain.

"Sabre," he gasped, his claws digging into her hips like tiny needles. "Move. Please move, baby."

Reaching for his hands, Sabre dislodged the claws and linked their hands together instead. Brax's eyes snapped open and she could see the wanton picture she made sitting atop of him reflected in the yellow depths. Lifting her hips a little, she gave an experimental rock, only to gasp and shiver as desire shot straight to her core. Still holding Brax's hands, she used her knees to push up higher this time, until just the tip of his huge cock remained buried inside her, before dropping all of her weight back down onto him in a rush. The snarl that rumbled through Brax's chest caused her sex to clench and her nipples to tingle. Unable to hold back any longer, Sabre got to work, repeating the same deep, fast movement over and over again until the both of them were a sweaty mess of pure sensation.

"Gods, baby. Yes!" Brax bucked from beneath her, his hips meeting hers with a resounding slap that was strangely erotic.

Moaning, Sabre shook the wet hair from her eyes and leaned over Brax's chest. Hovering over his mouth, she whispered; "Bite me."

Growling low, Brax grasped the back of Sabre's head and yanked her close so that her breasts were now rubbing against his chest, even as his hips continued to pump up into her. He licked her shoulder once in warning before his teeth sank into the tender flesh between her neck and shoulder. It didn't mean anything as far as a formal mating went. Angels and demons didn't mate like werecreatures and a bite, whether during sex or not, was not binding. *But it is erotic as fuck*, Sabre thought, feeling her eyes roll back in her head. The orgasm that swept through her body was swift and fierce, rising like a tsunami to flood every nerve ending with pleasure. She cried out, feeling Brax stiffen and groan beneath her, before he himself was swept away.

Sabre lay on Brax's chest, listening to the sounds of their hearts beating in sync and knew she was ruined. Thinking back to what Brax had said about her tattoo after the first time they had been together, Sabre realised he had been wrong. And so was *Dante's Inferno*. Paradise didn't begin in Hell, but Hell sure could be found in Paradise.

## CHAPTER TWENTY-TWO

"So ... what now?" Brax finally asked.

After knocking the world off its axis with their lovemaking, Brax had managed to half-drag, half-carry Sabre into his huge tub where he had proceeded to do the same thing all over again. Now, as the first hints of dawn were beginning to make their way into the room, he wondered what the two of them were supposed to do now.

Sabre raised her head where it had been resting on his shoulder, "With my hunt for the killer you mean? I actually have a bit more news to share about that," she admitted.

That wasn't what Brax had been talking about and he believed Sabre knew it, but he let it slide for now, continuing to pet her back as he asked, "What kind of news?"

"Well, I had a little chat with another one of my sources," Sabre admitted, sounding reluctant to divulge the information.

"Another one? You sure have a lot of sources for someone who claims to have no friends. You're worse than a gossip magazine, you know that?" Brax teased. For some reason, his teasing wasn't met with the smile or eye roll he was hoping for. Instead, Sabre frowned. "Hey, I was just kidding," he soothed, sitting up a little and leaning against the headboard.

Sabre looked up at him, giving him a weak smile, "I know. It's just ... I'm not sure how to explain this one to you. You see, this guy is kind of covert. And, well, he has this thing about protecting the royal line of Cerberus. I know it doesn't make a lot of sense and he –"

Brax covered Sabre's mouth with his palm to stop the babble, "Are you referring to Hound?"

Sabre's eyes widened and she looked more than a little shocked, "Wait, you know who Hound is?"

"Well, yeah. He's one of my contacts too, albeit a newer one. But he's given me a few leads that have panned out here and there. He's also in direct contact with a few of my Horde – soldiers I trust implicitly – and they say he's on the level. Actually, if it wasn't for him, we probably wouldn't be here," he admitted, the thought only just crossing his mind.

Sabre sat up now too, not bothering to cover herself with a sheet, completely unconcerned with her nudity. "What do you mean?"

"Hound was the one who suggested I hire you," Brax revealed.

Sabre's fists clenched in the pillow and she shrieked, "What?!"

"Shit! Sabre, what's with the banshee voice?" Brax leaned away from her.

"Hound told you to hire me?" Sabre demanded, voice still higher than normal.

"Well, not directly. Hugo, one of my lieutenants, told me to. But the suggestion was made to Hugo by Hound." He cast Sabre a side-eyed look, "Apparently even hobo-secret-spy-rebels know your reputation."

Sabre choked, "Hobo?" she laughed, "I really want to be there when you call him that one day. I can't believe he is the reason you hired me. That sneaky fucker!"

"Okay, I have no idea what you're talking about and I don't particularly care. But if you're worried about your association with Hound, don't be. It doesn't bother me."

Sabre gazed at him for a few seconds before smiling, "Good. I thought you were going to be mad when I told you. And I don't want you to be mad. I've kind of gotten used to seeing kindness in your eyes when you look at me," she confessed, damn near breaking his heart.

Pushing Sabre back down onto her back, Brax peered down at the beautiful, complicated, un-broken woman in his bed, and – not for the first time – felt his heart expand as warmth and joy and hope filled it up. Reaching out, he ran a calloused finger from her forehead to the tip of her perfectly pointy chin, shaping her face with hands and eyes, unable to get enough of her. He would never be able to get enough of her, he acknowledged. And having never been a coward even one day in his life, he decided to open his mouth, "Look into my eyes, Sabre, and tell me; is kindness the only thing you see there?"

An adorable frown appeared on her forehead as she appeared to think, even as her eyes dutifully searched his. "Uh, I see your beast I guess too. Your eyes reflect the light like a fucking predator," she volunteered, making him snort in amusement. She smirked at him, "Luckily, I'm not prey."

"Hmm, lucky," he agreed. "But that's not what I was talking about. I'm referring to love, my literal little assassin. There is love in my eyes when I look at you. I know it must be there because there is love in my heart every time I see you … or touch you … or think of you."

He watched the colour leech from her face and her eyes go wide and glassy. She even appeared to have stopped breathing. "Shit!" Brax exclaimed. "Are you having a stroke?" Sabre said nothing, simply pushed at his chest and slid from the bed. Feeling like his heart was turning to lead in his chest, he managed to croak out, "Sabre?"

Sabre shook her head, quickly bending to retrieve her clothes and hastily pulling them on. She snatched up her weapons and was almost at the door before he managed to get his body to catch up to his brain. Brax growled as he leapt across the room, blocking the assassin's hasty retreat. "Where do you think you're going?"

Sabre clenched her jaw, her gaze locked on a point just over his shoulder. "I know what I am, Abraxis. What I will always be. But that doesn't give you the right to be so cruel."

Brax felt his head snap back as if Sabre had physically slapped him. "What? What the hell are you talking about being cruel? I just told you I loved you, woman! You're the one walking away and breaking my damn heart!" Brax was yelling but he couldn't seem to make himself stop.

Sabre said nothing, but as he continued to study her, something about the way she held herself, as if she were made of glass and would crack at any second, caused his anger to evaporate. Searching her beloved face, it hit him that she genuinely didn't believe him. Instead, she believed she was the butt of some cruel practical joke. As if she wasn't fit to be loved. As if he would say the words just to watch her bleed out as he ripped them violently away from her. "Oh, Sabre …" he murmured, watching her flinch as if from a physical blow. Taking a slow, tentative step in her direction, he commanded softly, "Look at me."

Sabre stubbornly shut her eyes and responded through gritted teeth, "Go to Hell, Brax."

Brax felt his lips twitch despite the circumstances. "Maybe one day. I hear it's lovely."

Sabre's eyes popped open and she sneered at him, "You're hilarious. Now if today's part of the entertainment is over, I'm outta here."

She tried to nudge past him but he wouldn't allow it. "Sabre, please. I'm not being cruel. I'm not lying. This is not a trick. I just …" he broke off, running his hands through his much shorter hair in agitation. "I just … love you. I love you, Sabre. I don't know how or why or when it happened. But it did. I'm in love with you. And I don't see why I should have to keep the words locked away just because they might offend your delicate sensibilities," he added, hoping to remind her of when she had used those words teasingly herself. Too bad he didn't have a trachea handy to hammer his point home.

Sabre's eyes finally flew to his. This time they looked incredulous rather than blank. "You … you love me?"

Cupping her face, Brax said simply, "I do."

"And …" Sabre licked her lips, "this isn't a trick?"

Brax shook his head, "It is not."

"But, I don't understand," Sabre's eyes pleaded with him. "What do you see in me?"

His love sounded so genuinely confused as if she weren't worthy of love that Brax wanted to go and kick some arse. Someone somewhere must have pounded that insecurity into her head so hard that she had begun to believe it. Well, Brax was determined to show her just how worthy she was. Even if it took him a lifetime. He picked up her hand, "What do I see? I see life," he said kissing her on her first knuckle. "I see love," he kissed her second knuckle. "I see home," he stated, kissing her palm and laying it flat against his beating heart. The heart that now beat solely for her.

Sabre's eyes zeroed in on her hand, her fingers flexing on his chest, "But … why?" she still sounded incredulous.

Brax summoned a grin, "There's just something about a woman who can break a guy's nose with her pinky finger that really does it for me. Go figure."

Brax's response that time had her laughing out loud, and joy filled his heart, replacing the cold and loneliness he had allowed to enter over the past year. "Well, what do you say?"

"I say it's a good thing love is blind," Sabre stated, before gripping his head and pulling him into a kiss that ran the gamut from desperate to passionate to hopeful. But finally, oh finally, it slid into love and Brax cradled her face between his palms tenderly in thanks.

He pulled back, placing a chaste kiss on the tip of her nose, "I love you."

Sabre smiled at him, her whole face alight with happiness, "I love you more."

Brax felt his breath catch in his throat, his ears ringing with the confirmation of Sabre's love returned. "Whilst I love hearing that, you know it's not a competition, right?" he told her.

"Uh huh," Sabre nodded her head, "Whatever you say, my King. Whatever you say."

## CHAPTER TWENTY-THREE

"Shit, I'm nervous," Brax admitted. His companion didn't say anything, simply continued to stare at him in silence. "Well? Where are the words of wisdom? The support?" Nothing. Not so much as a hint as to what Brax was supposed to say to Draven. "You're useless, you know that?" Styx thumped his tail against the ground, the sound echoing throughout Brax's office like a sonic boom, causing him to wince. "Careful with the sledgehammer you call a tail, buddy. You know Draven doesn't approve of you being on these hardwood floors." And probably for good reason, Brax admitted. Styx's feet sported wickedly sharp claws that had ruined more than one antique floor covering over the years.

After Sabre had left that morning, Brax had retreated to his father's office in an attempt to actually do some kingly work. No matter how long it had been and the fact that it had also been used by Mikhail, the large room with the dark cherry wood flooring, the mahogany table and bookcases, and the dark green leather chair, would always be his father's office. Mikhail hadn't changed a thing in the forty years since their father's death, and Brax had likewise kept it the same. Although, that was probably largely due to the fact that he had barely stepped foot into the room since Mikhail had died. But whatever. He was there today and trying to step up his game. He wanted to be the type of king Sabre would be proud of. He knew most people wouldn't understand or believe him but Sabre really did make him want to be the best version of himself. Luckily, he didn't need everyone to believe him. Just one person. And that person was on their way now, hence why he was trying to get advice from a non-verbal hell hound.

"Brax?"

Draven's voice floated into the room as the office door opened and Brax knew he was out of time. Clearing his dry throat, he yelled, "I'm in here."

Draven entered the office looking confused, "I went to your rooms, but the guard on duty –"

"Hugo," Brax supplied.

Draven eyed him, "Right, Hugo. Hugo said you were in your office working. I know he's one of your closest friends from the Horde and I thought perhaps he was playing a prank of some kind. Yet here you are ... working."

Brax grimaced. Draven's assessment of the situation made him feel like a right arsehole. Hugo was indeed one of his closest friends as well as a lieutenant. Brax had seen very little of him and others since the death of his brothers, too consumed with uncovering the person behind their deaths. The only time he had seen them was to order them to do shitty jobs well beneath their stations. Brax had called Hugo up that morning and asked if he would be willing to be a part of the Royal Guard. Hugo had been thrilled and was going to be handpicking his own team. Brax had isolated himself so much that Draven was essentially the only person shadowing him. And although that was more than enough, it was decidedly against protocol.

Brax looked down at the dozens of papers on his desk, shuffling them around and messing them up even more. "I'm attempting to work," he offered. "But it isn't going well. The place is a mess. I don't even know where to start."

Draven walked over and placed an arm on Brax's shoulder, the weight was familiar – solid and comforting. "Looks like you already have," Draven squeezed him. "I'm proud of you."

The words caused warmth to spread throughout Brax's chest and he cleared his throat, "Thank you. I'm sorry I –"

"Stop. Don't apologise. You don't need to apologise for anything, you hear me? I'm just glad to see the old Brax back," Draven said.

"Yeah, well, you can thank Sabre for that," Brax stated in a rush, trying to rip off the bandaid.

Draven stilled, before moving to the other side of the desk, "Sabre?"

Brax pushed away from the desk too, standing so he and Draven were eye to eye. "That's right. She's given me so much, Draven. And I'm not talking about answers."

"Are you referring to orgasms?"

Brax choked, "What?!"

Draven eyed him drolly, crossing his arms over his chest, "I know you've been sleeping with her, Brax. I am your guardian. It is my duty and honour to know everything about you and all that you do. If you think the fact that you are having sex with Sabre has alluded me, you are mistaken. Although, I really wish it *had* alluded me. That is an image I could have gone my whole life without," Draven muttered.

"I – you – you knew?!" Brax was beyond shocked.

Draven rolled his eyes, "Oh, please. You forget I knew you

during puberty and your early twenties. I know what you look like when you're getting laid. It is most disturbing," he gave a delicate shudder. "And though I wish you were engaging in such activities with someone else, I can't say I'm opposed to the changes it has wrought in you. That's why I haven't said anything. I don't know how or why but she appears to bring out something in you that has been missing for the past year. I'm ... grateful to her," Draven ground out.

"Wow, that sounded like it hurt," Brax chuckled.

Draven levelled a stern look in his direction, "I assure you, it did."

Brax laughed again, slapping Draven on the back as he made his way to the comfy lounge before sitting down. "I have to say, I'm so relieved to hear you say that. Because ... well, I love her, Draven."

Draven seemed to choke on his own spit even as his crystal blue eyes damn near fell out of his handsome, angel head. "I'm sorry, what did you just say?"

Brax shook his head, amused at his guardian's antics. "I just told you I was in love with Sabre."

If it were possible, Draven became even paler upon hearing the words for the second time. "Abraxis ... you ... you can't really mean that," Draven stuttered. "I thought you were just fucking some of your grief and aggression out on her!"

This time, Brax frowned and he sat up straighter in his chair, "No ... that is not all I've been doing. I do mean it, Draven. Somehow, some way, Sabre has wormed her way into my heart. She's everything I never knew I wanted in a woman. She makes me happy, Draven."

Draven must have realised Brax was serious, for he squatted down in front of him, taking his hand, "As your friend, I am pleased to hear you speak such words, though as your guardian and advisor, I must urge you to reconsider."

"Reconsider? Draven, you're not listening to me. It's not a choice – it's an emotion. It's a connection. I can't reconsider." He pulled his hand from Draven's grasp, "And even if it was a choice, I would choose Sabre. Every. Single. Time. She's mine."

Draven remained on one knee, head bent and Brax started to feel sick to his stomach. He knew Draven and Sabre had a love-hate relationship, but he had been sure it was more for entertainment purposes than actual spite. He was sure the two enjoyed the hell out of their bickering. Brax wasn't sure what he would do if he was forced to choose between the two most important people in his world. "Do you really hate her that much?" he finally asked.

Draven sighed, raising his head and admitted; "Sabre asked me the same question just shortly after our acquaintance."

Brax swallowed audibly, "And what did you say?"

The angel stood up, shaking his head slowly, "I said yes. I said I hated everything she stood for." Brax felt his stomach swoop sickeningly. Draven, clearly seeing the look on his face, hastened to continue, "I just don't understand her, Brax. Every now and again I see glimpses of this person who is loyal and kind and strong beyond belief. She's funny and warm and generous … But glimpses aren't enough, Brax. Sabre hunts, tortures and kills people. That's what she does. I mean, that's exactly why you hired her in the first place! She's an angel. Every fibre of her make-up tells her to do good. To *be* good. Yet … she isn't. Sabre isn't good, Brax. Good versus bad must be a battle of wills she fights every day, yet the side she chooses is the side she has been trained for – not born for. That's a choice, Brax."

"Perhaps it is," Brax allowed. "But, Draven, I don't care. I don't care that she could crush me with one hand tied behind her back. I don't care that she'll come home to me at night covered in someone else's blood. I don't even care that she has a zombie as a best friend and a snarly, wounded weretiger as a protégé. I care about the way Sabre makes me feel; happy, in love … at home. I care that she makes me laugh because she is funny as fuck and the most sarcastic person I have ever met. I care about her loyalty and faith in her friends and the fact that she adores my hell hound and he adores her. I care about *her*, Draven. Everything she has done and everything she has been through has shaped her into the person she is today. And that is the person I love. The rest of it? It's all just details, Draven."

Draven's eyes roamed searchingly over Brax's face, his stance remaining rigid for another heartbeat before he slumped, "She's not what I would have chosen for you."

"Draven, I love you. You know that. But … you don't get a choice. Hell, I don't think even *I* get a choice. My beast has already decided she is ours. She feels like my mate, Draven," Brax admitted. And it was true. His inner beast, the part of him that was primitive and alpha and predator, had claimed Sabre as surely as if they were fated to be together.

"Demons don't have fated mates," Draven pointed out, searching for any and all straws to clutch.

There were many creatures in Purgatory who had fated mates; their bodies recognised each other on a biological level, causing them to be drawn to one another. Brax, as a demon, didn't experience that in the same way. Although, because he had a beast as a part of him – a part of his soul – he believed he could still feel that little *click* locking into place whenever he was near Sabre. Angels were the same as demons – no pheromones or blood connection to tell them when they had found the one. But Brax believed it made their choice of each other even more special. And the fact that they recognised each other in another way – with their hearts and with their heads rather than their senses, made the connection even more real.

"My body may not have recognised Sabre's on a biological level, Draven. But my heart recognises her, my soul does. She's mine. I am hers," was all Brax said in response. Draven was silent for so long, Brax was beginning to sweat. Was Draven really going to make him choose between the woman he loved and his best friend?

Finally, Draven spoke, "Does this mean I have to be nicer to her?"

Brax barked out a laugh, the relief plain to hear, "No. You two can carry on as you wish. I dare say Sabre won't be any nicer to you, so you had better stay on your toes."

Draven nodded his head, breathing in deep before releasing the breath harshly. His eyes met Brax's, "Abraxis, I am happy for you. Truly. If Sabre is yours then she is mine too. I will protect her with my life. You have my word."

Brax may or may not have felt all choked up as he grabbed Draven in a fierce man-hug. The two of them slapped each other on the back a few times because they were very manly, before clearing their throats and looking away until their eyes were clear once more. "Thank you, Draven. She's the best, you'll see. Sabre is —"

Brax was interrupted from extolling all of Sabre's virtues by a knock on the door. One of his new royal guards stuck his head in the door, apologising but saying Brax had a visitor who claimed to have information about the assassinations of the royal family. Draven became alert in an instant, exchanging a heavy look with Brax.

"Stay here," Draven commanded, before following the guard back outside.

Brax stood up to pace while Draven checked out the unexpected guest. Was this another long-lost witness crawling from the woodwork thanks to Sabre stirring up trouble? Or was it merely someone trying to make a quick buck? Brax and Draven had been approached by numerous concerned citizens, claiming to have information about the 'Royal Assassinations' as the newspapers had dubbed it. News had more than gotten around about his hunt for his family's killer. As such, there had been more than a few opportunists, willing to share their valuable information for the right price. Draven was always more than willing to test the validity of their claims – and then kick their arses to the curb when he discovered they were baseless.

When Draven came back through the door, he was pale. Brax saw his hands tremble as he ran them through his blond hair. "My King ..."

Brax walked over to him, "Draven? What is it? Is it really a witness?"

Draven swallowed audibly, "Yes. Yes, it is a witness. And you need to listen to them. I – this one is not lying."

Brax took in his guardian's pallid complexion and stuttering words, "I'm not going to like this, am I?"

"Brax ... I'm so sorry," was all Draven said.

Squaring his shoulders and standing up straight, Brax faced the door, ready to take on whatever came through. He wasn't expecting the lithe form of an elf to slip in, nor the terrible, damning words that followed.

"My King, you have been deceived," the elf said, voice light and humble.

Brax listened to the mysterious elf as he spun a tale so horrible and insane that he thought it might just be true. A deep, vicious snarl left his lips when the man mentioned a name, causing him to pause. With ice filling his arteries and going directly to his heart, Brax gestured at the man; "Continue."

## CHAPTER TWENTY-FOUR

Sabre was early. She wasn't due to meet Brax until that evening but after all the feels of the previous night, she'd found it hard to concentrate and even harder to slice and dice. So instead, she had decided to go and see how Brax had fared telling Draven he loved her. Sabre really didn't want to know how that conversation went. She was sure the other angel would have tried everything to convince Brax he was wrong. But Sabre had faith in her man. She may not have believed him at first when he had said those precious and startling words to her, but she knew Brax never lied. He loved her. A breathless laugh escaped her; someone loved her! Her! An angel rejected and reviled by her own kind, dragged through childhood with violence, and with more blood on her hands and sins in her heart than perhaps any other soul in Purgatory. Brax knew all that – he *saw* all that – and he loved her anyway. If all the years of pain and drama and blood was the price to pay for being gifted her demon king, then she was glad to have paid them.

Smiling to herself and plotting the best way to tell Jinx and

Gage, as well as Hound, that she was head over heels in love, she didn't notice the tense atmosphere as she approached Brax's office. That morning – after mutual orgasms in the now hair-free shower stall – Brax had informed her he would be working the day away in his office. Sabre couldn't be prouder. The door was open a crack, so she simply pushed her way in, grinning when she found the man of her dreams standing with his back to her in the centre of the room.

"Brax! I know I'm early, but ..." Sabre trailed off, her hands instinctively reaching for her weapons when two strong arms wrapped around her in a punishing grip. She cursed, unable to free her hands, resorting to delivering harsh kicks with her heels against hard shins. "Draven!" she screamed, "What the fuck are you doing?!"

Draven snarled in her left ear, "Quiet!" He then followed up with, "How could you?"

It was the second, low and pain-filled question that had her pausing right before she was about to headbutt him and break his nose, freeing herself so she could then kick his butt even more. She knew Draven wasn't going to take Brax and her relationship well, but she never dreamed he would physically attack her. And why was Brax letting him? "How could I what, Draven? How could I love Brax? It was really quite simple, I assure you." Draven still held her in an almost unbreakable grip and Sabre huffed, staring at Brax's back. "Brax? You want to call off your guard dog here? I don't want to have to hurt him."

Brax finally turned around and the look on his face would have dropped her to her knees had Draven not been holding her up. "Brax? What's wrong?" But he only continued to look at her with dead eyes and her heart began to pound a furious rhythm for a whole other reason. *Oh no,* she thought, *not now. Please don't let him know. Not like this,* she begged silently, praying to anyone who would listen. Which, given who she was, was very likely no one.

"I'm going to ask you this once. And Sabre?" Brax cautioned in a low, flat voice, "You better tell me the truth."

Sabre held his eyes, the pain in her chest making it difficult to breathe. Still, she raised her chin and nodded her head, "I won't ever lie to you. Let me go," she demanded to Draven, who surprisingly immediately released her.

"Were you the assassin hired to kill my brother? Did you kill Mikhail?"

Sabre heard herself whimper in her head. Brax knew. He knew and the look on his face and the hate in his eyes was something Sabre hadn't been prepared for, no matter what she had said to Jinx and Gage. Still, she answered the only way she could; "Yes," Sabre said, "I was the assassin hired to kill Mikhail."

Brax appeared to whither before her eyes and the sound that rose in his throat was part whimper, part snarl, "Get out," he then whispered.

"Brax, please, wait …" Sabre pleaded. She just needed a chance to explain. She could explain, she knew she could. If he would only give her a chance …

"I said get out, Sabre! Get out before I kill you!" Brax roared, the sound reverberating off the walls and causing a very docile Styx to whimper plaintively in the corner.

Sabre cringed against the onslaught, but tried again, "Just wait, Brax please. You don't understand. Let me explain."

Brax stormed toward her, his face thunderous. He gripped Sabre by the biceps and picked her up so her toes dangled on the ground, "Explain? Explain what?! I already understand! You killed my brother!" he snarled directly in Sabre's face, giving her a small shake before thrusting her away from him as if she were trash. "Get her out of here," he commanded Draven. "I really will kill her."

Draven grabbed Sabre again and began forcefully pulling her from the room. Sabre knew all sorts of moves to get away from the angel dragging her away from the heartbroken demon in the centre of the room, but she used none of them. The strong, noble warrior she had grown to love beyond anything she thought was possible was bleeding and broken as surely as if she had stabbed him with a sword. She had only a few seconds left to weigh up her decision. Hound had told her she would need to make a choice and he was right as usual. Although all the pieces weren't in place and the end game was not upon them, the time to choose was still now. She only hoped it wasn't too late.

She was at the doorway when she suddenly gripped it, forcing Draven to a stop. "The King lives!" she shouted, frantically trying to get the words out around Draven's arm across her throat. Sabre coughed, fingers clutching at Draven's forearm, "Mikhail lives!"

Brax choked on a sob, "The King lives? Are you forgetting I was the one who found his body? A single cross bolt to the heart with his life's blood spreading around him in a sticky puddle. My brother is well and truly dead. And *you* killed him! You just admitted it! Don't try to fucking backtrack now."

Sabre shook her head desperately, unable to form any more words as Brax turned away, dismissing her ... forever. She allowed Draven to drag her the rest of the way out and quite literally throw her out the front door.

"I'll give you twenty-four hours before I come for you," Draven warned, looking every inch the battle-angel he was.

The palace doors slammed with a finality that echoed in Sabre's heart. She was too blinded by the tears in her eyes to see the forgotten, long-lost witness grin in triumph before he melted away into the shadows of the palace grounds.

## CHAPTER TWENTY-FIVE

*A*rriving at the den, it was all Sabre could do to put one foot in front of the other. Draven had thrown her out of the palace – literally – spewing obscenities and dire threats. She wondered why he hadn't simply killed her outright but figured he was thinking of the potential information she held under lock and key in her mind. Besides, it wasn't like he didn't know exactly where to find her. She was obligated to return to the Blue Devil thanks to her contract. Draven no doubt knew all the ins and outs of blood and soul bonds and knew she was tethered to the assassin den. And if she wasn't there, she would be at Gage's warehouse. She had been tempted to go there and lick her wounds but she was simply too raw to be around her friends. Breathing in shakily, she began to make her way up the drive, her overwhelmed mind frantically trying to come up with a solution to her mess. If only she could get Brax to listen. Remembering the grief in his eyes as she had admitted to killing his older brother nearly felled her midstep. But what was worse was the look of hatred he had thrown at her as she was being dragged out of his domain.

The love he once promised with just a simple glance had been extinguished.

So caught up in her anguish, she didn't register the two bodies blocking her path until she almost ran into them in the foyer. Carlisle and an elf she had never seen before were blocking her way. "Move it or lose it," Sabre warned, quietly. She meant the statement quite literally.

Carlisle didn't budge, instead looking her up and down, eyes shining with something akin to excitement. "Sabre, my friend here has been telling me an interesting tale."

Sabre's eyes flicked to the elf for a brief second before locking onto Carlisle, "I am not in the mood, Carlisle."

"Oh, I believe that. Considering you've just ruined your chances of getting any more kingly booty," Carlisle laughed.

Sabre narrowed her eyes, feeling her fingers flex. She wanted to hurt the incubus so bad. "What do you want?"

"What? No surprise over me knowing you've been banging the new king?" When Sabre merely stared at him, Carlisle shifted uncomfortably but continued, "I knew. And I thought it was a genius stroke to be honest. Kings do make good bed fellows. So many secrets, so much power to manipulate. I was damn proud of you."

"Great. All my dreams have now come true," Sabre sniped, sarcastically.

Carlisle shook his head, "I know you hate me, Sabre. I hate you too. But you're one of my best assassins and one of my greatest achievements. I mean, how many Den Masters could boast they own the assassin who killed the last king?"

Sabre blew out a rough breath. The contract on Mikhail had been a private one but like a good little assassin, Sabre had kept her owner informed. He had known all along she was the one to kill Mikhail. Sabre had no idea what Carlisle was getting at.

"Do you have a point?" she snapped, patience more than eroded.

Carlisle's hand snapped out, locking around her throat and hauling her in close, "My point is that I thought you had fulfilled that private contract. Several of my vested acquaintances were well pleased by that. Now my friend here, he tells me he overheard something very interesting. Something that could be very damaging to me and my little den here."

Sabre didn't bother fighting the hand that was slowly cutting off her oxygen. For one, it wouldn't do any good. She couldn't harm Carlisle. For two, she was really interested in where this conversation was headed. She managed to wheeze out a, "What?"

Carlisle squeezed his fingers harshly before letting her go. Sabre fell to the floor with a crack and Carlisle followed her down, squatting in front of her. Tilting her chin up, he said, "My elf thought he heard you tell Abraxis that Mikhail was still alive. Now, you either killed or you didn't. How can both be true?"

Sabre smirked, "If you're so clever, Carlisle, why don't you figure it out yourself?" As the incubus swore and raged, giving her a few solid kicks to the ribs, Sabre tried to get a better look at the elf. What exactly was going on and why was Carlisle so invested in the deaths of the royal line? Perhaps he was more heavily involved than she had first thought. Sabre cursed herself for being so close to a source yet so fucking oblivious.

"Get her up. I want her questioned immediately," Carlisle commanded, gesturing to someone on his right.

Sabre tracked the sound of heavy footsteps right before Mercy moved in front of her line of sight. Once the personal torturer for Hades himself, the pain demon had been under the employ of Carlisle for over one hundred years now. He was huge and muscled – as most demons forged in the depths of hell tended to be. With slate grey horns that protruded from his head just behind his hair line and curved backwards, and pale grey, cloudy eyes that seemed to peer into your soul, Mercy was a disconcerting presence to say the least. The demon was the very definition of a sadist, literally feeding from the pain of others. Thus, the job of torturer was his cup of tea.

Jerking her to her feet, Mercy began hauling her down the hallway before pushing her into the room at the end. "I've got this," Mercy informed Carlisle, levelly.

The incubus pointed a finger at the demon, "See that you do. Sabre … have fun."

Sabre flipped Carlisle off, "Have fun," she mocked in a high-pitch voice after the door had shut with a bang, before muttering, "Stupid fuck."

"Stupid fuck," Mercy agreed, his face stoic.

Sabre rolled her shoulders, poking at her tender ribs and determining nothing was even cracked, let alone broken. She then roamed around the torture chamber, poking at various tools and accoutrements before finally hoisting herself up onto a bare, stone slab. Kicking her legs, she asked, "How much time do we have?"

"Carlisle gives me carte blanche, you know that. But he's particularly impatient this time. He wants to know what you know very badly. Still, he's aware of how stubborn you are, so I figure we have a good couple of hours," Mercy commented, casually walking over to her and taking a seat next to her on the same stone bench.

Sabre made to rise, but Mercy gestured her to stay there, "No, no. Stay there," Mercy urged. "We may as well be comfortable while you get me caught up."

Sabre smiled a genuine smile and pushed herself back so she was sitting with her back flush against the wall. Mercy was the second of the two people in the den she trusted and considered a friend. Carlisle, the moron, had no clue of course, and would be expecting Mercy to be removing flesh from her bones in an effort to get her to talk. Sabre knew Mercy would happily do it, but only because of his demonic nature. Not because he wanted to hurt her. He was loyal to Sabre and always would be. She had saved his husband and son from a fate worse than death over fifty years ago, cementing their friendship and ensuring his loyalty. He would do everything he could to stall, but when Carlisle came back, she knew they had to make it look like Mercy had tried. Otherwise his cover would be blown.

*And one cover going down the crapper was more than enough for one day*, Sabre thought, knowing that no matter what came from that day's antics, Carlisle would never trust her again. Although he couldn't know the full extent of who and what Sabre truly was, he had enough suspicions that Sabre knew her time at the den was over. She was more than a little relieved. She just had no idea what she was going to do considering the major clusterfuck that was in the process of going down.

"So," Mercy's deep voice drew her attention, "You've been fucking the new king, huh? What's that like?"

Sabre laughed before laughing some more. And then laughed so hard that tears ran down her cheeks. She thought maybe she was a little hysterical but considering she was about to be tortured by a good friend, had broken the heart of her one and only love, and had revealed a doozy of a secret, she felt she was entitled.

"That good, huh?" Mercy asked.

Sabre grinned, "Oh, Mercy, you have no idea."

Mercy's greedy grin matched her own, "Do tell. And leave nothing out."

"And then you fell in love with him?" Mercy asked when Sabre came to the conclusion of her tale.

Sabre snorted, not moving from where she rested her head comfortably on the demon's broad shoulder. "Yeah. Stupidest thing out of millions of other stupid things I've done in my life."

"Well, I think it's wonderful!" Mercy enthused, the lightness in his voice at complete odds with his terrifying appearance. "Wait until I tell Heath and Milo," he said, referencing his chimera husband and son.

Sabre groaned and Mercy laughed because Heath was an incurable romantic and had been trying to set Sabre up for years. Unfortunately for Heath, Sabre had ended up maiming or even killing the blind dates he had arranged. It seemed the chimera only knew arseholes. Other than his husband of course, Mercy was a real gem.

The shrill ringing of a phone interrupted their girl talk and Mercy's face went blank as he looked at the caller ID. "Yes, sir? Yes. No, not yet. Yes, sir. I understand."

Mercy lowered the phone and they continued to sit in silence for a few minutes before Sabre sighed and nudged Mercy away. Jumping to her feet, she dusted off her butt and looked around the room, "Okay. Where do you want me?"

Mercy groaned as he pushed slowly to his feet, "The chair I guess. You sure you don't just want to make a gaol-break? You know I hate the fucker as much as you do, right? I'm only here because I have a steady stream of victims to feed me and to repay my debt to you."

Sabre eyed the steel chair disdainfully. The thing was so cold on her butt, even through her leather pants. A fact she knew from more than one visit to the torture chamber in the past. The room didn't belong to Mercy and Carlisle liked to have a little fun in there as well as bring in outside interrogators. "I've already told you," Sabre grimaced as she sat down, her butt cheeks immediately chilled, "Mercy, you don't owe me anything."

"I owe you my world. Now that you're in love I'm sure you can understand that."

Considering she was about to be tortured by a man she considered a friend just to keep Brax and his family safe – and for the small chance that Brax might actually find out and forgive her – Sabre supposed she did understand. Shaking that off, she looked at Mercy, "Start with a shoulder."

"A finger," Mercy countered, causing Sabre to roll her eyes in annoyance.

"A fucking finger? Come on, Mercy. Carlisle will know something is up if you only break a finger. Dislocate a shoulder, crush a couple of fingers and then get a little stabby in places that bleed a lot," Sabre demanded.

Mercy huffed in annoyance but made his way over to the table and grabbed a ball hammer. "Fine. But let's come up with a plan to get your man back while we're at it, okay?" Before she could blink, Mercy slammed the hammer down onto her pinky finger, asking, "What if I killed the angel for you? Draven, right? He sounds like a real bag of arseholes."

Sabre gritted her teeth and shook her head, "You can't kill Draven. He may be a dick but Brax loves him. You know how demons are with their guardian angels."

Mercy grunted, bringing the hammer down a second time. He then scowled when Sabre didn't make a sound, "You're no fun, you know that? Can't even get a decent meal out of you because you're too hardcore to feel pain like the rest of us mere mortals."

"Oh, I feel pain," she replied, twitching a little when Mercy brought the hammer down for a third time on her middle finger this time. It hurt, sure, but she was able to acknowledge it and move on. A trick she had learned in the early years of her training.

But what she was finding hard to push aside was the pain in her heart from the look of absolute hatred on Brax's face when he had learned the truth. Nothing could have prepared her for what being in love felt like. And nothing felt as shitty as a broken heart.

Mercy sucked in a sharp breath, "Okay, that was a lot of pain. Yay for me; boo for you. Thinking of your man?" he inquired. Commiseration was sharing the flush of vitality from her emotional torment on his face.

Sabre nodded her head but didn't say anything further. And true to his name, Mercy went about breaking her body and left all further talk of her broken heart alone.

## CHAPTER TWENTY-SIX

"You dumb fuck! What have you done?!"

The angry words were accompanied by a rage-filled hiss as Jinx stormed into Brax's living quarters. As usual, Gage wasn't far behind the teen, and he looked as pissed as Jinx sounded. Draven immediately stepped forward to intervene but Brax held him back. The whole affair with Sabre just two hours before had brought little satisfaction and he was jonesing for a fight. Perhaps the pair in front of him could provide him with one. Brax subtly tested the strength in his legs before he stood up to his full, imposing height. The betrayal of Sabre had weakened his knees and crushed his heart. Brax was utterly and completely devastated.

"You aren't welcome here anymore. Remove yourselves before I have you forcibly ejected," he barked at the pair.

Jinx's bi-coloured eyes flashed in challenge, "I dare you to try."

Gage placed a restraining hand on her arm as she took an angry step forward. "What happened?" the man asked, sounding hostile as hell but with a more even tone than the spitfire next to him.

"I learned the truth," he stated simply, daring them with his eyes to come to Sabre's defence. If they tried, he would rip their words apart. Sabre had confessed. He had heard it with his own ears. Had seen the heart wrenching truth of it in her eyes. There was nothing they could say that would save her.

"Which one?" Gage asked, dark eyes staring directly into bright, yellow ones.

"Which one? How many do you think there are?" Brax asked, rhetorically. "There is only one truth. And that is that Sabre was the assassin who killed Mikhail!" his response ended on a roar.

Gage looked unimpressed and Jinx simply looked even more pissed. "You're wrong, Your Majesty. There happen to be many truths. Sabre –"

Brax cut him off. The sound of Sabre's name on his lips enough to make his stomach revolt, "Were you complicit in her crimes?"

The pair looked at each other, Gage raising an eyebrow at Jinx, who smirked, "Complicit? As in, did we know she was the one to assassinate your brother? Yeah. We knew."

"Then you both shall be punished as well. Murder of a royal is an automatic death sentence," he intoned, ruthlessly pushing down the part of him that had come to like the pair, especially the young Jinx. The hate and thirst for vengeance that had plagued him for over a year, but which had all but dissipated in the weeks of knowing – and loving – Sabre, was swiftly returning. He felt like a volcano ready to erupt. Draven, obviously sensing his rage, bravely placed a calming hand to his arm. Brax didn't bother to shake it off as even the angel's powers of comfort couldn't hold a candle to the storm raging within.

"Oh, get over yourself, Brax! You don't know the whole story.

Clearly you didn't give Sabre a chance to explain," Jinx fired back.

"Explain?! *Explain?!*" Brax all but roared, ignoring the flash of admiration when Jinx stood her ground, raising her chin like a little warrior – or a queen. "What is there to explain? She admitted she killed Mikhail." Saying his name now hurt as much as it had the day he had found his brother dead.

Jinx nodded quickly, "She did. But –"

"There is no but!" Brax literally roared, and he felt claws pierce the tops of his fingers even as his fangs grew in his mouth. "She made a fool out of me! All this time, I had her looking into the threat against the throne. And it was right in front of me. It was her!"

"You haven't acted like a moron before, now is not the time to start," Jinx scolded, apparently unaffected by his beast. "Sabre is *not* the threat to the throne. Yes, she was hired to assassinate Mikhail. But she wasn't the one who did the hiring. She also wasn't the one who killed your father, or your uncles, or your little brother. *That's* what you hired her to find out."

Brax laughed, the sound a hollow parody of humour, "Semantics. Don't get cute with words, Jinx. They will not save you."

Jinx growled in frustration, making a move as if to step forward. Gage wisely put his arm out in front of her. "We're not trying to save ourselves," Gage offered. "We're trying to save Sabre."

"Oh, well then. That's much fucking better," Brax's voice was heavy with sarcasm.

Gage ignored Brax's derision, "One of our spies contacted us to tell us Sabre is being tortured by Carlisle as we speak."

Brax couldn't help his body's visceral reaction to those words, even as his brain told it not to care – that the woman in question had murdered his brother and she deserved everything she got. "I don't care."

Jinx's blue and green eyes gentled for the first time since she had arrived, "Yes, you do," she said, gently. Then implored, "Think, Brax. Why would Carlisle want to torture Sabre? What could she possibly know that he would potentially kill his best asset for?"

"I don't care," Brax's response was immediate. But it sounded less sure, even to his own ears. Thankfully, Draven chose to step forward and commandeer the conversation. Or the argument. Or whatever the hell the fucked-up situation was.

"Was he unaware she held the contract for the assassination of Mikhail? Was it a private contract?" Draven asked.

"It was indeed a private contract," Gage confirmed. "But Carlisle still knew. He knows the names of every single heartbeat Sabre is tasked with stopping. Perhaps he wants to know *who* hired her, but that is doubtful. He's already in on the conspiracy to take down the line of Cerberus. Sabre figured that out and already told you that. Why would he care who hired her to complete a task he agreed with? No, it must be something else. What exactly happened?" Gage urged.

It was on the tip of Brax's tongue to tell them all to fuck off, but Draven stepped in front of him, forcing their eyes to meet. "Abraxis ... my friend. You know my feelings for the woman and I would be more than satisfied to see her rot for her crimes. But ... I know your feelings for her too. And for that reason ..." he turned back to Jinx and Gage, "I'm willing to listen."

Brax felt his eyes itch, breath stalling in his throat. But he allowed neither the tears to fall nor the pained howl to escape his lips. Falling back into the chair behind him, he listened with a detached ear as Draven explained the day's nightmarish events.

"Wait, who was this witness? And where is he now?" Gage demanded once the story had been told.

Draven sighed, "He was an elf. And he didn't divulge his name. He must have slipped out in all the confusion when Sabre was being ... evicted. We haven't seen him since and have no way to contact him."

Gage was frowning, "And you don't find that a little odd? Why would a witness suddenly pop up now? And not just any witness, one who could clearly identify Sabre? It doesn't make any sense."

Jinx was nodding, "Unless that was the whole point. To identify Sabre. To get you to turn on her," Jinx accused, glaring at Brax.

"Turn on her?" Brax was incredulous, "She killed my brother!"

Jinx dismissed his comment with a flick of her wrist. "Sabre never mentioned an elf," she said to Gage. "A new player?"

Gage nodded, then considered her words, "Or perhaps a very old one."

"What are you two talking about?!" Brax yelled, his fragile patience all but gone. He wanted to rage and rend and tear. He wanted to howl and cry and wallow. The two beings in front of him were denying him that.

"Don't you get it? That 'witness'" Jinx raised her fingers to make air quotes, "was a plant. Sent to discredit Sabre. No doubt because she was getting close to the truth. She's been working round the clock to figure out who the culprit is. Ever since you hired her. And before that —" Jinx quickly shut up.

Brax narrowed his eyes, "And before that, what?"

Jinx pursed her lips but Gage gave her a nudge to her shoulder, "Sabre loves him," the zombie said softly.

Jinx's shoulders drooped, "Before then she had been aiding

someone who wants to help. He goes by –"

"Hound," Brax finished. "Santa's secret little helper. Yes, I know. He's made himself known to me a few times in the past. Sabre mentioned he was a source of hers."

Jinx looked surprised, "She told you about him?"

Gage rolled his eyes, poking Jinx in the side with his finger, "Sabre loves him, remember?" He ploughed on before anyone could address those words, "It still doesn't seem like enough for Carlisle to turn on Sabre now. She's too valuable to him. Something else must have happened," Gage pressed.

"Nothing," Brax said, suddenly exhausted. He covered his face with his hands, "There's nothing. Just like Sabre is to me."

The silence dragged out for a few tense, depressing moments before Draven cleared his throat, "There was one other thing. As she was being dragged away, Sabre yelled that the King still lived."

Gage's dark skin turned alabaster as all the blood drained from his face, "She said that? And that fake fucking witness heard?!" he yelled. "Shit, shit, fuck and damn! This is bad, this is bad. No wonder Carlisle wants to tear her apart for information."

Brax stood up slowly, eyes intent but mind suspicious, "Why would her den master care about a careless statement thrown out in desperation to stop me killing her?"

"Duh!" Jinx snarked at him, turning her back and heading for the exit, "Maybe because it wasn't an act of desperation."

Brax growled, launching himself into the air and landing in a predatory crouch in front of the weretiger. He may have appreciated strong females but the bratty teen was beginning to piss him off in ways that had nothing to do with her association with Sabre. "I saw Mikhail with my own eyes. He had no heartbeat. He bled out. His heart was destroyed by that cross bolt. He was dead. Nothing you can say will change that."

"Fine. It's not my place to anyway. But aren't you at least curious as to why Carlisle is so interested? Don't you care at all that Sabre is likely getting torn apart as we speak? Because there is no way she would talk. Sabre is unbreakable."

"I don't care …" Brax's fallback response sounded lame even to his own ears.

"Well, I care. Gage!" Jinx pushed past him, Gage coming to heel like a good little dog. "We've put a call out to assemble the troops but it's going to take a few hours. What should we do in the meantime?" Jinx asked, eyes pleading.

What the hell were they talking about? "Wait, troops? What troops? Are you referring to my Horde?"

Jinx sneered at him, "Why would I be talking about your stupid demon army? I'm talking about Sabre's friends."

"Friends, plural? You make it sound as if there is more than one," Draven tossed out.

Both Gage and Jinx looked scornfully at the angel. Gage shook his head, looking almost pitying, "You really have no idea. Both of you don't. That's Sabre's fault. And she would be the first to admit that. Unfortunately, it was just one more cross she had to bear for the good of many." Before Brax could question what Gage meant, the man continued on, "Yes, Sabre has friends. Although, she wouldn't call them that. She likes to think she has none. And I suppose some wouldn't call themselves that either. Most of them owe Sabre a debt. We took the prerogative of calling them all in."

Draven and Brax exchanged a confused look, "Debts? What kind of debts could they possibly owe that they would be willing to storm the most notorious assassin den in Purgatory that is filled with brutal killers for?" Brax asked.

Gage's black gaze was unwavering as he met Brax's eyes, "Life debts. They all owe Sabre life debts."

## CHAPTER TWENTY-SEVEN

"What has she said?"

Carlisle stormed into the room, acting all macho and aggressive and it was all Sabre could do not to roll her eyes and snort over the display. Mercy was right; Carlisle was very impatient. Usually, he was happy to leave Mercy to his work for at least a day before barging in and demanding answers. But Sabre calculated that it had only been around three hours – with only about twenty minutes of that time taken up with a little slap 'n' tickle. Not that Carlisle knew that of course. Sabre was sure she looked just as pathetic and broken as her owner was expecting. Mercy had done a great job smashing fingers but had forgone dislocating her shoulder in case she needed it for later. He had instead sliced a few cleverly-placed cuts on her neck and upper chest, as well as some burns to her arms and legs. They looked particularly nasty but Sabre knew they weren't deep. They would heal in a matter of days.

"Nothing," Mercy answered Carlisle.

Carlisle spun on him, "Nothing? What do you mean nothing?"

"She hasn't said anything, sir. She's been sitting there quiet the entire time. It's like she's a mute," Mercy waggled his eyebrows behind Carlisle's back as he lied through his pointy teeth. Sabre barely restrained herself from laughing. It would be decidedly inappropriate.

Carlisle rounded on Mercy abruptly, "Are you losing your touch? Perhaps you just aren't trying hard enough."

Mercy drew himself up, "I assure you. I haven't lost my touch. I am all about pain and I assure you, that woman is in pain right now. She merely refuses to talk. She's stubborn."

"Stubborn!" Carlisle got right up into Sabre's face and snarled, "Listen here, bitch! You'll talk, even if I have to cut out your tongue."

Sabre moved her head back in shock, cocking her head to the side and scrunching up her nose, she then said; "What the fuck? Really, Carlisle? That's the best threat you can come up with? How the fuck am I supposed to talk if you cut out my tongue? You really are an idiot, aren't you?" Her response earned her several punches to the face and gut. It knocked the wind out of her, but she still managed a chuckle, "Wanker," she spat blood onto the floor.

Carlisle snarled, his pheromones leaving him in a rush, causing Mercy and Sabre to both groan – more in annoyance than in a sexual haze. "You won't talk? That's fine. I don't need you to talk. I'm bringing in Touma."

Sabre stilled at that. Touma was a satori – a being who could read minds. He was also a particularly nasty piece of work and had been hanging around Carlisle for years. Sabre had been forced to endure Touma's unique brand of torture a few times in the past and wasn't ashamed to say that she would rather have her fingernails plucked out than have someone invade the inner sanctity of her mind. Touma was also exceedingly expensive, Sabre knew. Carlisle really wanted what was in her head.

"What the hell is going on, Carlisle? Why do you care so much about a throw away comment I made in the heat of the moment?"

"Why? Because if it's true, it could well ruin years of careful planning! That's why!" Carlisle yelled in her face.

"Careful planning by you?" Sabre asked, wondering if Carlisle could be the mastermind behind the demise of the line of Cerberus. "Or your little elf friend?" *And just who was that little fucker, anyway?* Sabre wondered. Whoever he was, she was going to rip his pointy little ears out of his head and shove them fair up his butt when she caught up with him.

Carlisle's eyes roved over Sabre's face, but the man seemed to regain some of his control because he simply stepped back, saying nothing. A small beep from his phone had him grunting and striding from the room, "He's here."

Mercy made no move to close the door but quickly moved to her side where she was tied to the chair with wire bindings. "Don't worry, I had Phaedra sound the bat signal a couple of hours ago. Your team will be here soon. You've dealt with Touma's mind games before. You'll be fine."

Sabre summoned a smile, "I'm glad someone has faith in me."

Mercy placed a beefy hand on her shoulder, giving it a warm and sincere squeeze. "Always," he promised her.

Before she could say anything further, Carlisle sauntered back into the room, a small, slender man of Asian descent following behind him. The man looked innocuous enough but he could look you in the eyes and see into your head in seconds. It wasn't the same type of ability as Draven's empathic ones were. Sabre knew his were based on his ability and need to heal and they were a passive power. Touma's on the other hand, were an active power – and painful.

"Hello, Sabre. Always a pleasure," the satori murmured, dragging a chair in front of her and sitting down. "I'm going to dig around in your skull for a minute now."

Touma spoke casually as if they were taking a stroll in the park and Sabre realised how annoying she must sound when she did the same thing whenever she tortured someone. Luckily, Sabre was now just as adept at blocking mental torture as she was blocking physical pain. With the amount of secrets crashing around in her head, it had been absolutely integral and she had worked damn hard to ensure nothing and no one was getting inside. That included the smarmy, Japanese man of myth in front of her.

Instead of tensing up when Touma put his hands on her head, Sabre relaxed. She found the happy place she was looking for in a nano-second, listening with a half-ear to Touma's running commentary for Carlisle's benefit.

"That's it, almost there … just a little bit. Uh huh! She's thinking of …" Touma abruptly shut his mouth.

"What? What is it?" Carlisle asked greedily.

Touma glared at Sabre, before clearing his throat, "She's thinking of the Stay Puft Marshmallow Man," he admitted.

"Excuse me?" Carlisle's voice was frigid.

"You know, like from *Ghostbusters*. At the end when they're not supposed to think of anything but Ray can't help himself and he thinks of the Stay Puft Marshmallow Man? No? Well, anyway, then it comes to life and tries to kill everyone. I can understand why Ray thought of it. It just popped into my head too," she assured Carlisle innocently. Her words were met by stunned silence. "I take it none of you have seen *Ghostbusters*? I mean, I know it's a human movie from the other middle realm but come on! It was practically a documentary!"

Carlisle popped her in the eye with a fist, causing Sabre to grunt – but not succeeding in wiping the smug look off her face. "Try again!" he demanded.

Touma clenched his jaw, pressing bony fingers into Sabre's temples and closing his eyes. The only sound in the room for several minutes were the harsh, impatient breaths of Carlisle. Presently, a strangled noise came from Touma's throat.

"Now what?" Carlisle demanded.

Touma dropped his hands and cleared his throat, looking decidedly uncomfortable as he gazed at Carlisle and Mercy, "Now she is thinking of gay porn." Touma's eyed her sideways, "*Lots* of gay porn."

Mercy choked on a laugh and Sabre couldn't hold herself back anymore, laughing uproariously. It took several blows with a bat for her to even realise Carlisle had lost control of his flimsy patience and was attempting to beat the shit out of her. "What's the matter? Gay porn is hot. Hotter than hetero porn," Sabre pointed out. And it was. Mercy's quick nod told her the pain demon was on her side.

Unfortunately, Carlisle really wasn't amused and Sabre soon found herself hanging from a hook in the ceiling like a slab of meat. He then proceeded to tenderise her like one. Mercy stood back and watched the show, no doubt gorging on the waves of pain emanating from her now severely abused and injured body. But the pain demon took no pleasure in it, Sabre knew. The murderous look in his eyes directed at Carlisle and Touma – who had stayed to help out – and the fisted hands demonstrated the man's desire to put a stop to the torture. With a few small shakes of her head and a couple of microscopic finger twitches, Sabre had ordered Mercy not to interfere.

Not only was she aware that Jinx and Gage would be planning a rescue attempt – nothing would stop the dynamic duo, not even Sabre's direct orders. But she also wanted to know how deeply involved Carlisle was in the conspiracy against the throne. Unfortunately, Carlisle was lost in his rage and Sabre hadn't been able to learn anything of value, other than the fact that the incubus was stark raving mad. The man hadn't even asked her any questions.

Even with her ear canals filled with blood, Sabre still heard the moment the fighting began outside. Carlisle wasn't one to soundproof his torture chamber. Oh no, he wanted others to hear exactly what was going on inside the room. And to fear it. The abrupt noise had Carlisle turning to the door with a curse, and Sabre took the time to take stock of herself and the situation.

Believing she was too injured to do any real damage let alone attempt an escape, Carlisle had not seen fit to bind her feet. Her arms were unfortunately still tied with titanium to a hook secured in the ceiling. But her dangling feet were blessedly – and stupidly on Carlisle's part – free. They were also bare because Carlisle had gotten a little slap-happy with a cane to the soles of her feet. Still, Sabre rolled her eyes internally, unable to do so externally due to the heavy swelling of her orbits. She could make a kill with her little toe. *Well, maybe,* she amended, before swiftly following it up with, *challenge accepted.* Her primary issue was not the mangled state of her body but the fact that she couldn't cause the den master bodily harm thanks to her fucking contract. Luckily for her she had a very pissed off pain demon hovering in the shadows, ready and willing to cause some agony and inhale the fumes.

"What the fuck is that?" Carlisle yelled.

Sabre licked her lips, "Looks like your day just went FUBAR," she informed the piece of shit incubus. And with those magic words, Mercy sprang into action. FUBAR was their pre-agreed codeword for when Mercy – and Phaedra – would show their true colours, and their true allegiance. And that just happened to be to Sabre.

Mercy literally jumped on the incubus, his huge weight sending them crashing to the floor, where Mercy then pummelled Carlisle with nothing more than a closed fist. As much as she wanted to enjoy the show, Sabre had a satori to kill with nothing more than her toe. Whistling sharply to gain his attention, Sabre quickly flicked her foot out, her big toe catching the side of Touma's mouth and hooking it. Yanking, Sabre reeled him in like a fish, only releasing her toe's grip on the inside of his mouth when he was close enough to wrap her thighs around his neck. One quick twist to the right and Touma's neck snapped, the sound reverberating in the room with a satisfying crunch and grind.

Mercy looked up from the prone and bloody man on the floor, and Sabre gestured him over. He made quick work of her bonds, lowering her carefully to the floor. Sabre remained on her feet – just – rubbing her sore wrists where the wire bindings had cut into the skin deep enough to need stitches. Sabre kicked at Touma with her toe, "Do you think that counts as killing somebody with my toe?" she asked Mercy.

Mercy snorted, already moving about the room, grabbing weapons. "Not quite."

"Damn," Sabre muttered, promising to try again in the future. But for now, she followed Mercy from the room.

From the sounds of it an epic battle was taking place on the grounds at the front of the den. There were a few noises coming from various rooms but the bulk of the fighting appeared to be outside. Sabre wondered how Gage and Jinx had managed to draw the entire assassin den outside where the cavalry would have a better chance at winning. Sabre had no doubt the pair had called in some of her chips to help get her out of Carlisle's clutches. But Sabre figured it had only been a little over six hours and the number of people who owed her within a small radius wasn't huge. Typically, those who owed her a debt tended to move far, far away from her. *Go figure.*

Sabre pushed herself off the wall and picked up her pace. A handful of untrained supernaturals would be no match for Carlisle's elite assassins and mercs. With nineteen other killers bound to the Blue Devil Den, there was often more than half there at any given time, plus another dozen guests or visitors who were just as deadly. Add in all the servants whose help could go either way, and Sabre knew her friends would be majorly outnumbered.

The front door was conveniently open and Sabre charged through it ... only to come to a surprised stop. The fight taking place was as fierce and as bloody as she expected. But it was a lot more evenly matched. For some reason, there were soldiers bearing the Horde insignia on their tactical gear. Only about a dozen, but still. *What the fuck ...?* Sabre thought eyeing the skilled men and women facing off with some of the arseholes from the den.

"Are those soldiers?" Mercy asked coming up behind her.

Sabre simply shook her head. It made no sense. Why would there be – and then she heard it. A pissed off growl that seemed to rumble up from the depths of Hell itself. Sabre watched in wonder as Brax literally picked up a six-foot goblin by the hair, shook him like a ragdoll and tossed him aside like he weighed nothing at all. The goblin in question was built like a brick shithouse and judging by his shattered sword, had no doubt made the mistake of trying to stab Brax in the back – no doubt the cause of the angry growl. Harvey – said goblin – landed on top of a satyr with a nasty thump. Neither got back up. Presently, Brax's head whipped up and his piercing amber eyes, aglow with his inner beast and battle-lust, locked onto hers. The man looked mad enough to rip off her head. She wondered if that was why he was here; to kill her himself. Well, he was going to have to get in line, because at that exact moment, Wade jumped in front of her.

"You fucking bitch! What have you done?! This is all your fault!"

Sabre was burned to shit, with multiple broken bones and dripping blood from a few decent cuts but she still summoned a smile, giving her usual reply; "Fuck you, Wade."

The response seemed to enrage the werewolf, for he lunged at her, shifting mid-leap. Sabre dodged the hairy beast easily. Werewolves were strong and fast – but when in their shifted form, their animals tended to take over. It meant human thinking and strategising went out the window, replaced with animal instincts and need. And the animal in front of her needed to chew off her arm if the look in his eyes was anything to go by.

Obligingly, Sabre lifted her arm and waved it around, "You want this, huh? Doggie want a bone? Yeah, you do. Look at it; it's all bloody and torn. Fresh meat …" she taunted Wade, hearing Mercy's snort of amusement before he lunged off the deck to join the fray. Wade leapt at her and Sabre allowed the momentum from his weight to push her onto her back. She then kicked with her legs, sending Wade soaring over her head and off the porch. Pushing back with her heels, she scooted quickly on her butt until she felt a blade under her hand, thankfully left there by Mercy. Palming the small throwing knife – and cursing Mercy for not leaving something bigger – Sabre stood up before taking a running leap onto Wade's hairy back. The werewolf snarled and snapped but couldn't dislodge Sabre where she was stabbing the small blade repeatedly into his thick back muscles. When a clawed hand raked down her spine, Sabre swore viciously and stopped fucking around. Reaching around the front of Wade's face, she plunged the blade straight into his eye. The werewolf screamed for a second before collapsing in a heap, Sabre sprawled out on top of him.

"Sabre! You walking cunt! I'm going to kill you!"

Sabre huffed but pushed herself to her feet and whipped her head around at Carlisle's voice – just in time to see him launch a freakin' spear in her direction. Feeling exhausted, Sabre barely managed to bend her knees in preparation of batting the huge missile out of the way, when a blur of white appeared in front of her, effectively blocking her view and preventing the wickedly sharp object from impaling her. The white moved and Sabre realised she was staring at a wall of pristine feathers. Draven turned to her then, spear clutched in one hand and a pair of brass knuckles on the other. Sabre stared at him in shock. Of all the people to save her from a healthy disfigurement by spear, Draven would have been the last on her list. They locked eyes for a split second, neither saying anything, before Draven spun back around and raised his arm. He was clearly intent on sending it back to its owner.

"No," her words had Draven hesitating, "We need him." Sabre then looked at Carlisle, who was a good distance away – the coward. "Carlisle, you piece of shit," was all Sabre stated. But it was enough.

Carlisle spat on the ground and made a gesture with his hands, calling in his troops. More than half of those who were still conscious moved to stand next to him. But Sabre was pleasantly surprised to see a couple of fellow assassins and about a dozen household staff slowly began to make their way in her direction instead. Not being an idiot, Sabre kept a wary eye on them, nodding in thanks as Gage, Jinx and a few other familiar faces converged on them. Carlisle was all but vibrating in rage, pretty blue eyes now bloodshot, taking in the scene. Sabre saw his eyes widen when he also began to pick out some familiar faces and she felt herself smile from the realisation on his face. She was sure it wasn't a pleasant look.

"You know, I always hoped I would be able to see your face when the truth finally came out," Sabre taunted. She could feel the heavy weight of Brax's stare as he came to stand by Draven, who was still at her side. Ignoring the love of her life was one of the hardest things she had ever had to do. But the events of the day had set wheels in motion that couldn't be undone. And if she were being honest, she didn't want them undone. She had been working behind the scenes for years and she was tired. Bone-weary exhausted actually. So, she was going to seize the day and take the bull by the horns and all those other wonderful clichés.

"What ... what the hell?!" Carlisle yelled. "Is that Sampson? And Rory? And that's motherfucking Shiloh! Lieutenant of the Demon Horde!"

Sabre saw Brax jolt upon hearing that last name but she continued to ignore him for now, "Why yes, Carlisle. It is. I gotta hand it to you, you never forget the face of a hit."

"But they're all dead!" The incubus screamed. "They all had contracts taken out on them and they were killed by –" he broke off mid-sentence.

Sabre grinned, ignoring the sting in her split lip, "Me. They were all by killed me. That's what you were going to say, isn't it?"

"I don't understand," was Carlisle's reply. And damn if he didn't sound like a whiny little bitch.

For some reason, his words caused over one hundred years of suppressed rage to bubble up and Sabre felt herself step forward, hands clenched, "You don't understand? Really? It's not that hard, you stupid fuck! I am an angel. I don't kill; I protect!" Sabre screamed so loud her throat hurt. And though it may have not been completely accurate – she had indeed killed hundreds of people – she had only killed the guilty. Only those deserving of her wrath.

"But ..." Carlisle looked around at the dozens of faces she had been hired to kill over the years. "You did kill them. I saw proof of death."

Sabre had no doubt Carlisle had sent spotters after her whenever she had a mission. And although she knew it wasn't every single time, it must have been enough that the den master was satisfied with the authenticity of her kills. She also knew that the bodies of her hits were found and all the proper funerary arrangements made. Yes, there was certainly a lot of proof of death. But death didn't have the same meaning to her that it did for others. Death was merely a pause – not an end. If she so chose it to be, that was. The itch in her back that had been making itself known since laying her eyes on Draven's, admittedly amazing wings, was getting worse. Seeing no need to continue hiding and knowing it would make her point like nothing else would, Sabre allowed her wings to unfold.

Stunned gasps and curses filled her ears as her massive three-metre wings emerged from her back, ripping their way past her battered shirt. She allowed them to expand, going so far as to give them a couple of flaps before she tucked them back against her spine. Because her primary feathers brushed the ground and arched over the back of her head, Sabre had no doubt she made a heavenly picture of red and gold.

"But you're fallen. You shouldn't have wings. You have no Grace!" Carlisle yelled, but he was beginning to look panicked.

"Oh, there's nothing wrong with my Grace, I assure you. I am *not* fallen." Sabre raised her chin, her wings flexing out behind her as she levelled her eyes on her tormentor, "You didn't break me, Carlisle."

The incubus's face twisted in rage, all hints of beauty eradicated. He went to take a step forward, only to be stopped by Bevin. Carlisle hissed in frustration but the sphinx whispered something harshly in his ear that had him gritting his teeth and nodding his head. Before Sabre could do no more than swear, the whole group winked out of existence. As a sphinx Bevin was capable of teleporting on a mass scale. Sabre was going to have to hunt the prick down. *But not today,* she thought. Today, she was going to go and have a very long nap.

"Sabre! Are you okay?" Jinx cried, suddenly petting an unblemished spot on her arm.

Sabre felt like roadkill, but she simply said, "I'll be fine, Jinx. Thanks for the rescue."

Gage came up behind the weretiger, handsome face grinning, "As if you really needed us."

Sabre shook her head, making eye contact with her two closest companions, "I will always need you."

Jinx sniffed, blinking quickly, "Aww, blood loss always makes you sappy."

Sabre laughed, turning to the throng of creatures watching wide-eyed and confused, "Thank you. I appreciate your help more than I can say." She received a few murmurs and smiles, and a lot more stunned looks at her wings, before Sabre bit the bullet and turned to Brax and Draven; "Thank you. For, you know, coming here. And stuff," she kicked at the ground with her toe. Jeez, could she be any more lame?

Draven was eyeing her wings with something akin to awe. "You ... you're a resurrection angel."

Sabre winced, hunching her shoulders a little. Yes, she was a resurrection angel. The crimson feathers that looked like they had been dipped in gold were a dead giveaway. Despite what the entire population of Purgatory believed, her wings had not sickened and eroded away with the passing of time. Instead, they were healthy, shiny, and feathery. Sabre sighed, the feeling of having her wings on display for the first time in a hundred years was something akin to an orgasm. Well, she amended, maybe not an orgasm with Brax. They were all kinds of awesome.

Movement from the corner of her eye caught her attention and the next thing she knew her sight was blocked by one very pissed off, yellow-eyed demon. Brax had his claws out – which were dripping in blood – and somehow his shirt had gotten ripped off. The man was now magnificently and conveniently bare from the waist up. His corrugated abs moved harshly as the breath sawed in and out of his chest in angry bursts and his lips started moving as if he were speaking. But Sabre couldn't focus on the words because there were rivulets of sweat dripping down the dips and valleys of his eight-pack like her own personal river. She wanted to follow their path, especially when their journey ended in the waistband of his pants.

"Golly, Sabre. You've been fucking *that*? No wonder you thought you were in love with him and his magic dick."

Jinx's awe-filled voice snapped Sabre from her lust-induced haze, and she promptly elbowed her younger friend in the ribs. Sabre smiled in satisfaction when Jinx oompfed loudly; clearly her ribs were tender from the fight. Brax took a single step closer and Sabre was forced to raise her chin to see his face. It was blemish free – the man didn't have a single scratch on him thanks to his gift from Cerberus. But his handsome face was carved into an angry network of lines. Sabre wondered if he was going to let her explain or if he was just going to behead her where she stood. To be honest, the endorphins from the fight and her wing reveal were rapidly leaving her and her injuries from the torture session were making themselves known once again. She wasn't sure she could even lift a feather to defend herself. Not that she would, she knew. She would give everything she was – even her life – to the demon standing in front of her. Her heart hurt just looking at him.

"When you said, *the King lives* …" Brax's voice was rough with emotion. "You really meant …?"

Sabre nodded her head slowly, "That he is alive," she stated, boldly. Sabre then looked Brax straight in the eye; "Yes, I killed your brother … but I also brought him back."

## CHAPTER TWENTY-EIGHT

Brax paced, Styx whining at his side, trying to understand his master's agitation. At a loss for anything else to do, Brax reached a hand down to pat the hell hound. Styx leaned his considerable weight against Brax's leg, causing him to grunt and brace himself. The hound really was a huge beast, "She'll be okay, boy. Don't worry." Brax wondered who he was trying to convince; himself or the hound. Still, Styx gave a rumble as if in agreement before his dark blue tongue licked over the back of Brax's hand.

"Brax …"

Draven's soft call had his head whipping up and he looked behind the angel frantically, his eyes seeking out even a small glimpse of the woman bruised and battered within the room. It had been Draven rather than Jinx, Gage – or any number of other supernatural creatures currently awaiting news in the living area of the palace – who had gently pushed Brax outside one of the guest rooms so he could heal Sabre from her terrible wounds using his angelic gift. Draven had been in there a long time. At least it felt that way to Brax. It was unusual. Draven's ability was usually very fast – sometimes instantaneous – thanks to his Grace. The minutes ticking by was why his hall rug would be worn out down the centre thanks to his incessant pacing.

"Is she all healed?" Brax asked, frantically. Swallowing as much as his dry mouth would allow before asking his next question; "Will she let me see her?"

Draven clenched his jaw, looking frustrated and pained at the same time, "She is not healed. At all."

"What? Draven! What have you been doing in there! Get your arse back in there and make her better, damnit!" Brax yelled, causing Styx to jump then growl.

"She won't let me," Draven revealed.

"She ... what?!"

Draven dragged a hand through his hair, messing up his usually perfectly tousled locks, "She won't let me! The darn woman is even more stubborn than you! She won't let me near her. Brax, I don't know what to do," Draven's blue eyes pleaded with Brax to somehow fix the situation.

Cursing women's stubbornness in all the realms, Brax pushed past Draven and into the room, "Sabre! What are you thinking? Let Draven heal you!" he yelled at the bruised and bloody woman on the bed.

Sabre gritted her teeth, "No."

"No? Surely your stupid feud isn't worth your health!" Brax realised he was practically shouting and made an effort to tame his tone, "I'm sorry. It's just ... Sabre, you're really hurt. Please –" his voice cracked and he had to turn away from her. The sight of his love covered in blood and burns and cuts was almost too much for him. His guilt was eating him alive.

"I'm an angel. I heal quickly. Don't worry, it's not like I'm going to die or anything," Sabre sounded sardonic.

Brax rounded on her, "Don't even joke about that!"

Sabre sighed, exhaustion present in every line of her body. "Just ... relax, Abraxis. I've had worse. This will heal. Truly."

"There is no need for you to be in pain, Sabre," Draven said softly from where he still stood just inside the door as if unsure of his welcome.

*That makes both of us,* Brax thought. Wondering if Sabre would ever forgive him for not listening to her. For not giving her a chance to explain. All of the carnage at the Blue Devil – all of Sabre's current pain – could have been avoided had he simply listened to her when he had the chance. Sabre was quiet, having not responded to Draven's gentle words. Taking it as tacit encouragement, Draven slowly moved forward.

"I would heal you, if you will let me. Please. I know we do not have the best of history. But, I ... I would heal you, angel," Draven's words were gentle but formal.

Sabre's shoulders slumped where she had been sitting rigidly against the upholstered headboard. "It's not you, Draven," she paused, a small twitch moving her lips up at the corners, "It's your face."

The ridiculous teasing that never failed to piss Draven off had them all chuckling in surprise, the levity much needed and very welcome in the tense room. Brax found himself brave enough to look directly at Sabre and found her staring back at him. She gave him a small nod, which he had no idea how to decipher. Did she forgive him? Did she want to slice his throat open? Did she want a cup of apple tea?! *Fuck, I am absolutely losing it,* Brax thought. Still, he trembled over the possibility that Sabre maybe wasn't picturing him in a shallow grave in that instant.

"Sabre ..." Jinx began. But Sabre quickly shook her head. A hiss escaping from between her teeth from the movement.

"No. He can't. In all seriousness, I thank you for the offer, Draven. But you really can't."

"Why not?" Draven sounded just as frustrated and confused as Brax felt.

"Because you're not just a healer. You're also an empath. One who can read thoughts with the touch of your hand. I was able to keep Touma out of my mind because I wasn't injured and because he's a fucking moronic dickweed. But I can admit I'm damn tired. I also trust you. I'd have a hard time not spilling my mental guts," Sabre admitted.

Brax opened and closed his mouth silently a couple of times before looking at Draven. Even the revelation that Sabre had even more secrets locked away in her brain other than the mammoth one of her being a resurrection angel and his brother being alive, didn't seem important right then. In fact, Brax could care less what she knew about what. He just wanted her whole again. "Sabre, I don't care if you have the meaning of life stored in that brain of yours. Just …" he trailed off, knowing he wasn't entitled to ask anything of her under the circumstances.

"I assure you I have great control over my abilities. As well as a code of ethics. I would never pry into your mind. I can heal you and keep your secrets intact. I promise," Draven said, sincerely.

Sabre opened her mouth only to be cut off by the huge, horned demon in the corner of the room. "She accepts," the man grumbled, jabbing a finger in Sabre's direction. "No more arguments, young lady. I'm so full on pain right now I probably won't have to feed for months. Let the walking stiff heal you."

Draven stiffened at the insult but quickly relaxed again when he heard Sabre snort out a laugh. "Now that is cleared up. May I?"

Sabre eyed the other angel in front of her before finally

reaching out with a bloody hand containing three broken fingers, "Fine. Thank you."

Draven wasted no time, sitting down on the edge of the bed and grasping her hand gently. He placed his other hand on her chest just below her throat and Brax felt the entire room exhale in relief as Draven's healing energy began to do its job right before their eyes. It took almost thirty minutes for Draven to be satisfied that he had healed all of Sabre's wounds and Brax had done nothing but stare at the woman the entire time. He didn't care how creepy he was coming across or that it was probably making Sabre uncomfortable. All he cared about was watching the porcelain perfection of her skin return inch by inch. When Draven finally let go of Sabre and sat back with a sigh, Brax rushed forward only to stop before he made the mistake of touching her. Because he knew his touch would never be welcome again. Sabre surprised him when she said;

"It's okay, Brax. Go ahead. Just ask."

"Ask what?" he questioned, genuinely confused and revelling in the fact that Sabre was at least speaking to him.

"You've been incredibly patient when I know you must be busting at the seams to ask about your brother. He –"

"That's not what I want to ask." Sabre looked beyond confused. It wasn't a look he had seen on her face before and it was endearing as hell.

"But Mikhail ..." she began.

"Can wait," Brax interrupted. "Apparently he's been waiting for over a year. A little bit longer won't hurt him." Brax tried to keep the resentment from his voice when he said that. Shaking off his anger to deal with in another time and place, he focused on what was most important to him, "Will you forgive me?"

Sabre frowned, "Forgive you? For what?"

"For not listening to you this morning. You tried to tell me there was more to the story and I wouldn't listen. I am so sorry, Sabre. So, so sorry. I –"

"Hold up, beastie-boy," Sabre held up a hand for silence as she rose gracefully to her feet.

*So,* Brax thought in abject misery, *she isn't even going to let me beg.* Sabre walked over to him, pausing only when he could feel the warmth from her body against the line of his. He wanted nothing more than to grab her, throw her down on the bed and spend the next fifty years or so worshiping her body and grovelling. But he did none of that. He simply awaited his fate.

"Why are you apologising? You have nothing to apologise for. *Of course* you didn't listen to me. Why would you? You had just learned I was the assassin hired to kill your brother – the then king. A job I really did perform. I *did* kill Mikhail. If anyone has anything to be sorry for it's me. Not you. So, just, you know – shut up."

Brax felt his mouth drop open in shock, "Nothing to apologise for?"

Sabre nodded once, crossing her arms over her chest, "That's right."

"You don't hate me?" Brax ventured, voice filled with hope.

Sabre's mouth fell open this time and she blinked rapidly as if trying to compute his words, "Hate you? Why would I hate you? I love you."

"You … you love me?" Brax choked.

Sabre narrowed her plum eyes at him before turning to Draven, "Is he okay? Did he get hit on the head during the fight?"

Draven covered his quick smile with the palm of his hand, "I do not believe so, no."

"Huh," Sabre turned back to Brax. "Yes, Brax. I love you. We already had this conversation, remember? You said you loved me and then I said I loved you more. Because I'm a winner," Sabre pointed out, "So of course I love you more."

Brax clutched at his chest, wondering how his heart was still inside his rib cage because it was thumping so loudly. It was all he could do to hear Sabre's words of love. She loved him. Sabre still loved him!

"You're not saying anything," Sabre pointed out, "Do you not still love me? Is that your problem?"

"Yes! Of course, yes. How could I not love you? I will always love you. You are mine," he was quick to say, bounding forward to snatch up her hands. The smile that spread across Sabre's face was truly angelic and took his breath away with the sheer beauty of everything she was. He cupped her cheeks before he offered a peck to her lips, confessing, "I was so worried you wouldn't want me anymore. The very first test of my love for you and I believed a stranger's words over yours. I should have trusted you. I'm sorry."

"Not want you anymore? Why? It was one little blip in our otherwise great relationship. I mean, sure, we've only been seeing each other officially for like, fifteen hours. But I think we've been doing really well. Okay, I have nothing to compare it to because, let's face it, I'm not a shining beacon for healthy relationships considering most of my friends are people that I've been paid to kill. Then secretly brought back to life. It's complicated," Sabre finished her banal chatter with a shrug of her shoulders.

Brax stared at her for a heartbeat before he laughed so hard he was forced to bend over at the waist to catch his breath. Then he was on her between one heartbeat and the next, crushing their mouths together and tangling their limbs, trying to get as close to her as possible.

"I hate to interrupt, but is now really the time for the two of you to fornicate?" Draven's voice was dry as a desert when he interrupted their interlude.

"Oh my Hell. Did you just say *fornicate*?" Sabre laughed as she pulled away from Brax's ravaging mouth – but not his questing hands. "Say it again," she urged.

Draven sniffed, raising his chin, "I most certainly will not."

Sabre looked back up at Brax, eyes twinkling merrily, "Make him say it again. If you order him to do it, he's duty-bound to obey."

"Is that why you killed Mikhail?" Draven's words were like a bucket of cold water – and just as abrupt.

The smiling, flushed, well-kissed woman in his arms of just seconds ago, suddenly stiffened and pulled out of his grasp. Brax grumbled in displeasure, hauling her back against his chest. This time with her back to his front so she could accost the other angel at her leisure. As much as Brax wanted to know everything about Mikhail and Sabre's part in his death – and resurrection – he wanted to hold the assassin more. In fact, he may never let her out of his sight again.

"Wow, way to kill the mood. Douche," Jinx narrowed her odd eyes at Draven, and if looks could kill, Brax's angel would be well and truly incinerated.

## CHAPTER TWENTY-NINE

Sabre relaxed back against the broad chest behind her, trusting Brax's strength to keep them both upright. She went one step further and clutched at the forearms holding her so securely. She couldn't believe Brax was worried about *her* forgiving *him*. She was the one who had gotten all stabby with his big brother and then omitted that titbit every time she saw him. Sabre had been sure their relationship, only in its infancy, had been doomed. One of the reasons why she held back from Draven's healing hands was because she didn't want to be fit enough to have to deal with Brax kicking her butt to the curb. But, if the strong arms currently wrapped around her like an octopus were any indication, her butt was well and truly safe.

Turning to Draven, she asked point-blank, "What do you think you know?"

Draven arched a perfectly manscaped eyebrow, "Everything I'm pretty sure."

Sabre narrowed her eyes at him, "Oh I doubt that. And if you did, I'd have to kick your arse for snooping in my mind when you promised me you wouldn't."

Draven shook his head, "I didn't snoop. I would never do that. I am an angel of integrity, unlike some –" he abruptly broke off, clearing his throat.

"Unlike some angels? Is that what you were going to say?" Sabre prodded, relishing the flush creeping up Draven's neck. To her shock, Draven bowed in her direction, placing a palm over his heart.

"I apologise. Obviously, I – *we* – have been mistaken in our thinking. Though, I am sure that was your intention so I don't really know if the apology is necessary."

"Wow. You can't even apologise right," Gage spoke up from where he was leaning next to Jinx and Mercy in the corner of the room.

Sabre chuckled, finding the lame apology funny as well as more than sufficient. Besides, his actions spoke volumes more than his words. Sabre couldn't deny it felt good to finally be vindicated – somewhat. Jinx, Gage, Mercy and Phaedra had been the only people to know – other than those she had resurrected of course – that Sabre was still an angel in full possession of her Grace. They had also known that she was a resurrection angel. But that was the extent of their knowledge. The rest of her secrets weren't really hers to share and she had kept them locked behind several layers of impenetrable steel in her mind and in her heart. She desperately wanted to unload all of her burdens but wasn't sure she was allowed to.

Draven, who had been watching her face carefully during her self-reflection, had pity in his eyes when he asked; "How much can you tell us?"

"Nothing," Sabre shook her head and glanced up at Brax. "I'm sorry. I can't tell you anything else."

Brax didn't look angry, simply curious when he questioned; "Why? Are you afraid of something – or someone?"

"Afraid? No." And that was the truth. She was no more afraid of her true employer than she was of her own shadow. Without thought, she said as much to Brax.

"Your true employer?" his forehead wrinkled as he looked down at her.

Sabre snapped her mouth shut. She had said that out loud? Over a hundred years of lying and hiding and she suddenly gets a case of verbal diarrhoea? "Fuck me …" she muttered.

Jinx laughed from the corner. "Wow, Sabre. Look at you giving away trade secrets. It must be all those sexy sex pheromones Brax is releasing."

"I don't have sex pheromones," Brax quickly rejected.

"Oh, Your Majesty. Believe me, you most certainly do," Mercy purred, eyeing Brax as if he were a piece of meat – tenderised of course because that was just how Mercy rolled.

Brax eyed her torture-happy friend before giving himself a discreet sniff. He cast a questioning look at Draven who simply shrugged and shook his head. Sabre stood on her tip toes in order to place a kiss to the tip of her guy's nose because he really was just too adorable for words. But his endearing ways were still not enough for her to talk. Some bonds exceeded even the heart. But, oh how she yearned to open up to her lover. Draven, seemingly taking pity on her once more made a suggestion and Sabre was just desperate enough to latch onto the flimsy worth of it, that she agreed readily.

"What if we guess? Or make statements that you can then confirm or deny?" was Draven's suggestion.

Sabre worried her bottom lip, nails digging into Brax's arm where she still clutched it like a life preserver. "It's a technicality and a loophole ... but I'll take it. Okay," she decided. Besides, what was Mikhail going to do? Kill her?

"Did Mikhail hire you to kill him?"

Draven's abrupt – and perceptive – question had her demon finally releasing her. Brax's arms dropped and he looked at his guardian in shock, "What the fuck, Draven? What kind of a question is that? Why would my brother ..." his words trailed off as he stared at Sabre's face. "Mikhail hired you to kill him?"

Testing the strength of their love once more, Sabre answered simply; "Yes."

Breath exploded from Brax's lungs, "Why?" He began to pace in the confines of the guest suite, arms waving in the air, "Why would he do that? Why would he take himself away from me?"

The pain in Brax's voice made Sabre want to kick Mikhail's arse the next time she saw him. She had no doubt that time would be soon. Word spread quickly in Purgatory and she knew he would be hearing of the day's events very soon. He might even know already. Sabre stood in front of Brax's path and placed her palm over his frantically beating heart, looking into his beloved yellow eyes as she answered, "Because he wanted to save you."

"What? Save me? I don't understand."

Brax's eyes pleaded with her to make sense of something nonsensical. To make everything right again in his world when everything had been turned topsy turvy. The trust and faith that showed caused Sabre's knees to wobble a little. So, throwing word games to the wayside, Sabre explained the best she could, all the while tracing the frown lines on her demon's forehead.

"The conspiracy to wipe out your family started well before Mikhail. You were right to think it began with your father and uncles. After your father was killed, you know Mikhail tried for years to identify the killer. Hell, *I* tried for years. I still can't believe Phaedra had information all this time. I suppose it hardly matters now, but it still pisses me off," Sabre muttered. "Anyway, after your brother was killed, Mikhail was determined the same thing wouldn't happen to you. He didn't want to lose another member of his family, so he ordered me to kill him – and to bring him back of course. He thought he could work better from behind the scenes. Hunt the person down and put a stop to the killing."

"He left Brax exposed," Draven frowned, sounding almost angry. "Abraxis was the last direct family member left. Mikhail being gone only caused Brax to be in more danger."

"Hey, don't shoot the messenger," Sabre raised her hands in supplication. "We're talking about man-logic here. I just did as I was told."

"How did he even know you were a resurrection angel? Because, babe, I have to tell you; that is just fucking amazing. Your wings are the most magnificent things I have ever seen. They are so beautiful – just like you," Brax enthused. "But that is one huge secret in itself. The last resurrection angel seen in Purgatory was thousands of years ago and gifted from the Heavens to my great-times-a-hundred grandfather to be his guardian as the direct offspring of Cerberus and the first King of Purgatory."

"Mikhail knew the same way that you know everything about Draven," Sabre admitted.

"Huh?" Brax still looked confused.

"Oh, don't be so daft, Abraxis!" Draven scolded, "Sabre is obviously Mikhail's guardian angel."

"What? That's impossible. Mikhail doesn't have a guardian …"

Sabre winced when Brax's words slowed down before stopping altogether. He spun her around so she was facing him and she could see the heavy, very displeased frown on his face.

"You're his guardian angel," Brax stated.

"Yes."

"You've always been his angel."

"Yes," Sabre confirmed.

Brax threw his hands up in the air in defeat, complaining, "How come I didn't know about you? How come *nobody* knew about you?"

Sabre was worried about the next part of the story because it was just plain crazy. "Well, this is where it gets a little tricky. You see, your dad knew about me. You know how your father was a little clairvoyant? Yeah, well. He knew who I was the moment he laid eyes on me when I was fourteen."

Brax was already shaking his head, "Fourteen? What?"

"I know this is a lot to take in, but just let me explain. Please?" Brax obligingly nodded his head, but Sabre thought it was probably more automatic than anything else. She had a funny feeling all forms of higher functioning had currently shut down in Brax's overwhelmed brain. "Remember I told you I met your father once? I was there to kill a visiting dignitary at the time. Maliq caught me in the act but like you said before, he let me go. Because he knew who I was to Mikhail. He knew I was his guardian. Mikhail was only two at the time. Actually, all three of you were only two. But I knew who Mikhail was the moment your father placed him in my belligerent, bratty, teenage arms." Sabre smiled, remembering the tiny dark-haired toddler with the shining green eyes reflecting the light and growling like a little beast from Hell. Sabre had fallen in love with him in that very moment. But it was a very different type of love than she had for Brax. She hoped she wasn't going to have to make that distinction to Brax – that he understood the bond between guardian and demon. Knowing that was a potential issue for another time and not wanting to borrow trouble, Sabre continued on for her captive audience, "Maliq knew my powers of resurrection were going to be needed in the future. It was his greatest regret that his sons were going to be plagued with death and hardship and he fought to make sure it wasn't so. Unfortunately, we can't fight fate – even the great Kings among us."

Sabre knew she was overwhelming Brax with a lot of information. Information he would be well within his rights to disregard and simply not believe in. Unfortunately, everything she had just told him was the truth. She kept her eyes on his, begging him to believe her, and was relieved when he gave a tiny nod of his head and a quirk of his luscious lips.

"You're a freaking guardian angel like Mr Stick In The Mud here?"

Jinx's voice broke off the silent conversation, making Sabre chuckle, "I am. Though, given my other vocation, I don't think you should be comparing me to him."

"Absolutely not," Draven sniffed in disdain.

"So, you really do kill people too? I mean, I know you've brought some of them back – which is super amazing and something I want to talk to you about more. Because, well, my girlfriend can bring people back from the dead! How cool is that?"

Brax's words had the room laughing but had Sabre ducking her head. He had sounded so proud when he said that. It had been years and years since anyone other than Mikhail had been proud of her and she loved the warm-fuzzies she was feeling. Still, she felt it best to be honest; "Yes, I really do kill. And maim. And torture. But only those with stains on their souls and trespasses in their actions. Full disclosure; I kind of like it." Draven coughed and Sabre glared at him, "Fine. I love it. I love it, okay? And I'm damn good at it!"

Brax chuckled and drew her in close once more, "Ah, my murderous little sugarplum. Still, all those lives saved. One miracle after another – and each and every one of them kept your secret. That's a hell of a lot of loyalty there, Sabre."

Sabre shrugged, yawning wide, "I always explained the situation; that I was forced to kill them but that they were good peeps so I made the executive decision to bring them back. I also threatened them with a more eternal death if they didn't keep quiet. Most of them joined Hound and his merry band of men, aiding you in secret."

"Hound? That guy again?" Brax scrunched up his nose, "I gotta be honest, other than a few pieces of miscellaneous information here and there, the guy hasn't been all that effective."

Brax's words startled a laugh out of Sabre, "Oh, I dare you to say that to his face," she snickered.

Brax ran his eyes over her for a moment before sighing, "Hound is Mikhail, isn't he?"

Sabre grinned and pinched his cheeks, "Look at you; not just a pretty face. Yes. Hound is Mikhail."

"I'll kill him," Brax snarled, baring his fangs.

"That's fine," Sabre agreed. "I can easily bring him back."

The room lapsed into a comfortable, yet contemplative silence. It was inevitably broken by Jinx, because what teen could stay quiet for long? "Now what?" she asked.

Everyone looked to Brax because whether or not Mikhail was still alive, and therefore the rightful king, Brax was still the one currently with his arse on the throne.

"Now we find Carlisle so I can kill him," Brax eventually said.

"I like this plan," Sabre enthused.

"I thought you would," Brax grinned down at her. "Then we find that mysterious, sinister, motherfucking elf so I can kill him."

"Even better," Sabre agreed.

"And then … we go find my brother so I can kill him," Brax said in conclusion.

Sabre clapped her hands in glee, "There's so much killing in this plan. This is the best plan ever!"

Draven rolled his eyes, muttering, "Of course you think that."

Raising her middle finger and firing it at the rude angel, Sabre turned to Brax, smoothing her palms over his chest and tweaking his nipples on the way, "Hmm, that plan is deliciously violent. I'm not rubbing off on you, am I, my demon?"

Brax groaned, clutching her hips in a steel grip, "Not yet, you're not. But I really wish you were," he rumbled, seductively.

And just like that, all Sabre wanted to do was wrap herself around him – naked of course – and never let him go. Boosting herself up, she ignored the other occupants in the room and proceeded to maul Brax's handsome face.

"Annnd that's our cue to leave," Gage made a gagging sound in the back of his throat.

"Dear Heaven. They look like a couple of seals slapping up against each other. I think I just threw up a little in my mouth."

The room went silent, Sabre and Brax stilling. Sabre pulled her mouth from her man's and turned incredulous eyes to Draven, "Did you just make a joke?" She was beyond shocked.

Draven sniffed and picked an imaginary piece of fluff from his sleeve, "I did not. I was serious. You two look ridiculous." And with that, he spun and left the room.

Sabre stared blankly at the space he left behind, hearing Jinx giggle as she walked past, patting her arm. "I'm glad you're not dead, Sabre."

"Yeah. Glad you're not dead," Gage repeated, hooking an arm through Jinx's as they continued to leave the room.

Mercy gave them both a jaunty salute as he too, left. And then they were blissfully alone. Sabre, still being clutched by the butt cheeks by Brax with her legs locked tightly around his waist, grinned up at him. "Now ... where were we?"

# CHAPTER THIRTY

Brax was breathing and sweating as if he had just run a marathon. He was gratified to see the assassin was in no better condition, even in her currently half-comatose state. The pair of them had wasted no time in getting to the make-up sex. Brax was pleased to note make-up sex was as good as all the movies and romance books would have you believe. It had been a day of ups and downs that was for sure, and it was starting to take on a surreal quality as he lay entwined with the mate of his choosing. Sabre was in fact *not* a fallen angel. She probably had more Grace in a single feather than Draven did in his entire wing set. Not that Brax would ever be stupid enough to say so to the angel in question. But resurrection angels were so rare and a gift given directly from the Heavenly plane, that they were practically a thing of legend. Add in all those gold feathers that Brax saw and he figured Sabre was not only the most powerful angel in Purgatory, but also the most righteous.

Said legend suddenly gave out a decidedly indelicate snore and Brax cringed when drool hit his chest. "Oh, yes. A rare jewel indeed, sent directly from the Gods themselves," he muttered. He was not sorry in the least when Sabre bolted upright, hastily wiping at the drool on her chin.

"Huh? What? What do I need to kill?"

Brax laughed, "Down, tiger. Nothing needs to die. I was just thinking out loud."

"Oh," Sabre pouted, her short hair sticking up like she'd stuck her finger in a power socket.

Grinning, Brax reeled her in for a long, tongue-filled kiss. Pulling back, he marvelled at Sabre's blemish-free skin. Draven may have been a bit of a tight-arse, but he was the best healer in all of Purgatory. Brax knew the other angel would have worked hard to ensure not even a scratch remained on Sabre's body after finding out they had so badly misjudged her. "I'm not dreaming am I? Mikhail is really alive and you are his guardian?" Brax couldn't help but ask again, perhaps for the tenth time that evening. Sabre didn't seem to mind his repetition, leaning forward to cup his cheek as she replied patiently;

"Yes. Your brother is alive and well. I really am his guardian. And I really do love you," she added.

Brax swallowed tightly, "Thank all the Gods."

After some serious heavy petting that resulted in mutual orgasms, Brax relaxed back against the sheets, content to hold and be held. He was in a mild state of doze when Sabre surprised him by talking.

"You really don't mind? About me being me and everything I've done?" she asked, rather abruptly.

Knowing truth was the foundation he wanted laid in their relationship, Brax rolled to his side to face her before he answered, "I wouldn't say I don't mind, I mean … you shot a cross bolt through my brother's heart." Sabre winced, ducking her head, but he wouldn't let her hide. Lifting her chin with his thumb, he nudged her head up. "But I understand duty more than most. So, if there is one thing you can count on, Sabre, it's that I understand you. I *know* you. And I love you anyway." Tears rushed to Sabre's eyes and the fact she didn't bother to hide them from him, spoke volumes. "Still, I can't believe even my lieutenants didn't contact me to tell me they were alive," Brax mused, thinking of the two dhampirs who had been killed at the same time as Mikhail. They had been unlucky enough to be on guard duty. Brax grunted, "Especially Shiloh."

Sabre tilted her head and narrowed her eyes, "Especially Shiloh? Why her *especially*?"

"Ah, well ..." Brax made an effort to stay very still, like prey hiding from a predator.

"You were lovers!" Sabre accused, her fingers twitching as if imagining a weapon between them.

Brax stifled a laugh, lest she decide to use her imaginary weapon on him. The fact that she could literally kill him and bring him back from the dead made her all the more dangerous. *And sexy,* he added, *definitely more sexy.* "Very briefly in our youth. Before I was even General of the Horde. It was one night and exactly two times," he rushed to explain.

Sabre harrumphed at that, "Only twice in one night? Woman has no stamina. No wonder she was so easy to kill," she muttered.

Brax could no longer contain his laughter and he fell onto his back, his hilarity shaking the bed. "You know, green looks good on you," he pointed out between gasps. He suddenly gasped for an entirely different reason when the vixen climbed onto his chest. Her knee slipped between his legs and nestled against his balls. Brax quickly shut his mouth.

Sabre tapped his chin with a wicked finger, "I am not jealous. Such fickle emotions are beneath me. I simply wish I didn't bring her back, that's all. Should have left her all stabby and stuff."

Brax ran his hands along the outside of Sabre's thighs, before trailing them up her back and hooking them over her shoulders. Dragging her down so he could feel the heat of her breath against his own, he said, "Sabre?"

"Yes?" she whispered.

"I love you."

Sabre's lips smiled against his before moving across his face like a blessing; "I love you more."

Sabre and Brax will return in Reluctant Royals, book two, *Reluctant Assassin*

MORE BY MONTANA ASH

The Elemental Paladins Series (paranormal/urban fantasy romance)
WARDEN
PALADIN
CHADE
RANGER
CUSTODIAN
REVOLUTION

The Familiars Series (paranormal reverse harem/polyamorous romance)
IVORY'S FAMILIARS

With T.J. Spade
(paranormal/fantasy reverse harem/polyamorous romance)

FORBIDDEN HYBRID
FORBIDDEN HEX

TINK AND THE LOST BOYS

## MEET MONTANA

Montana is an Aussie, self-confessed book junkie. Although she loves reading absolutely everything, her not-so-guilty pleasure is paranormal romance. Alpha men – just a little bit damaged – and feisty women – strong yet vulnerable – are a favourite combination of hers. Throw in some steamy sex scenes, a touch of humour, and a little violence and she is in heaven! She is a scientist by day, a writer by night, and a reader always!

Printed in Poland
by Amazon Fulfillment
Poland Sp. z o.o., Wrocław

# RELUCTANT KING

## RELUCTANT ROYALS, BOOK ONE

### MONTANA ASH

Published by Paladin Publishing

Reluctant King
Copyright © 2019 by Montana Ash

All rights reserved

This is a work of fiction. Names, characters, businesses, places, events, and incidents are either the products of the author's imagination or used in a fictitious manner. Any resemblance to actual persons, living or dead, or actual events is purely coincidental.

This book or any portion thereof may not be reproduced or used in any manner whatsoever without the express written permission of Montana Ash, except for the use of brief quotations embodied in critical articles and reviews.

Cover design by: Jennifer Munswami, J.M Rising Horse Creations

Cover character render by: Rebecca Poole

Formatting by: Glowing Moon Designs

ISBN: 9781687424990